MUSIC FOR THE DUKE

Suddenly a Duke Series
Book Two

Alexa Aston

ARE YOU SIGNED UP FOR DRAGONBLADE'S BLOG?

You'll get the latest news and information on exclusive giveaways, exclusive excerpts, coming releases, sales, free books, cover reveals and more.

Check out our complete list of authors, too!

No spam, no junk. That's a promise!

Sign Up Here

www.dragonbladepublishing.com

Dearest Reader;

Thank you for your support of a small press. At Dragonblade Publishing, we strive to bring you the highest quality Historical Romance from some of the best authors in the business. Without your support, there is no 'us', so we sincerely hope you adore these stories and find some new favorite authors along the way.

Happy Reading!

CEO, Dragonblade Publishing

Additional Dragonblade books by Author Alexa Aston

Suddenly a Duke Series
Portrait of the Duke
Music for the Duke

Second Sons of London Series
Educated By The Earl
Debating With The Duke
Empowered By The Earl
Made for the Marquess
Dubious about the Duke
Valued by the Viscount
Meant for the Marquess

Dukes Done Wrong Series
Discouraging the Duke
Deflecting the Duke
Disrupting the Duke
Delighting the Duke
Destiny with a Duke

Dukes of Distinction Series
Duke of Renown
Duke of Charm
Duke of Disrepute
Duke of Arrogance
Duke of Honor
The Duke That I Want

The St. Clairs Series
Devoted to the Duke
Midnight with the Marquess

Embracing the Earl
Defending the Duke
Suddenly a St. Clair
Starlight Night (Novella)
The Twelve Days of Love (Novella)

Soldiers & Soulmates Series
To Heal an Earl
To Tame a Rogue
To Trust a Duke
To Save a Love
To Win a Widow
Yuletide at Gillingham (Novella)

The Lyon's Den Series
The Lyon's Lady Love

King's Cousins Series
The Pawn
The Heir
The Bastard

Medieval Runaway Wives
Song of the Heart
A Promise of Tomorrow
Destined for Love

Knights of Honor Series
Word of Honor
Marked by Honor
Code of Honor
Journey to Honor
Heart of Honor
Bold in Honor
Love and Honor
Gift of Honor
Path to Honor
Return to Honor

Pirates of Britannia Series
God of the Seas

De Wolfe Pack: The Series
Rise of de Wolfe

The de Wolfes of Esterley Castle
Diana
Derek
Thea

Also from Alexa Aston
The Bridge to Love
One Magic Night

PROLOGUE

Parkwood—1794

FIA LEFT THE schoolroom and headed downstairs. Her governess had gone to her bedchamber for a nap. At least that's what she'd said. Fia knew Miss Blankenship would drink the funny-smelling liquid from the little tin she kept with her. Anytime Miss Blankenship did that, she would grow silly and then sleepy. She would give Fia a task to complete and then go to her room. Sometimes for hours.

Fia always finished what she was supposed to do and then found something to entertain herself with. She knew what Miss Blankenship did must be wrong, but she felt sorry for the governess. Once, she had come across Miss Blankenship crying after she had been drinking from the tin. The governess told her just how alone she was. How she had no family and no friends and went from position to position. She begged Fia not to say anything to her parents before she drifted off to sleep. Fia had watched the governess' drool pooling in the corner of her mouth and then dribbling down her chin. When she was feeling well, Miss Blankenship was a good teacher to her. Fia did not want to be the one who would tattle on the woman so she would be forced to leave.

Downstairs, she first went to the drawing room, thinking she might practice the pianoforte. She had just started taking lessons and felt alive every time she sat and played. Three maids were cleaning the room, though, so she retreated to the library, retrieving Papa's atlas. The atlas fascinated her. Papa had showed her where England was and told her it was the greatest country in all the world. He showed her the many places England and its king ruled. Papa told Fia that one day he would take her to all of them.

She doubted that would ever happen. Or if it did, they would have to leave Mama behind. Mama always seemed to be sick. She would tell Fia a babe was coming, and Fia would grow happy at the prospect of being a big sister. Sometimes, Mama's belly swelled large, and Fia could place her hand atop it, feeling the soft kicks against her palm.

But no babies ever arrived. Mama would grow ill and take to her bed for weeks. When she emerged, she would tell Fia the babe had gone up to Heaven. Fia had finally stopped getting excited at the idea of having a little brother or sister. At least she could get out on the estate with Papa and walk and ride. With Mama, she would read and draw pictures. After a while, Mama would stop being sad and once more spend time outside her bedchamber with Fia.

She took the atlas to the large window seat and sat in it, her back against the wall and her legs stretched out in front of her. Opening it, she looked at different countries in Europe and then the Far East. She was distantly aware of two maids who entered the room to dust, but she tuned out their chatter.

Until she heard her name.

She realized the maids did not know she was in the room with them. Papa would have told Fia to make her presence known. He had said listening to others when they were unaware you were present was called eavesdropping. He claimed eavesdroppers sometimes learned things they did not know, but oftentimes heard things they wished they would not have.

Fia closed the atlas and started to slip from the window seat but froze at the conversation.

"They say the countess can no longer try for a baby," one maid said. "That the doctor warned her if she did so, it would cost her her life."

"But the earl needs an heir," the second maid said. "Else his brother—and that bratty boy of his—will become the heirs."

Fia did not like her uncle or her cousin. Theo was eight, two years older than she was, and lorded over her. He was mean to her—pulling her hair, pinching her sides, even kicking her shins. She had grown increasingly afraid of Theo but tried not to show it.

"It won't matter. His lordship worships the ground his wife walks upon. He will not let her become with child again."

"I heard his brother and nephew are arriving later today. Best we finish in here and report to the housekeeper."

Fia curled up and sat silently while the maids finished their work and then left the library. No one had told her they had guests coming. No one had told her anything.

She did not want Mama to die. She also didn't want Papa's title to go to her uncle or Cousin Theo. Fia wished with all her heart that she could have been a boy and realized by being a girl, she had been a disappointment to both her parents.

Two hours later, her uncle and cousin arrived. She saw the carriage pull up in the drive and watched it, her insides twisting, making her want to retch. Miss Blankenship, who had finally roused herself, called Fia away from the window and had her copy spelling words onto a slate. She tried to think about the letters, but it was hard, knowing Cousin Theo would be here any minute.

A maid arrived and told Miss Blankenship, "Her ladyship wishes for Lady Fia to come down to the drawing room for tea."

Relief swept over the governess' face. "Ah, I see. Your cousin must have arrived. Go along, my lady. We will continue with this lesson tomorrow morning."

Reluctantly, Fia followed the maid downstairs and entered

the drawing room. This was the first time Mama had left her bedchamber since the last babe didn't arrive. She was pale but smiling.

"Ah, Fia, my darling. Come say hello to your uncle and cousin," Mama encouraged.

She moved slowly across the room and stopped, dropping a curtsey. "Hello, Uncle."

She ignored Cousin Theo.

"It is too bad she is your only one," her uncle said, causing her mother to flinch and her father to wince.

Papa slipped an arm about her waist, pulling Fia closer to him. "We are blessed to have Fia," he said firmly.

She sat on Papa's lap for tea though she knew she was too old to do so. She didn't listen to what the adults said and avoided looking at Cousin Theo, who ate seven scones and two pieces of cake. Fia thought he would be very fat by the time he grew up if he kept eating so many sweets.

"I do think it is the right thing," Uncle said, his gaze landing on her. "What do you think, Sophia?"

She didn't want to admit that she hadn't been listening, and so she shrugged. Her uncle smiled broadly.

"See, Fia will be happy to have her cousin with her all the time. Of course, he will go away to school soon. Still, it will be good for Theodore to spend his holidays at Parkwood."

Her belly clenched. She stopped breathing.

What had she missed?

Papa said, "It will be good for Theodore to learn about Parkwood."

Fia heard the resignation in Papa's voice. At once, she understood that he accepted that there would be no new baby. No heir. That his nephew would one day inherit the estate and title.

"I am glad you think so," Uncle said jovially. "Of course, there is always the possibility that I might become the Earl of Parkhurst after your passing. After all, I am younger than you. I do believe it is the right choice to allow Theodore to be brought up at Parkwood, though." He turned to his son, who was stuffing yet another scone into his mouth. "You will like living here at Parkwood with your uncle and aunt, won't you, Theodore?"

Cousin Theo shrugged and continued chewing.

"I will come to see you during some of your holidays," Uncle continued.

Fia realized that her cousin would live here from now on. The thought of him terrorizing her on a daily basis made her feel both fear and sadness. She looked to Mama, whose eyes were bright with tears.

"I am so sorry to have let you down, Parkhurst," she said, her voice a whisper.

Papa took her hand and lifted it to his lips, kissing it tenderly. "You have not disappointed me, love. You have given me Fia. We will be happy," he promised.

But she knew things would never be the same again. Cousin Theo would always be around. They would no longer be a happy family of three.

"Stop eating those scones," barked her uncle, startling all of them. "Go and play with your cousin. Think of her as your sister now. We adults have matters to discuss."

She gripped her father's tailcoat, not wishing to leave with her cousin.

"Go on," Papa urged, lifting her from his lap and giving her a slight nudge.

Quickly, Fia left the drawing room. She hurried up the stairs, hoping Cousin Theo wouldn't follow her.

He did, though, dogging her heels. "Where is your bedchamber?" he demanded.

She took him to the top floor and showed him her room and the schoolroom. "Miss Blankenship's bedchamber is behind that door. She's my governess."

"I don't need a governess," Theo proclaimed. "I am going away to school. And then I will come here."

He backed Fia into a corner. "You will have to always do

what I say," he bragged. "One day, I will be the Earl of Parkhurst since your mama can't have a son. You will have to listen to me and do everything I say."

"I won't," Fia said stubbornly. "You cannot make me, Theo."

He stepped menacingly toward her, his hand spanning her throat. Theo began squeezing, tighter and tighter, until Fia could not breathe. She did the only thing she could think to do. She thrust her knee violently into his tender parts.

Theo screamed and released her.

Fia fled the schoolroom, running blindly down the corridor, trying to think of where to hide. She knew she couldn't go to her parents. Mama would believe her, but Papa would tell her she and Theo had to get along now because Theo was the new heir.

Pausing at the top of the stairs, Fia frantically wondered where she could go. Where she might hide.

Then she was violently yanked back by her lone braid. Her cousin had followed her and now wrapped the long braid around his hand. His eyes were shining, looking so scary that she could not breathe.

Theo held her in place, his face coming so close his nose almost touched hers.

"You *will* do what I say," he told her.

"Let go," she pleaded. "You're hurting me. You're going to pull out my hair."

"I will jerk it all out until you are bald if I want," he threatened. "You are no one. I am the favorite now because I am a boy. Girls can't inherit anything. I get it all." He smiled gleefully. "You don't get anything. You will have to depend on me."

Tears rolled down her face. "All right," she agreed, wanting him to release her.

He did so, slowly unwinding her braid until he only held the tip of it. His tone menacing, he said, "From now on, you will do whatever I want."

Defiance filled her. Fia placed fisted hands at her waist. "I don't have to until you are the earl."

Theo slammed his hands into her chest, knocking her backward. She sailed through the air, panic filling her, knowing she had no control. Then she landed hard, hearing the crack as pain rocketed up her left leg, and she screamed.

Theo stood gloating at the top of the stairs. Quickly, he raced down them, bending close.

"You think you hurt now? I will hurt you more if you tell on me. I will sneak in and smother your worthless mother and stupid father."

Through the radiating pain, she shook her head. "No, please, Theo. Don't."

"Then swear you will obey me."

Fia looked up as he loomed over her, tears rolling down her cheeks. "I promise."

"Good."

Then her cousin began shouting, "Come quick! Cousin Fia fell. She's hurt."

He kept on shouting as she lay there. Servants appeared. Her parents and uncle, too. Papa lifted her, and Fia screamed, her leg hurting so much she wished she were dead.

And Cousin Theo stood off to the side.

Smiling all the while.

CHAPTER ONE

London—Spring 1811

HENRY VAUGHN, VISCOUNT North, awoke and rang for his valet. Ripley arrived soon after with hot water, first shaving Henry and then assisting him in dressing. He made his way down to the breakfast room, knowing he would find his parents there despite the ball they had hosted ending in the wee hours of the morning. Neither his father nor mother liked to lie abed, and Henry greeted them as he entered the room and went straight to the sideboard, placing eggs and ham on his plate before taking his usual seat at the table.

"My, *our* ball will be talked about throughout the Season," Mama remarked. "Thanks to the Duke of Westfield's proposal to Lady Margaret Townsend."

Henry had danced with Lady Margaret and even called upon her twice, finding her rather interesting. He wasn't sure, though, about her desire to paint others in Polite Society. Because of that, he had shied away, sending her flowers but not certain he wished to court her.

The Duke of Westfield, on the other hand, had taken the proverbial bull by the horns and made his intentions quite clear with a public declaration in front of the entire *ton* in the Strumbull ballroom last night. Henry knew the first dance was not supposed to be a waltz and had been looking about, curious as to why the musicians began playing one. When he saw Westfield take Lord Audley's place and began dancing with Lady Margaret, Henry had an idea His Grace had somehow had a hand in the change of music.

Sure enough, Henry stopped dancing with his partner—as did every other couple in the ballroom—watching an incredible scene unfold. The duke wanted to wed Lady Margaret and she obviously was having none of it. Henry couldn't hear quite everything His Grace said, but he saw the look in Lady Margaret's eyes and knew the duke was swaying her opinion.

Then Westfield had dropped to one knee and proclaimed his love for the lady. She had accepted his offer of marriage. Rising, the Duke of Westfield had embraced his new fiancée and given her a kiss the likes of which no one had ever seen in public before. It was long, passionate, and truth be told, made Henry just a bit jealous, seeing how much this man loved this woman.

Then in a grand gesture, the Duke of Westfield had swept up his betrothed and carried her from the ballroom. The sea of voices rose in gossip, which had not ceased the entire evening.

"Yes, Mama, you will be the most famous hostess of this Season, I daresay."

She looked at her husband and smiled fondly. "I do not recall any grand gestures from you on my behalf, my lord," she said.

"Shall I make one now, my dear?" the earl asked.

Mama tittered and Henry smiled, happy he had parents who genuinely loved one another. They hadn't at the start of their marriage. Theirs had been an arranged one, but over the years, they had grown very close and fallen in love. Henry was their sole child, the only disappointment in their marriage. He knew they would have liked to have had many more. Because of that, he tried to be the best son he could be, earning high marks at school and university and not playing the rogue as so many of his schoolmates did. In fact, he was at a point where he would like to settle down. Perhaps this Season would be the one he took a bride. He would not share this with his parents now, though, else Mama would be after him every single day, shoving girls making their come-outs into his path and trying to help him find a bride. Henry decided he could do so on his own, without help from anyone else.

Because of the circumstances of his parents' marriage, he also knew love wasn't necessary at the beginning. True, it would be wonderful to find a woman to love and have those feelings before their wedding, but he would simply look for someone who was kind, generous, and a lively conversationalist. It would help if she preferred the city over the country. Though he enjoyed time spent at his father's country estate, he preferred the amenities of the city. In fact, he even thought he would like to do a bit of traveling once he did take a wife. There were places he longed to see. Perhaps he could take his bride on a honeymoon and visit some of them. Of course, with the war with Bonaparte still going on, he would have to watch where they traveled. Paris would be out of the question, though Henry did wish to see it someday.

He finished breakfast and said, "I think I will go up and see Linberry now."

His mother frowned but said nothing. His father said, "He is becoming harder and harder to control. I am thinking we may have to hire additional help. Bosley is no longer able to manage him strictly on his own."

Henry excused himself and went up the stairs. His grandfather, the Duke of Linberry, had gone into a steep decline several years ago when he reached his mid-sixties. Now seventy-one, Linberry needed watching around the clock, due to what the doctors called senility. His grandfather rarely knew who his family was anymore and sat staring into space for long periods of time. He had no memory of events in recent years but sometimes would speak of things from decades ago with clarity. Henry hoped this dotage did not run in the family. His father was in excellent health. Henry hoped he had many years before succeeding Father as both earl and finally duke.

He reached the bedchamber and rapped softly on the door, knowing that loud noises sometimes startled Linberry and set him on edge.

Henry heard the lock thrown, and the door opened. Bosley opened the door and quickly ushered Henry in.

"How is he today?"

The former valet to the duke shook his head. "Today is not one of His Grace's better days," Bosley said diplomatically. "I hope seeing you, my lord, will calm His Grace some."

He stepped further into the room and saw his grandfather pacing back and forth, something he did when he was agitated. He had begun doing it so often that he was wearing a path into the Aubusson carpet.

"Good morning, Your Grace. How are you feeling today?"

His grandfather turned, his eyes wild. "Who are you?" he demanded.

"I am Henry, your grandson, Your Grace. My father is Lord Strumbull. He is your son."

"Son?" the duke scoffed. "How can I have a son? I am but twenty years of age. I should be meeting with my tutor now."

His grandfather often thought he was back at Cambridge. Those must have been happy years for him. He rarely spoke of anything beyond them and never mentioned his wife.

"Why don't we have a seat, and you can tell me what you are studying."

Henry moved to a chair, hoping Linberry would do the same. Instead, his grandfather continued his frantic pacing and ignored everyone. Bosley shrugged, standing ready in case he needed to step in.

Then the pacing ceased, and the duke moved to sit in a chair near Henry. He looked blankly at him. "Who are you?"

"I am your grandson, Your Grace," he repeated. "My name is Henry. I was named after you."

The duke snorted. "Henry is a terrible name. I don't like it at all. It couldn't be my name." He thought a moment. "A-ha! It's not. Or rather, it is—but I go by Harry. That's it."

It was at times like these that he discovered small nuggets about his grandfather.

"You do look like a Harry, Your Grace."

Linberry nodded. "I never liked the name Henry. I always went by Harry. My sister used it immediately." His face soured. "My brother was another matter."

Knowing his great-uncle's disposition, Henry did not doubt it.

"Why, I had to box his ears but good before he agreed to call me Harry." The duke sniffed. "He was always a troublemaker, that one. Couldn't keep his cock in his breeches. Spread his seed everywhere."

Yes, the duke definitely described the man Henry knew.

"What does it take to get something to eat around here?" his grandfather asked.

Bosley stepped forward. "I have breakfast for you, Your Grace. I will fetch it now."

Henry knew at times Linberry could be quite finicky about food and hoped this wouldn't be one of them.

Bosley rolled a cart in front of the duke and lifted the silver cover, revealing a breakfast of porridge and scrambled eggs. The duke could only eat soft foods now, having lost several of his teeth.

As he ate, Linberry told Henry several amusing stories about his childhood, most of them casting him in the light of hero and his brother as villain. He did have a few nice things to say about his sister. Suddenly, the duke burst into tears and looked into Henry's eyes.

"She's dead, isn't she?"

He nodded. "Yes, Your Grace. She died five years ago."

"She was a good woman," Linberry said, sadly shaking his head. "She should have had a better life."

Henry had liked his great-aunt quite a bit. She had never wed and had lived with her older brother her entire life. Her death seemed to be the catalyst which had plunged the duke into this darkness of senility, where he remembered few people or events of the present and preferred to live in the past.

His grandfather spoke at length about childhood games he played with his sister and brother before he jumped ahead again to his university years, telling a few bawdy stories which left Henry blushing.

"Do you go to university?" the old man demanded.

"I attended Cambridge as you did, Your Grace. I have finished my studies there."

His grandfather nodded sagely. "Then I hope you are enjoying your life." He held up a finger and warned, "Don't ever wed, young man. I was forced to do so and hated the woman who became my wife."

How ironic that his grandfather had an arranged marriage and despised it. Yet he had turned around and done the same thing to his own son. Fortunately, his father and mother had found love.

"I say a mistress is always best," the duke declared. "I used to juggle two or three at a time. My wife couldn't stand that. She was a dried-up old prune by the time she was twenty. She gave me two boys, and I didn't like either of them."

Linberry's face went slack again and then he asked, "Who are you?"

Henry decided to take his leave with that question and rose. "It was nice visiting with you, Your Grace."

A worried look shone in his grandfather's eyes. "You will come back tomorrow? You will visit me again?"

He nodded reassuringly. "Of course, Your Grace. I come to see you every day."

The duke seemed to lose interest and returned to picking at his food as Henry moved to the door. Bosley followed.

"Thank you for your calming influence, Lord North. Even though His Grace doesn't seem to know you anymore, you are a good influence upon him. I know this is difficult for you to see."

It was—and it wasn't. Henry had never been close to his

grandfather, who refused any affectionate names and demanded his grandson call him Linberry. He knew, however, that Bosley had been extremely close to the duke for decades, serving as his valet.

"This is most likely harder on you than me, Bosley." He studied the servant's graying hair and wrinkled face and realized just how fragile Bosley was. It would be wise for his father to hire additional help to manage Linberry and his mercurial moods.

He left his grandfather's rooms, going to the library where the newspapers awaited him. A footman brought coffee, and Henry spent the remainder of his morning perusing them. The war news seemed positive, with the government believing they had Bonaparte on the run. It was only a matter of time before the British and their allies defeated him. War seemed to be the only thing he could recall since England had been at it for so long with the Little Corporal.

The economic news was bleak, and he skipped over it, turning to the gossip columns. As expected, they were full of reports regarding the Duke of Westfield's very public marriage proposal to Lady Margaret Townsend. For a moment, Henry was a bit jealous of the pair, again, having seen the love they held for one another as they gazed at each other while Westfield carried his betrothed from the ballroom.

Finally finished with his reading, he folded the newspapers and set them aside, downing the last of his coffee. He thought he might go to his club now and went downstairs. In the foyer, he thought he might see if his father wished to join him and asked a footman at the door, "Do you know where Lord Strumbull is now?"

"I believe his lordship has gone to visit with His Grace, my lord."

Henry did not want to interrupt that visit and decided to depart alone.

Suddenly, he heard shouts from above and looked up, seeing his grandfather at the rail. To be as old as he was, Linberry agilely climbed atop the rail and stood, his arms stretched wide. Fear filled Henry, knowing within seconds his grandfather would lose his balance and fall to his death.

Shouting up, he cried, "Linberry! Get down from there!"

The duke stared down to the foyer, and his gaze met Henry's from that distance.

In that moment, he knew the man would jump before he fell.

Then the earl appeared, slowly moving toward Linberry. Henry could only catch a few words since he was at such a distance, but he knew his father begged for the duke to come down.

The duke was having none of it.

Linberry's gaze again met Henry's, and he knew his grandfather was about to leap. That there was nothing he could do to stop the action. His father, though, must have realized the same and reached out, latching on to his own father's legs to prevent him from jumping, just as the duke hurdled over the railing.

Taking his son with him.

Henry saw it unfold as if in slow motion, seeing the gleeful smile on his grandfather's face as his banyan billowed wide, while his own father's look of terror sliced through Henry's heart.

Then both men landed on the marble floor merely feet in front of him. Immediately, he rushed to them, hearing the moans of his father, who had landed on his back. Agony shone in Strumbull's eyes.

"Fetch the doctor!"

Servants appeared, scurrying about.

Henry took his father's hand, clasping it gently, his other hand stroking the earl's brow.

"Help is coming, Father," he said reassuringly, though he believed his father beyond it.

Strumbull's eyes fluttered and then closed, and Henry looked to his grandfather. He, too, had landed on his back, spread-eagle. A pool of blood seeped from beneath him, his eyes wide in death.

Henry swallowed the bile that threatened to spew from him.

With his free hand, he reached and brushed his grandfather's eyes until they were closed.

The next few hours were a blur. His mother coming out and shrieking, falling to her knees at her husband's side, weeping profusely. The doctor arriving. The duke's body being removed, and the new duke's body taken gingerly up the stairs. Henry led his mother to her bedchamber and put her to bed, a maid watching over her. Returning to his father's rooms, he asked the doctor to provide a sleeping draught.

The doctor took something from his satchel and gave it to Henry, explaining how to administer it. He left and returned to his crying mother, having her drink it and staying with her until she fell asleep.

Going again to his father's bedside, he joined the doctor, who said, "His Grace's back is broken, my lord. Other bones, as well. I have administered morphine."

"Does he feel any pain?" Henry asked anxiously.

"At this point, no." The doctor gazed at Henry in sympathy. "You must be strong, Lord North. The duke has very little time to live. I will stay and continue administering the morphine to keep him as comfortable as possible."

Dully, he nodded. "Will he regain consciousness?"

"It is possible but not likely," the physician told him.

Thus, the vigil began, with Henry sitting at the new duke's beside, his hand covering the duke's cold one.

Late that afternoon, his father's eyes opened. Immediately, Henry saw the agony in them.

"It is all right, Father. You had a fall, but the doctor is here. You will get better. It will take time."

Sadness filled Strumbull's face. "I have never lied to you, Henry. I would ask . . . for the same courtesy. Tell me, what is it?"

"Your back is broken, as is your left leg and shoulder."

The physician had determined those, and he told Henry there was no reason to try to set or stabilize them because in all likelihood, the fall had paralyzed his father.

"How long do I have?" the duke asked, his voice low and weak.

"Not long," he said, deciding honesty would be best as his throat thickened with tears.

"You . . . have been the best son . . . a father could ever wish for." The duke coughed, his face scrunching up. "Take care . . . of your mother. This will be hard on her."

With those words, the Duke of Linberry took his final breath.

Horror filled Henry.

He was now the Duke of Linberry.

CHAPTER TWO

London—Spring 1812

LADY SOPHIA SAWYER awoke in the cramped, windowless room and remembered she was back in town at her cousin's residence. Parkhurst had exiled Fia to the top floor of the servants' quarters after her parents' deaths. They had both taken ill and passed away shortly after her seventeenth birthday. Her uncle had already been gone for five years, making her cousin Theodore the heir. Theo had immediately left university and come to Parkwood, ordering everyone about before he left for London. It had been a relief to see him go and allowed Fia to mourn in peace.

Little did she know those months spent alone at Parkwood would be the last peaceful ones of her life, months where music became her solace and refuge.

Once her year of mourning ended, Theo had summoned Fia to town before the start of the Season. Fool that she was, she thought he had sent for her to outfit her with a new wardrobe and see her make her come-out. She went into their meeting knowing she would have to tolerate him for a short while, but hoped she would wed and be able to leave his household.

Instead, he sentenced her to a life where he had absolute control over her.

Fia was to always call him Parkhurst. Never Cousin Theo. She would not make her come-out as planned. Rather, she was to earn her keep by giving music lessons to the children of the *ton*. Theo asked how many instruments she had mastered and listened to her play a selection on each one before making his announcement. While Fia loved music, she had thought to wed and begin her own family, teaching her children how to play the piano or violin.

She was exiled to the attic room, which held a single bed and a trunk to store her clothing. Thankfully, she did not have to share it with another servant because the rest of the room was filled with the various instruments she played. Her violin and viola. Her flute and cello. And for a time, her harp. The harp had finally been moved to the drawing room because Parkhurst would call upon Fia to play it for his dinner guests.

Dinners which she never attended but only entertained at.

For four years now, she had given lessons to children, most often starting them on the pianoforte and if they showed any talent, moving them to the violin or flute. Fia never saw a farthing from the lessons she gave. Parkhurst had told her it was gauche for a female in Polite Society to discuss money. He was the one to accept new clients and charge whatever he saw fit, pocketing every penny of the money.

He did give her pin money, as a husband would a wife, but it was so little that she could not afford to see a modiste or milliner. Fia had learned to sew from Millie, one of the household maids who had served as Mama's lady's maid. Parkhurst emphasized that Fia must always look presentable when she entered the houses of her students and she did, thanks to buying fabrics that were neutral and sewing her gowns herself, changing the trims to update them from year to year. She also learned from Millie how to craft her own bonnets.

Fia thought if she could take the money earned from the many lessons she gave, she might be able to live on her own. She had even brought it up once to Parkhurst on one of the rare occasions she saw him. The cold look he gave her was like a slap in the face. He told her never to address the subject again.

Millie appeared now, helping Fia to dress.

"It's good to see you again, my lady. Did you enjoy your time at Lord Capwell's estate?"

She taught both of Lord and Lady Capwell's daughters, girls who were nine and ten years of age and the most talented students she had spent time with. Because the Capwells thought their daughters held promise, they had asked Fia at the end of last Season if she might return to the country with them and tutor the girls until the next spring when the Season began. She had told them she must check with her cousin, Lord Parkhurst. Lord Capwell had said he would handle the matter.

The next thing Fia knew, she was packing to go Oxfordshire.

She had relished the months spent with the Capwells in the country. Parkhurst never went to Parkwood, preferring his steward manage the estate in his absence. That meant Fia, too, stayed in town year-round. To be able to take long walks in the country, breathing in its fresh air, had been the most she had enjoyed herself since her parents' passing. She had remained in Oxfordshire throughout all the holidays, accompanying the family back to town and arriving only yesterday.

It had been hard to part from Maisie and Daisy, but Lady Capwell had assured her daughters that they would continue their lessons with Fia. She only wished she could have remained in their household instead of returning to her cousin's residence.

"My lady?"

She realized she had been woolgathering and apologized to Millie. "Yes, my time in the country was most enjoyable. Maisie and Daisy both show true promise. It is unusual seeing ones so young with their talent."

"You are also talented when it comes to music, my lady," Millie said. "Why, I remember all the times hearing you practice when we were at Parkwood. And you would bring your violin or cello to her ladyship's rooms and play for her to soothe her." The servant grew misty-eyed.

Fia took Millie's hand and squeezed it. "I know you miss Mama. I do, too."

"His lordship told me when he weds that I can serve as a lady's maid again to the countess," the older woman revealed. "I think he's ready to look for a wife this Season."

She didn't really care what her cousin did. Any woman Parkhurst wed would probably be just as selfish as he was. Besides, her cousin's marriage would have nothing to do with her. Her only involvement, if any, would be to play for his guests at his wedding breakfast.

Millie excused herself, needing to get back to her duties. Fia brushed her hair and pinned it up, leaving her room to head down to the kitchens for breakfast.

When she arrived, the housekeeper said, "Lord Parkhurst wishes for you to breakfast with him, my lady."

"I see," she said guardedly.

Parkhurst must want something. Fia was never allowed to dine with him, having her breakfast and tea with the servants and eating from a dinner tray brought to her room at night.

She made her way to the breakfast room and steeled herself before entering, determined not to let her cousin chip away at any confidence she had gained while outside his presence during the autumn and winter months.

"Good morning, my lord," Fia said formally, moving toward the table.

A footman seated her as another brought her a cup of tea. A third brought a plate to her, removing its silver cover after he set it before her.

She began buttering her toast points, ignoring Parkhurst. If he wanted to speak with her, he would need to initiate the conversation.

She didn't have to wait long. He came directly to the point.

"I received a note from Lord and Lady Capwell. They are quite pleased with the progress their daughters made during your months with them. I have already set up twice weekly lessons with both girls."

He paused, sipping his coffee. "Now that you have returned to town, I will begin booking other lessons for you to give. There are several who wish for you to start up lessons with their children again. I am certain new ones will also want to come onboard. I will provide you with a schedule."

Fia knew she had no say in the matter. Parkhurst would schedule multiple lessons six days a week, giving her little free time to do her own practicing. She decided to address that now.

"In the past, you have had me giving lessons six days a week. I wish to cut it to five."

He scowled at her, not used to her speaking up. "That is not for you to manage."

"I need a day of my own to practice, Parkhurst. I must keep my skills fresh. Many times, parents ask to hear me play before they agree to allowing their children to study with me. If I misplay, they will think me untalented. Word will spread—and that could lead in a drop of people engaging my services. It would also give me not only time to practice on my various instruments, but I could also plan my lessons for my pupils with greater care. Surely, you can understand this."

She paused and added, "It would also make my playing for your guests more enjoyable. I would never wish to embarrass you by stumbling through a piece. Practice is important to a musician. We must never slack off or our playing will suffer the consequences."

She saw him considering her words before he grumbled, "It would mean less students."

"Then charge more," she told him. "You say that I am in demand. Have people pay what I am worth."

He stroked his chin, which was already doubled. Fia thought he had put on another stone since she had last seen him. Of course, he would not have trouble securing a bride. He was an earl. A wealthy one, at that. Some doting mama in the *ton* would find Parkhurst a suitable husband for her daughter, despite his ill-humor and girth.

"All right. You may have Saturday as your day for practicing and planning your lessons." He sipped his coffee again and added, "Lady Capwell asked for you to begin lessons this afternoon. She does not wish for either of her daughters to lose a step. You should arrive at one o'clock."

"Yes, she had mentioned that to me in the carriage yesterday."

"Lord Capwell compensated you well for your time at his estate," Parkhurst said. "You must keep him happy."

Fia wanted to point out that she had not been compensated at all, and that every bit had gone into her cousin's pockets. Still, she kept silent, not wishing to bait him and grateful that he had agreed to her sojourn with the Capwells in Oxfordshire.

"Then I will go to the Capwells' home this afternoon and begin again with the girls' lessons," she said lightly. "You will provide me the new schedule of lessons as clients are booked?"

"My secretary will. I will pass along to him which members of Polite Society wish to engage your services. You can meet with Bibby early tomorrow morning. As more return to town during the next two weeks before the Season begins, Bibby will add to your diary."

She liked Mr. Bibby, who worked with her on scheduling her pupils. Bibby was most efficient and tried to make certain lessons were given with adequate traveling time between houses. He also grouped pupils from the same area together so Fia would not have to travel far to each lesson on a daily basis.

Taking a bite of her eggs, Fia paused to savor sitting in the breakfast room again. She remembered dining here with her parents. A wave of sadness engulfed her.

"You are dismissed," Parkhurst said. "We have concluded our business."

"I have not eaten all my breakfast," she protested.

"Take it with you and finish elsewhere," he said airily, opening the newspaper that sat next to his plate.

Her cheeks grew hot as she rose, picking up her plate and saucer. A footman rushed to help her.

"I can take it myself. Thank you," she told him, trying to maintain her dignity as she saw pity in his eyes.

Another footman opened the closed door, and Fia moved toward the kitchens, her appetite now gone. She handed the plate and saucer to a scullery maid and went up the servants' staircase to her room. It was always either too cold or stifling hot. Today was a cold day even though it was the beginning of April. Soon, the days would grow warm and the heat would become unbearable.

For now, though, she had the morning to herself. She did not mind beginning the Capwell girls' lessons so soon. She knew Lady Capwell would look in near the end, which she looked forward to. The countess treated Fia with respect, and a friendship of sorts had formed between them during Fia's time in Oxfordshire.

She decided to go for a walk in Hyde Park. After spending several days in the carriage traveling back to London, she was ready to stretch her legs a bit. Returning to her room, she donned her bonnet and slipped her reticule onto her arm before heading down the stairs and leaving the house.

As she walked to the park, she thought of how she did have small bits of freedom. Other young, unmarried ladies would have required a chaperone to take a walk in the park. Fia came and went as she pleased without having to worry about that. When Parkhurst had not wanted to provide funds for her to hire hansom cabs to travel to each of her lessons, she had demanded he supply her with some kind of transportation. She had instruments she brought to different lessons and sheet music, as well, and she couldn't very well carry all that each day. He had relented, allowing her the use of a horse from his stables and a small cart. Again, she took no chaperone with her when she drove it from residence to residence and lesson to lesson.

Fia cherished these small things since so much of her life and position had been taken from her by Parkhurst. She doubted she would ever have the opportunity to wed or have children of her own because she was so busy giving music lessons. At least her work allowed her to be around children, whom she adored.

Reaching the gates of Hyde Park, she entered it and walked briskly, enjoying the movement and freedom of being on her own. She came upon Rotten Row, where so many of the *ton* rode, and saw but a few horses there. Not everyone had returned to town just yet, which might account for the sparseness of riders.

Fia did stop and admire two of the riders, one on a chestnut horse that must be sixteen hands, the other riding a black which might be seventeen hands. Both men rode with great skill, a grace about them and the movement of their horses. They flew by her, racing against one another. She only got a good look at the rider on the chestnut horse since he was closer to her. He was quite handsome, with brown hair and broad shoulders.

She hurried along, recalling how she had enjoyed riding with Papa. She hadn't been atop a horse in years and wondered if she even remembered how to ride.

Her left knee began troubling her, and she realized she had walked too fast after many days of no exercise at all. She had broken both the knee and lower left leg eighteen years ago.

When Theo had pushed her down the stairs.

No, Parkhurst. She mustn't forget to call him that, even in her thoughts. He had punished her the only time she had referred to him as Theo, sending her to her room before supper one night. Fia had been locked in her bedchamber without food or water for three days.

She had never made that mistake again.

It worried her that she might have grown soft, having spent so many months in Oxfordshire, away from Parkhurst. She must remain on her toes at all times. She hardly saw him as it was so any time she spent in his company meant she must always be on her guard.

Reversing direction, Fia crossed paths with the two riders again, glancing up and acknowledging them. They walked their horses this time, and she took in their appearances quickly. The man riding the black sat very tall in the saddle. He had coal-black hair and gray eyes. The other rider's brown hair shone in the sunlight. His warm, brown eyes regarded her with interest.

Fia moved on, leaving the park and returning home. She went to the kitchens and got a cup of tea and a biscuit from Cook, sitting in a corner and eating it before returning upstairs to her room. Once there, she took out her viola and played for a good hour before switching to her cello and finally her flute. Her fingers finally tired, she changed her gown and touched up her hair before leaving for the Capwells' townhouse.

Lord and Lady Capwell only lived two blocks away, and she walked to their townhouse, arriving only a few minutes later. No cart was necessary since both girls had their own instruments. A footman showed her to the drawing room, where only Maisie and Daisy were present.

"Lady Fia!" they cried in unison, coming to give her a hug.

"We missed you," Daisy told her.

"We've been practicing," Maisie added. "The Bach."

"Then why don't you play it for me? Or better yet, I shall accompany you."

Moving to the piano, Fia took a seat on the bench. "Invention Number Eight?" she confirmed, her hands hovering over the keys.

"In F Major," Maisie said, smiling brightly as she picked up her viola.

Daisy lifted her violin and bow, readying herself.

Fia counted and then they began playing together, continuing to do so until they finished. Surprisingly, she heard applause and glanced over her shoulder.

Lady Capwell had entered the room, as well as her mother-in-law, the Dowager Countess of Capwell, who had also been present during Fia's stay in the country. With them was another woman she did not know. She was elderly and yet held herself regally. Fia thought in her day, the woman must have been a great beauty.

"Come, girls," Lady Capwell said. "I want you to meet your grandmother's friend, the Dowager Duchess of Westfield."

CHAPTER THREE

Fia watched as Maisie and Daisy set down their instruments and moved toward the guest. Lady Capwell supervised the introductions, looking pleased at the curtseys dropped by her daughters.

Then the countess indicated for Fia to join them. She rose from the bench, her heart racing. She had never met a dowager duchess before, and this one looked increasingly intimidating as Fia approached her.

"Your Grace, this is Lady Sophia Sawyer," Lady Capwell shared. "She teaches music to my girls."

The dowager duchess studied Fia with interest. Turning to her friend, she said, "This is the one who traveled to the country with you?"

"Yes, Your Grace," the dowager countess confirmed. "Lady Sophia spent countless hours with my granddaughters."

The dowager duchess turned her gaze back to Fia. "What little I heard just then was lovely. Might you and the girls play something else for us?"

Fia's cheeks warmed. "We would be happy to, Your Grace."

She motioned for the girls to return to their instruments, and they briefly discussed what to play for the dowager duchess. They settled on Mozart and played the piece for their audience of three. Pride filled her as the last note sounded. The girls had done an excellent job on the composition.

"Brava!" cried the dowager duchess, causing the girls to giggle as the other two women applauded politely.

Fia nodded to Maisie and Daisy and both girls curtseyed in recognition of the praise.

"Why don't you go to the schoolroom now, my sweets?" Lady Capwell said. "Your governess is waiting."

"When are you coming next?" Maisie asked Fia.

"I will discuss our schedule with your mother," she told the eager pupil.

The girls placed their instruments in their cases and told the visitor goodbye. Fia moved toward the three seated women.

"Lady Capwell, I believe you have arranged with my cousin when lessons are to be held."

They briefly discussed the days and times, confirming Fia's next visit. "Then I will be off. It was good to meet you, Your Grace."

"Stay a bit, Lady Sophia," the dowager duchess said. "I wish to know a bit about you."

She hesitated, looking at Lady Capwell, who nodded subtly.

"Of course, Your Grace," she replied, taking a seat. It was rare she had an opportunity to sit with ladies of the *ton*, and she was out of practice in conversation, which led her to what most would have thought a faux pas.

"Are you the same dowager duchess who had her portrait painted by Lady Margaret Townsend? I read about it in the newspapers."

The dowager duchess smiled. "The very one. And Lady Margaret is now my grandson's wife. I think you should meet her."

"Meet a duchess?" Fia squeaked.

"Well, you have met me. That wasn't so bad, was it, my lady?"

Her cheeks burned. "No, Your Grace. It has been a pleasure meeting you."

"Tell me about yourself. I find it highly unusual, a lady of

Polite Society giving musical lessons to others. I do not recall seeing you at any events of the Season."

Fia bit her lip, knowing she danced a fine line now. "I do not attend the Season, Your Grace. Before I was to make my come-out, both my parents passed away. After my time of mourning, I made myself useful to my cousin, Lord Parkhurst, who inherited my father's title. I began giving lessons to children. I have always enjoyed music and learned to play the pianoforte and violin when I was a child. Eventually, I picked up other instruments and taught myself how to play them, as well."

"How interesting," the dowager duchess mused. "What does the rest of your family think of you ignoring social commitments in order to teach?"

"I must give lessons," Fia said and then realized she had revealed too much. "That is, I have the opportunity to teach young people how to play," she corrected.

"Lady Fia has done a marvelous job with my girls," Lady Capwell interjected.

Gratitude filled her at the countess coming to her aid. "The pleasure of teaching pupils such as Lady Maisie and Lady Daisy far outweighs my participating in *ton* events. Marriage isn't for everyone, Your Grace."

"I see," the dowager duchess said. "What instruments do you play—or teach others to play?"

This was familiar territory, and Fia relaxed. "I always start pupils on the pianoforte. It is the best instrument to learn from. If I see promise, I move a student to the violin. From there, students might take up the viola, flute, or cello."

"Lady Fia also plays the harp," the dowager countess noted.

"Oh, yes," seconded Lady Capwell. "I had not mentioned it to you, my lady, but we are hosting the opening ball this Season. I was hoping that I might persuade you to play the harp at it."

A rush of excitement spread through her. She had always longed to play at a ball, be it her harp alone or playing alongside other musicians. If she could do so one time, the possibility of playing on a regular basis might occur.

But would Parkhurst allow such a thing?

She swallowed. "I would have to discuss this with my cousin, my lady. Parkhurst would have to give his permission for me to do so."

Lady Capwell waved her hand. "Oh, I will have Capwell dash off a note to Lord Parkhurst. He can be quite convincing, you know."

"Yes, it was his efforts which allowed me to accompany you to Oxfordshire." Hope filled her. "Would you please have Lord Capwell do so, my lady? I would be most eager to play my harp—and even other instruments with the musicians you hire for the ball."

"I will do so when he returns from his club," promised the countess.

"In the meantime, I wish for you to accompany me home, my lady," the dowager duchess said. "We can have tea. You can meet the Duchess of Westfield."

"Now?"

The duchess gave her a haughty look. "Yes, now, Lady Sophia. Or do you have other lessons to teach this afternoon?"

"No, Your Grace," she said, mortification filling her.

Why did this woman wish for her to meet the Duchess of Westfield?

"Very well." The dowager duchess kissed the dowager countess' cheek. "It was good to see you, my dear." She smiled at Lady Capwell. "I enjoyed meeting your girls and hearing them play."

Rising, the dowager duchess said, "Come along, Lady Sophia."

Fia gathered her sheet music and said goodbye to the other two women, following the Dowager Duchess of Westfield from the room. They descended the stairs together, no conversation between them. She wondered if Parkhurst would miss her if she did not return home soon and decided he wouldn't. Besides, it would be difficult to pass up such an opportunity. To be in the company of not one—but two—duchesses. To share a bit of conversation with adults. She spent all of her time either with children or alone, and had days where she craved the company of others.

They left the townhouse and a gleaming carriage sat waiting for them.

"It is lovely," Fia said in wonder. "From the horses to the carriage itself. I have never ridden in anything so grand."

The dowager duchess smiled. "I do love a good carriage and matching horses. This is for my own personal use. My grandson's carriage is far superior to this one."

A footman opened the door and aided the dowager duchess and then helped Fia enter the carriage. She sat opposite the older woman.

"We are alone now, my dear. Be truthful with me. Are you being forced to give music lessons?"

Fia winced at the direct question. "I enjoy music and children, Your Grace," she responded carefully. "Matching the two together is a wonderful way for me to spend my time."

The dowager duchess frowned. "You did not answer my question, Lady Sophia. Or may I call you Fia as the girls did?"

"Please do so, Your Grace. My given name is Sophia, but my parents called me Fia from the cradle."

The dowager duchess' brows arched, waiting.

She interlaced her fingers, gripping them in her lap. "I have never spoken of such things, Your Grace, but I will simply because you asked me to do so." Swallowing, she said, "My parents died when I was seventeen. I grieved greatly for them. I was close to both. I had no siblings, and my cousin inherited my father's title and lands."

"Parkhurst."

"Yes, Lord Parkhurst. I thought . . . well, shall we say that Parkhurst and I did not get on well as children. He came to live with us during school holidays since he would one day be my father's heir."

"He was cruel to you," stated the dowager duchess.

"How did you guess?"

The old woman shrugged. "Continue."

"I thought I would have my come-out Season and find a husband. I knew my cousin did not want my presence in his household, as he never cared for me. Instead, he refused to find a sponsor for me. I never made my come-out."

"He put you to work," the dowager duchess said flatly.

Fia nodded, shame filling her.

"He uses your talent." The woman reached over and took Fia's hand. "You should find your own place, Lady Fia. Use your earnings from the lessons you give and break from this cousin of yours. I know something of Parkhurst. He is a horrible man. Disliked by many. You would do well to be away from his influence."

She burst into tears. Pulling her hand from that of the dowager duchess, Fia opened her reticule and found a handkerchief. She mopped her eyes and cheeks.

Sighing, she said, "I cannot do that, Your Grace."

The dowager duchess frowned. "You feel a loyalty to a man—a blood relative—who refused to do right by you and introduce you into Polite Society?"

"Truth be told, I despise Parkhurst, Your Grace. But I have no funds of my own. You see, the earl makes all the arrangements as far as the lessons go. He agrees as to which children I will teach and then collects whatever payments their parents make." She paused. "Frankly, I have no idea how much he charges for my time. I have no funds of my own, so it would be impossible for me to strike out on my own. Besides, I am certain if I did, Polite Society would look down upon me. A woman, living alone, earning a living? I would most likely lose what clients I do have, and then I would be out on the streets."

She shook her head. "No, I cannot cross Parkhurst. I simply won't do it."

The dowager duchess did not say anything the rest of the

short trip. She was helped from the carriage and looked into the vehicle.

"I give you a choice now, Lady Fia. Come in and have tea with me and the duchess—or I will instruct my coachman to return you to Lord Parkhurst's townhouse. What will you choose?"

Torn, Fia's thoughts were in a jumble. If she went inside, she feared what might happen if this dowager duchess shared any of Fia's story. Parkhurst would be furious at any gossip involving him. Yet she was so hungry for companionship. Just to speak to two women for an hour over a leisurely tea was so tempting.

Determination filled her. She would control the conversation. She did not have to share anything further. She could politely sip her tea and talk about the weather before she made her way home.

"I will come to tea, Your Grace."

The Dowager Duchess of Westfield smiled. "That is the spirit, my lady."

The footman handed Fia down, and the dowager duchess slipped her hand through the crook of Fia's arm. She couldn't recall the last time she had been touched by someone, other than Millie helping her dress. The contact comforted her, and she blinked away the sudden tears that sprang to her eyes.

They entered the townhouse, and the dowager duchess asked, "Where is Her Grace?"

The butler said, "She has finished painting for the day, Your Grace, and has gone to the drawing room for tea." He smiled. "I believe she has Lady Lenora with her."

"Excellent, Hampton. Please let Cook know we have a guest for tea this afternoon. Lady Sophia Sawyer is joining us."

"At once, Your Grace."

The dowager duchess led Fia up the stairs. "Tea won't be for another half hour or so. That is plenty of time for Cook to prepare. Oh, I do hope lemon cakes will be a part of it. You simply must have one. If there are none on the tea tray today, then you must come back another time to sample them."

Fia didn't say what was on her mind. That there would be no other teatimes with the dowager duchess. She rarely ate a proper tea because she usually was giving lessons during teatime.

They entered a drawing room with elegant furniture, rich paintings, and plush carpeting. She spied the duchess, a stunning redhead, who held a babe in her arms. The duchess caught sight of them and smiled.

"Who have you brought for tea today, Gran?" As they approached, she added, "I am sorry I cannot rise to greet you properly." She smiled down at the sleeping infant. "This is Lenora. We call her Norrie. She was born eight weeks ago and already has her papa and me wound about her smallest finger."

Fia dipped into a low curtsey as the dowager duchess said, "This is Lady Sophia Sawyer, Margaret. Fia to her friends—and I am hoping you and I will become that to her."

As she rose, Fia felt the blush stain her cheeks. "Her Grace is too kind, Your Grace."

"Please sit, Lady Fia. Tell me how you met Gran."

She placed her sheet music and reticule onto a nearby table and settled into a chair, as did the dowager duchess, and said, "I was giving a music lesson to the daughters of Lord and Lady Capwell when Her Grace arrived with Lord Capwell's mother. Her Grace was kind enough to insist we play for her."

"The girls were quite good for ones so young," the dowager duchess stated. "Lady Fia accompanied them on the pianoforte as they played their stringed instruments."

"Lady Maisie was on the viola, while Lady Daisy played the violin," she supplied. "Both girls have talent. I traveled with Lord and Lady Capwell after the end of last Season and spent the autumn and winter tutoring their children with daily music lessons. They improved mightily in such a short time."

The Duchess of Westfield's smile was genuine, lighting her face. "How remarkable! A lady of the *ton* who teaches music to others. I hope one day to teach Norrie—and any other children we have—to paint. I had not thought to give art lessons, though." She bent and kissed her daughter's forehead. "I think besides art that you will need to have music in your life, my little love. Perhaps Lady Fia will be able to teach you the pianoforte."

"I would be happy to do so, Your Grace," she replied.

"I took a little time away from my painting once Norrie was born," the duchess confided. "I only started up again a week ago."

"Margaret has sat with the babe in her lap as she painted," the dowager duchess said, smiling indulgently at the pair. "I thought the two of you had the arts in common and wished for you to meet. Lady Fia has agreed to stay for tea."

"Then we will have two guests," the duchess said. "Daniel ran into Lord North—I mean, the Duke of Linberry—this morning. He asked His Grace to tea this afternoon."

Two duchesses and two dukes? This was too much.

Fia shot to her feet. "I do not mean to intrude, Your Grace. I should be going anyway. My cousin will be expecting me."

"Sit down," commanded the dowager duchess sharply. "You heard me."

She sank into the chair again. "Yes, Your Grace."

"Lord Parkhurst will not be looking for you, my lady. We both know that."

A single tear trickled down Fia's cheek. "No, I suppose not."

The Duchess of Westfield reached and took Fia's hand. "Talk to me, my lady."

"Tell her what you told me," the dowager duchess urged, her tone soft now.

"That I am a prisoner in my own home?" Fia asked bitterly. "That I have not a farthing to my name?'

The duchess squeezed Fia's hand. "Tell us whatever you wish."

"It won't make any difference," she said stubbornly.

"It may not," agreed the duchess. "But you will feel better for getting it out."

And so Fia repeated to this duchess what she had told the

dowager duchess in the carriage. How she had been an adored only child who had a talent for music. How the deaths of her parents had led to her cousin inheriting the title. How Parkhurst had told her to give up on her foolish dreams of having a Season and marrying and having a family of her own.

"I give music lessons to children of Polite Society," she concluded. "My cousin arranges all of this. I have no say in which pupils I take on. He—or rather, his secretary—sets my schedule and collects the fees paid. I am given only a few pounds a year. I have learned to sew my own clothes and make my own hats so that I am presentable enough to call on my students in their homes. I will never escape Parkhurst, though. He has a hold on me which he will never relinquish."

Fia turned to the dowager duchess. "Are you satisfied now, Your Grace? I have told my humiliating story to the both of you. I have no family who has intervened. No friends I can take refuge with. I am not certain why you have forced this from me."

Tears of anger now streamed down her face. Tears of frustration because she had no control over her life and could see no way out of her unusual circumstances.

"At least Parkhurst did not kick me from my home. I do have a roof over my head and food to eat."

The duchess handed the babe to the older woman and took Fia's hands, pulling her to her feet.

"You and I have more in common than you realize, Fia. I was able to move out and live on my own, thanks to the fees I collected from the portraits I painted. Art was my world. I never thought to wed, though I did wish for children. You, too, are talented in the arts. The musical arts. You are already earning far more than I did, only you are not seeing those profits.

"I think it is time you do receive the monies from those who have hired you to teach their children. I want to help you do this. Will you allow Gran and me to help you? The support of two duchesses can be a powerful thing."

Fia thought of the many years still ahead of her, years she

would be dependent upon Parkhurst. Years she would be beholden to him for allowing her to remain under his roof. What if she could break away and live on her own?

"Yes," she said fervently. "Please . . . help me escape and live my own life."

The Duchess of Westfield smiled. "We will be honored to do so, Fia. Please, call me Margaret. I think the first step should be that you move in here."

CHAPTER FOUR

HENRY AWOKE EARLY, having gotten very little sleep the previous night. He didn't think he had a decent night of sleep since his father had perished in the violent fall a year ago.

He had to assume so much, so fast. With both the death of his father and grandfather on the same day, Henry was elevated from Viscount North to the Duke of Linberry. He had grieved deeply, missing his father terribly, a man who had been Henry's closest friend. Mama had been flattened by her grief, and Henry had thought it best for them to return to the country and remain there to mourn, missing the bulk of the Season.

He had spent the past year learning all the responsibilities that came with his ducal title. Of course, he had visited Linfield but had never lived there. Now, he was responsible for his country seat, as well as his father's property of Brookwood and three other ducal estates scattered throughout England. He had buried himself in the ledgers of each of these estates, traveling from one to the other, getting to know the stewards who managed them and the tenants who lived upon the lands. He had hoped to take his mother with him, but she fell into a deep melancholy and begged to be left behind. When he finally did return to Linfield, he found she had left for his childhood home. Henry had gone there, and she told him she felt closer to her dead husband being at Brookwood. They had buried his father in the village churchyard, and she said she went daily to his gravesite.

He insisted she return to Linfield with him so that they eventually spent the Christmas holidays together, quietly, on their own. Mama had gone back to Brookwood after that, while Henry had remained at Linfield, taking up the mantle of his responsibilities. He now had a clear understanding of how his estates ran and had spent a great deal of time out on the land, getting to know the farmers and their needs. He did write to his mother, telling her that he would call for her come the spring. He let her know they would return to town for the Season in early April.

When he had reached Brookwood, Mama balked at accompanying him. She said nothing brought her joy anymore, while he told her it was wrong to wallow in such grief and that Papa would not have wanted that for her.

She told Henry if she went to town, she would be miserable—and she had been the three days they had now spent in London. He needed to find a doctor who could address her tremendous grief and help her push past the melancholy which consumed her.

He also needed to take a bride.

Having been an only son, Henry knew the importance of providing an heir. How quickly life could change. He would go into this Season aware of the need to wed and get his heir as soon as possible. Perhaps once he married, Mama would take to his wife and be happy when grandchildren came along. She had always wanted more children of her own. Hopefully, Henry could give her as many grandchildren as she wished for.

He decided to go riding in Rotten Row. It was still early and riding always brought him solace. He dressed on his own without the aid of his valet and skipped his morning shave, which he could have upon his return. In the past, Mama would have chided him for doing so, but she rarely rose before noon and even more rarely left her rooms. Henry made a point of going to them to visit her, much as he had done with his grandfather when the duke's senility had begun.

He cut through the kitchens, nodding to Cook, and went out the back door to the stables. A groom saddled Artemis for him, and Henry swung into the saddle. He clicked his tongue, and the horse took off at an easy gait.

Minutes later, he reached Hyde Park and made his way toward Rotten Row. He saw a couple of early morning riders, nodding to them but keeping to his path. He gave Artemis his head and raced down the row, his mind a blank as he pushed aside his worries for a few minutes.

When he reached the end of the row, none other than the Duke of Westfield awaited him, sitting atop a beautiful, large black. The last time he had seen Westfield, the duke had been carrying Lady Margaret in his arms, the couple newly betrothed. Henry almost choked on the emotion that gathered in his throat, remembering talk of the duke's betrothal being the last conversation he'd had with his parents before his father plunged to his death.

"Good morning, Lord North," the duke said in friendly fashion.

Henry supposed Westfield had not remained in London for the Season, marrying and taking his bride home to the country with him. He did not know of Henry's status.

"It is Linberry now, Your Grace," he said brusquely.

Westfield's brows arched. "Is that so? Then I am very sorry, Linberry. That must mean not only your grandfather, but your father has passed, too. I was not aware of that fact. I left town a couple of days after attending the lovely ball your parents hosted. I am not one to keep up with news of the *ton*."

"I understand, Your Grace. Good day."

Henry turned Artemis and Westfield called out, "Would you care to race a bit?"

"I recall from school that you are quite competitive."

Westfield looked puzzled. "We knew one another at school?"

Henry finally smiled. "I knew you, Your Grace. Every boy at school knew you. I believe I was a good six or seven years behind you. I think all boys in my form wanted to be you."

The duke grinned. "Flattery will get you nowhere, Linberry. If you think I am feeling sorry for you and would allow you to win, you are sadly mistaken. Now, shall we race or not?"

He nodded.

Both men immediately urged on their horses, and the world became a blur as they raced down the entire length of Rotten Row. Henry nudged out Westfield by less than a nose. He pulled up on his reins and slowed Artemis to a walk.

They each turned their horses and began walking them up the row.

Westfield said, "That is some horse you have there, Linberry."

"Artemis loves to race. Thank you for issuing the challenge, Westfield. I hope it was not a pity win."

The duke arched one eyebrow. "Never. How long have you been in town?"

"Just a couple of days. I returned with my mother. She has not handled my father's death well. I am trying to find a doctor who can help her overcome the melancholy which has descended upon her. I hoped if I brought her back for the Season, she could be around friends and try to begin to live again. Now, I am having doubts as to the wisdom of that."

"Bring Lady Strumbull to tea this afternoon," Westfield suggested. "I know Margaret would enjoy seeing you. You were one of the few men who made a favorable impression upon her last Season. If I had not literally swept her off her feet, you might have had a decent chance with her."

"That is kind of you to say, Your Grace. Perhaps I could rouse Mama and she would be interested in tea with you and the duchess. Thank you for the invitation."

Henry glanced to his left and saw a woman walking toward them along the path. She was uncommonly pretty, with golden blond hair and delicate features. As they reached her, he was drawn in by her blue eyes. She might be an eligible young lady.

He didn't really care whom he wed anymore. He had decided love was the last thing he wished for in his life. True, his parents had enjoyed a long and loving relationship, but seeing the horrendous grief his mother had at losing the love of her life made Henry wary of ever falling in love. He did not want to suffer as he had seen Mama do. Better to wed a woman and keep his distance from her.

The two men reached the end of Rotten Row and the Duke of Westfield said, "Until teatime, Your Grace."

Henry nodded. "Until teatime," he agreed.

He returned home and breakfasted alone. Once done, he informed his valet he wanted a bath. It would not do to show up at the Duke and Duchess of Westfield's residence this afternoon still smelling of horse and stale sweat. His valet bathed and shaved him and after Henry dressed, he went to his study to await the doctor who was coming.

Half an hour later, Dr. Carson was shown in. Henry wished to speak to the physician before Dr. Carson saw his mother.

"It is good to see you again, Your Grace," Dr. Carson said. "Your note said that Her Grace is still ailing. Please tell me about her condition."

Henry launched into a quick explanation of how Mama had never rallied after her husband's death, falling deeper and deeper into melancholy.

"There are a few things we can try, Your Grace," the doctor said. "Bleeding her would be one."

"No. Our village doctor tried that. It only left her weak and lethargic. If I thought it would work, I would have you continue the process, but I have seen it do no good."

"What about laudanum?" the physician asked. "I know I prescribed it to her in those early days after His Grace's death."

Again, Henry shook his head. "We tried that for a few weeks after we arrived in the country. It left her confused and sleepy," he shared. "She has always been a vibrant, alert woman, Doctor. I did not like what it did to her."

The physician gazed upon him with sympathy. "She may never again be the woman you once knew, Your Grace. I know Her Grace was quite close to her husband."

"I do not expect her to be exactly as she was before, Dr. Carson. I merely want her to exhibit at least some will to live." He frowned and added, "There have been times I have been afraid that she might take her own life."

There. He had admitted it. Voiced his greatest fear.

"I see. If bleeding and laudanum are not effective then, Your Grace, I am not certain how to advise you. If Her Grace is not interested in living, then you must give her a reason *to* live. She needs to become involved in something or with something. Grandchildren would certainly help. Have you considered marriage?"

"I plan to do so by the end of this new Season," he confirmed. "I, too, believe grandchildren would give Mama a new lease on life. In the meantime, would you at least see her?"

"Of course, Your Grace. I will go to her now."

Henry took the physician up to Mama's rooms and saw how she seemed to possess no energy. Left to her own devices, she might not have even dressed or combed her hair. At least she had a wonderful lady's maid who had been with her many years and took excellent care of her mistress.

After a short visit, Henry accompanied Dr. Carson into the hallway.

"Physically, she is in decent health. Mentally and emotionally? She is in a bad way, Your Grace. The sooner you can wed and produce those children, the better chance you have of bringing her back."

Dr. Carson hesitated and then added, "I am afraid if that doesn't help her recover, you might have to institutionalize her."

"What? No, I will never have her put away. Never."

Henry signaled a footman and asked that the physician be shown out. He then returned to his mother.

"Mama, we have been invited to tea with the Duke and

Duchess of Westfield this afternoon," he said brightly, hoping that might rouse her.

She did not bother to meet his eyes. "I do not feel like socializing over tea. Pasting on a smile and chatting with people I do not know, Linberry, is not something I wish to do."

"Well, that is the point of tea, Mama. We can get to know them. Remember how the duke so gallantly proposed to Lady Margaret at the ball you and Papa hosted?"

Henry thought the memory of that night might stir Mama, but it seemed the mention of his father only made her grow more agitated.

"Go without me, Linberry," she said. "I do not wish to keep you from your friends."

"Mama, you must rouse yourself," he told her. "The Season will be starting soon. You need to see your friends again. Have some new gowns made up."

"If you say so," she said dully, resignation in her voice. "For now, though, I wish to be left alone."

He took his leave, sadness filling him. Frustration, too, built within him. It would take time to find a woman and plant his seed in her belly. At least a year before a child might arrive. What was he to do with Mama between now and then? Even worse, what if even a grandchild did not stir her?

No, he had to find something now that would help occupy her time and bring her back to the land of the living. He would ask the Duchess of Westfield for help. She had impressed him with her intelligence. Surely, she would have an idea how to help his mother.

Henry went and buried himself in work until it was time to leave for tea. He summoned his butler and asked that the carriage be brought around, then gave his coachman instructions where to take him. They arrived at the Duke of Westfield's townhouse, and Henry was greeted by a butler who took him not to the drawing room but the duke's study.

Westfield put aside what he was working on and said, "Sit,

Linberry. You look as if you could use whisky instead of tea."

"I would hate to go to your duchess with spirits on my breath, Your Grace."

"I thought you were bringing Lady Strumbull with you this afternoon."

"Actually, she is Her Grace. And I tried to get her here and failed. Dr. Carson came and examined her today. Mama is generally in good health, but her overwhelming grief at my father's death has her in a bad way. Carson recommended what our village doctor had—bleeding her or dosing her with laudanum. Neither have been effective this past year. He did suggest that she find something that might interest her. If her interest is sparked, then she might have a reason to live."

"If you do not mind, we can discuss this at tea. My grandmother and wife are my most trusted confidantes and two of the wisest people I know."

"I will admit I am desperate, Westfield. Yes, you may share with them my mother's state. Hopefully, they will have sage advice for me."

The duke rose. "Then come along, Linberry. We'll get a good tea in you."

They ventured upstairs to the drawing room and upon entering it, Henry saw not only the duchess and dowager duchess, but also a third woman present. As they approached, he recognized her.

She was the woman he had spotted this morning while riding in Rotten Row.

CHAPTER FIVE

"WHAT?" FIA EXCLAIMED. "You just met me, Your Grace. I could never impose... Parkhurst would never allow..." Her voice trailed off.

"Margaret," the duchess reminded. "And you will be Fia to us." She looked up. "Ah, darling. There you are. And Your Grace. How good of you to come to tea this afternoon."

The duchess rose, as did the dowager duchess. Fia realized she was the only one sitting and leaped to her feet. When she did, she recognized the rider from Hyde Park this morning.

He was probably a foot taller than she was, with medium brown hair and brown eyes the shade of melted chocolate. His athletic frame was shown to perfection, his long legs encased in tight, fawn breeches, and his impeccably tailored coat displaying broad shoulders.

The other man smiled genially. "You know my wife, Your Grace, but may I present my grandmother? This is the Duke of Linberry, who recently came into his title." He smiled and took the infant into his arms. "And this Lady Lenora, our daughter. We call her Norrie."

The duke took the dowager duchess' hand and bowed, then did the same to the duchess. "Thank you for your kind invitation, Your Grace."

The duchess smiled. "And I have someone to present to you

and my husband." She indicated Fia. "This is Lady Sophia Sawyer, my new friend. My husband, the Duke of Westfield, and his new friend, the Duke of Linberry."

Her host took Fia's hand. "Delighted to meet you, Lady Sophia. Linberry, Lady Sophia."

The second duke took her hand. Fia felt a tremble run through her at his touch. He gazed intently at her, causing her cheeks to heat.

"Good afternoon, my lady. I believe I saw you earlier this morning near Rotten Row."

She swallowed, trying to force down her nerves in the presence of two dukes and two duchesses. "Yes, Your Grace. You were racing and rode a magnificent black."

"That was Artemis," the duke said, a twinkle in his eyes. "I am never happier than when I am on a horse."

"Linberry barely edged me out in our contest," Westfield grumbled good naturedly.

"Oh, do have a seat," the dowager duchess said. "All this standing is tiresome. And the teacart has arrived, along with the nanny."

The nanny claimed the babe from the duke and left the room.

"I should go," Fia said, uncomfortable with the situation. "I did not know that you had a guest coming, Your Grace," she told the duchess. "You should spend your time with His Grace and not me."

"You'll do no such thing, Lady Fia," the older woman said sternly. "I invited you. You are my guest. My grandson invited Linberry. You are both welcome." She looked pointedly at Fia. "Please, have a seat."

Knowing further protests would only draw unwanted attention to her, Fia sat, gripping her hands in her lap, trying to still the trembles that still ran through her. Parkhurst would be furious if he learned she had taken tea with two dukes and two duchesses. She should never have allowed the dowager duchess to talk her into coming to meet the Duchess of Westfield. Moreover, she never should have spilled her secrets to two women who were practically strangers.

"Sit with Lady Fia, Your Grace," the Duchess of Westfield said, her husband taking a seat beside his wife.

Then the duke captured her hand and kissed her fingers. Fia saw the heat in the man's eyes and felt her own widen. She had read in the gossip columns of the pair. How the duke had proposed in a dramatic fashion to Lady Margaret Townsend at Lord and Lady Strumbull's ball last Season, shocking Polite Society as he swept his betrothed off her feet in a romantic gesture and carried her from the ballroom. It had read like a fairy tale. Fia hadn't truly believed it occurred as was written—but seeing the couple together now changed her mind.

The teacart was brought close, and the duchess poured out, awarding Fia the first cup of tea.

"Do try the blackberry tarts," Westfield urged. "They are a specialty of Cook's."

"I have already told Lady Fia she must have some of the lemon cake," the dowager duchess said, taking a plate and placing a slice on it before handing it to Fia.

As she sipped her tea and sampled the items on her plate, Fia hoped neither duke would speak to her. That they would have their tea and then she would be allowed to escape. That the duchess would forget her scheme of having Fia move into this household.

Instead, the Duke of Westfield turned to her. "How did you and my wife meet, my lady? We have only recently returned from the country."

He looked at her so friendly and open that she relaxed. "I teach music lessons, Your Grace. Your grandmother was visiting the household where I was giving lessons today. She insisted I come to tea and meet Her Grace, since we both enjoy the fine arts."

"Lady Fia plays beautifully, Westfield," the dowager duchess said. "And she has the two Capwell girls playing better than orchestra members at balls."

"Lady Maisie and Lady Daisy possess a rare talent," Fia said. "I was fortunate enough to work with them daily for several months. Lord Capwell requested that I accompany his family to the country after the Season ended. I stayed in Oxfordshire until we came back to town this week." She paused. "I returned to my cousin's household."

"Who is your cousin?" Linberry asked.

"Lord Parkhurst," she said neutrally. "I have lived with Parkhurst since my parents died several years ago."

"I am sorry to hear of your loss, my lady," Linberry said quietly. "I lost my own father last spring. He was my closest friend and the best man I have known."

"My sympathies to you as well, Your Grace," she said, understanding his grief. "To lose a parent is difficult, especially one you are close to."

"Lady Capwell would like Lady Fia to play at their ball, which is to open the Season this year," the dowager duchess said.

"You play at balls?" Linberry asked, frowning.

Fia realized most of the *ton* would not believe it appropriate for a lady to play with the hired musicians.

"No, Your Grace. I have never done so. However, I believe it would be a great honor. I have never played in public, only at gatherings my cousin has hosted in his home."

"But you cannot dance and play at the same time, my lady," the duke insisted.

Her insides churned. She could not disparage Parkhurst in front of two dukes.

"I do not attend the Season, Your Grace," she said dismissively. Let him think her rude or unkind.

It was better than him knowing the truth.

"My husband tells me you are in town for the Season, Your Grace," the Duchess of Westfield said smoothly, turning the focus from Fia. "I hope you will attend the ball we will host."

Linberry directed his attention to the duchess. "I would be

happy to, Your Grace."

"The invitations will go out soon," the duchess promised. "Have your secretary look for it."

Then the duchess began speaking of taking up painting again. "I am a bit out of practice doing portraits since I took time off while I increased. The odor of my paints did not sit well with me. Now that Norrie has arrived, I am eager to pick up my brushes again."

Fia knew about the painting duchess, who had taken the *ton* by storm last year, with many begging for her to paint their portraits. Millie would retrieve the newspapers thrown out and bring them to Fia's attic room. She enjoyed reading the gossip columns and learning about the parents of her pupils. It was the closest she would ever get to learning about Polite Society.

The duke took his wife's hand. "I know the *ton* is ready for you to begin again. Perhaps you might start with Linberry here."

"No," the duke protested. "I have no need of a portrait."

Westfield said, "Of course, you must at some point, Linberry. Every duke should have his portrait made to add to his family's gallery. Future generations will come and stand before it, wondering about the man in the painting. No one could do you better justice than my duchess. Her talent is immense."

The duchess brought her husband's hand to her cheek. Again, such an intimate gesture moved Fia. The love between the two was obvious, causing a wistfulness to run through her. She would never have a husband or children. Never find love.

"Actually, darling, I think I would like to start by painting Lady Fia first," the duchess announced.

"What?" she cried. "No, that's impossible."

Westfield grinned. "Don't use that word, Lady Fia. My duchess will only see that as a challenge. She will wear you down until you agree to her proposal."

"I cannot," she said, shaking her head. "Parkhurst would never allow such a thing."

The duke frowned. "Why not?"

"I . . . you see, Your Grace . . ." She began wringing her hands, fumbling for words.

"I am out of practice," the duchess declared. "You would be doing me a favor, Lady Fia. That is why I had offered for you to move in with us just before my husband and His Grace arrived. If you are living here, it will make it so much easier to paint your portrait."

Fia noticed the puzzled expression on Westfield's face, which he quickly hid.

"If that's what you wish, my love, then we will make it happen," Westfield proclaimed. He turned to Fia. "I will speak to your cousin, my lady. It won't be a problem. You can come stay with us as soon as your maid can pack your things."

"No, Your Grace," she said, rising. "It would create a disastrous situation. One which I prefer not explaining to you. I hope you and Her Grace will respect my feelings regarding this matter. I cannot have my portrait painted. I cannot leave Parkhurst's townhouse and live here, even for a short time."

She faced the duchess, pained at what she was saying. "You are a lovely woman, Your Grace. I wish I could be your friend. But there are even problems a duchess cannot solve. Please, do not speak of any of this to my cousin. It will only cause grief for me—and I have suffered enough as it is."

Fia curtseyed. "It was lovely meeting you, Your Grace," she told the dowager duchess. "Thank you for your kind interest in me. Please, continue with your tea. Good day."

She hurried from the room, tears blurring her eyes as she moved along the corridor and down the stairs. She reached the bottom and raced across the corridor, the footman stationed at the door barely making it to his feet and opening the door for her.

Moving down the street, she took in her surroundings, figuring out where she was. It was another six blocks to Parkhurst's townhouse. Fia took a few calming breaths and slowed, walking at a more normal pace. As she did, she cursed inwardly, berating herself for ever having accepted the invitation to tea. It had been wrong to do so. She should have known better. She wasn't meant to make friends or mingle freely in Polite Society. If Parkhurst learned of her activities this afternoon, he might toss her onto the street—and then where would she be? No roof over her head. No way to provide for herself.

No, that wasn't true. She had become clever with her needle. While the *ton* might not wish her to teach music to their children, with Parkhurst poisoning them against her, she could go to work for a dressmaker. She wouldn't be destitute.

The idea appealed to her. It would be a hard life, but one of her own making. She loved creating gowns for herself and sprucing them up, changing them from season to season. True, she would have to give up music to do so. Or would she? She had talent and could play several instruments. Perhaps she could play along with other musicians at balls, though she doubted any of them were women. But what of the opera? Might she have the ability to join an orchestra?

With these new possibilities filling her head, she decided now was the time to break with Parkhurst. Or at least soon. She would wait until the end of next week to receive her quarterly pin money. That would help pay for a room for a short while. In the meantime, she could scour the newspapers and see about finding a room and if anyone might be advertising for help at a dress shop. With the Season almost here, she knew modistes would be busy for the next few months.

Having a plan to break free gave Fia new purpose. She reached her destination and went to the rear of the house, entering through the kitchens, as usual. Cook greeted her and she paused to talk with the old woman a moment, wishing she could tell her about the delicious blackberry tart she had consumed for tea.

Going to her attic room, Fia saw the latest newspapers lying on her bed. Millie must have placed them there. She began poring over them, circling ads that interested her with a pencil.

Then she realized she had left both her reticule and sheet music at the Duke of Westfield's residence.

However would she get them back?

CHAPTER SIX

"WHAT IN THUNDER just happened?" Westfield asked his wife.

Henry was wondering the exact thing himself as he watched Lady Fia race out the drawing room door. Oddly enough, he felt a powerful urge to follow her.

"Oh, dear," the duchess said. "I have made a mess of things."

"No, you haven't," snapped the dowager duchess. "It's that odious Parkhurst. Lay the blame where it rightfully should be, Margaret. You were only trying to help the poor girl."

"I am utterly confused," Westfield admitted. "Straighten things out for me, my love."

The duchess said, "I don't wish to betray any confidences Lady Fia shared, Daniel."

Her husband brushed his fingers against her cheek. "If Lady Fia is in trouble and needs our assistance, I must know of the fight ahead. Linberry, too."

"What?" he asked. "I don't truly know the woman, other than our brief time at tea," he protested.

Westfield gazed at him steadily. "She needs our help, Linberry. And two dukes are better than one, don't you agree?"

"I am not certain I should involve myself in the matter," he said, thinking how Lady Fia had mentioned teaching music to children and wanting to play at a ball, not dance at it. She seemed too unconventional for his tastes. Whatever scheme the duchess had up her sleeve, Henry did not think he should become a part of it. After all, he needed to find a bride this Season. Becoming involved in some kind of scandal involving a woman he'd only met did not appeal to him.

Even though Lady Fia was quite appealing.

"Then you are not the man I once believed you to be, Linberry," the duchess said, judgment in her tone. "The Lord North I was fond of would definitely have offered his help."

"See here, Your Grace," Henry said, bothered by her words. "I am a good man. I am doing my best to be a good duke. One far better than my grandfather ever was."

The duchess studied him silently, her disappointment clear. Henry had no idea what he had done or said to have her behave in such a manner.

The duchess rose. "Thank you for coming to tea, Your Grace," she said formally.

Knowing he was being dismissed, he came to his feet. "Thank you and His Grace for your generous invitation."

"Oh, would the two of you sit?" the dowager duchess said, her irritation obvious. "My grandson is correct. The power of two dukes far outweighs that of one. If you are trying to live up to your title, Linberry, then you need to help those in need. And Lady Fia most certainly falls into that category." She looked to the duchess. "Tell them, Margaret. Then we can put our heads together and see if we can come up with an answer. If we don't, I fear the poor girl is doomed to a life of indentured servitude."

Henry wanted to tell the old woman that she was exaggerating but held his tongue. He was a guest in this home—probably for the first and only time—but he would do his hosts the courtesy of hearing what the duchess had to say.

He waited for the duchess to seat herself before he did so himself. The duke took her hand. "Go on, love," he said encouragingly.

With tears brimming in her eyes, the duchess explained how

Fia Sawyer's parents had passed away and her cousin, whom she seemed terrified of, had taken up her father's title.

"I remember Lord Parkhurst, her father," Westfield said. "He was a good sort. Jovial and kind. All I know about his heir is that he spends more time in gaming hells than in *ton* ballrooms."

"We all have known men such as Parkhurst," Henry pointed out. "While I am sorry Lady Fia lost her parents, she should have mourned her year and then taken her place in Polite Society. She could have then wed and be out from under Parkhurst's thumb."

"He would have been her guardian, though," Westfield pointed out. "He might have refused her permission to wed."

"But she never made her come-out," the duchess told them. "She thought after her mourning period ended and Parkhurst summoned her to town, she would do so." The duchess frowned. "Instead, he did not allow that to occur. She is a gifted musician, and so he has her giving lessons to children of the *ton*."

"And the earl keeps all her earnings," the dowager duchess added. "Poor Lady Fia has no money and no friends. Parkhurst keeps her isolated and dependent upon him."

That made Henry's blood boil.

"I wanted to help her, Daniel," the duchess continued. "I thought we could ask Parkhurst to allow her to stay with us in order for me to paint her. It would get her away from him for a while."

"But you always sketch your subjects and paint from those, not from having a person sit for his or her portrait."

"Parkhurst wouldn't have to know that," the duchess said. "And maybe . . . Gran and I could introduce her into society while she stayed with us. It's a thought."

The duke brought his wife's hand to his lips and kissed it. "It is a start. Of course, Parkhurst would have to allow it. As her guardian, he has complete control over her until she is of legal age. Do you know how old she is?"

"No, but that would be easy to find out," his wife said. "Perhaps you could write to the earl and ask if we could call upon him. I think he would find it rather hard to refuse a request from a duke and his duchess." She looked to Henry. "Might Your Grace wish to accompany us? You could also agree what a good idea it would be."

Though he hadn't wanted to become involved, it looked as if that would happen. Besides, he thought it cruel of Parkhurst not to have allowed his cousin to make her come-out, much less the fact that he forced her to give lessons and not receive any of the compensation. Guilt flooded him, as he had surmised it was Lady Fia who was resisting becoming a full member of Polite Society, when instead it had been her cousin preventing her from joining in what she was due by her birthright.

"I would be happy to accompany Your Graces to Lord Parkhurst's for a chat." He glanced at the nearby table and stood, picking up the items that Lady Fia had left behind in her haste. "And you can return her reticule and sheet music when we do."

"I don't think that wise," the dowager duchess chimed in. "Lady Fia was adamant that her cousin not know about her coming to take tea with us. I gather she is not allowed to socialize with others in any manner. She indicated that she would be punished if he found out. Better to wrap these up and have them delivered to her instead of handing them over in front of Parkhurst."

"I agree, Gran," the duke said. "But how will we approach the earl if Lady Fia has not met any of us?"

"I did meet her at Lady Capwell's. I am friends with the dowager Lady Capwell and visited her today. Margaret can say she accompanied me. We heard Lady Fia play there."

"And I decided I must paint her," the duchess said. "It is flimsy—but it will allow us entrée into the earl's home." She beamed. "After all, an earl would be honored to have a duke and duchess call upon him. Actually, two dukes if you are agreeable to going, Linberry."

"Make that two duchesses," the old woman said. "I wouldn't miss this for the world."

"Then it is settled," Westfield said. "I shall write to Parkhurst immediately and ask that we be allowed to call tomorrow afternoon for tea. Linberry, we shall pick you up at a quarter till."

"I will be eagerly waiting," Henry promised.

The duchess smiled at him. "Thank you, Your Grace. I know you are under no obligation to become involved in this matter. However, I do appreciate your willingness to do so."

"I see you have taken to Lady Fia. You will be a good friend to her, Your Grace. If I can play a small role in helping her take her rightful place in Polite Society, then I am your humble servant."

FIA LEFT HER last lesson and climbed into the cart, driving home through the busy London streets. She guided the horse to the Parkhurst mews and left to return to the house, cutting through the kitchens. Cook was giving orders as scullery maids bustled about.

"Do you mind if I make myself a cup of tea, Cook?" she asked. "I promise to stay out of your way."

"We have guests coming for tea, my lady!" Cook exclaimed. "A duke and duchess. And Lord Parkhurst wants everything to be perfect for their visit."

A sick feeling grew within her. She had received a parcel an hour after she had returned home yesterday. In it, she found her missing reticule and the sheet music she had carelessly left behind after fleeing the drawing room of the Duke and Duchess of Westfield. The duchess had included a brief note, saying she had been delighted to make Fia's acquaintance and hoped to see her soon.

But she didn't realize that meant the duchess—and duke— would try to call upon her.

Fia never took tea with her cousin. Often, he entertained his friends at tea or dinner. The only time her presence was requested was after a meal. She would provide the entertainment for Parkhurst's guests. If the Duke and Duchess of Westfield showed up expecting her to be present at tea, they would be sadly mistaken.

What if they demanded she come down? Oh, Parkhurst would be livid. Naturally, he would send for her. After all, it wouldn't do to offend a powerful duke and his duchess. But Fia dreaded the punishment Parkhurst would come up with once his guests left.

She had to stop this before it happened.

But how?

Leaving the kitchens, Fia returned to the rear of the house and then made her way to the front. If she could intercept the Westfields before they arrived, she could explain that she wouldn't be at tea. Thinking of the direction she had walked yesterday in returning from their townhouse, Fia moved down the block in that direction. She couldn't wait for them in front of Parkhurst's townhouse. He might very well be looking out the window, if only to watch for their carriage and see its splendor.

She reached the end of the square and waited for several minutes, her belly gnawing with nerves, anticipating their arrival. The dowager duchess had said her grandson's carriage was even more splendid than hers. When a gleaming black carriage laced in gold appeared, being drawn by four coal-black horses, Fia knew this had to be the one. It was the most magnificent vehicle she had ever laid eyes upon.

Quickly, she stepped into the road, waving at the coachman, hoping he would stop in time. He spied her and pulled up on the reins.

"Thank you," she called up to him. "I must speak to Her Grace for a moment. Please, don't start the carriage," she pleaded.

Looking perplexed, he nodded. Fia ran to the door and knocked. Without waiting for an answer, she opened the door, floored to find not only the Duke and Duchess of Westfield within, but also the dowager duchess and the Duke of Linberry. Speechless, she could only look at them, her mouth open.

"Lady Fia," the duchess said brightly. "Why, what are you doing?"

Snapping out of her trance, Fia said, "I will not be at tea, Your Grace. I have just learned from Cook that you are coming to see Parkhurst. I beg of you, do not ask for me. Do not have my cousin send for me."

The duchess' brow knitted in confusion. "What is wrong?"

"I . . . I do not take tea with Parkhurst. Ever. If you are to ask for me, he will grow quite upset. He would not show it then but . . ." Her voice trailed off, shame filling her.

"He would mistreat you, my lady?" the Duke of Linberry asked sharply.

"I did not say anything of the kind, Your Grace," she said quickly. "But it would not be wise for me to be asked to tea. Promise me you won't." Tears filled her eyes.

Linberry climbed from the carriage and handed her his handkerchief. "Dry your eyes, my lady," he said gently.

Dabbing at them, she thought him so kind—which caused a flood of new tears to leak from her eyes.

"I'm sorry," she apologized, wiping them away.

"You have nothing to be sorry for," the duke said gently. "Return home, Lady Fia. And do not worry."

"Thank you," she said softly, offering his handkerchief to him.

"Keep it," he told her.

Nodding, she turned and hurried away, going back the way she had come, praying the four would make their visit and never return.

She moved through the kitchens again, seeing the food being placed onto plates, her stomach growling as she passed. Going up the servants' staircase, she went to her attic room, removing her bonnet. She bathed her face with water in the basin and dried it.

Then Fia sat on the bed, her belly still churning. She hoped her wishes would be taken into consideration. Then again, who was she to tell a duchess what to do? Fear gripped her then, followed by worry as to what might happen to her if she were called to the drawing room.

A knock sounded on her door and a maid opened the door. "You're wanted downstairs, my lady. In the drawing room."

Resignation filled her. Fia rose and hurried to her destination, knowing Parkhurst would be angry if she tarried. Bile rose in her throat, and she forced it back down. Her life would be miserable now. Then resolve filled her. She had already found a few rooms to let in the newspapers that might be suitable. There had also been a few advertisements looking for help in dress shops. If she could hold out for a bit longer, she would leave this place of misery. After all, she was of age.

Leaving, though, meant never returning. If she failed, she could not come crawling back to Parkhurst. Fia vowed she would rather starve to death than do so.

She paused a moment outside the drawing room to collect herself—and then bravely put a smile on her face and entered.

CHAPTER SEVEN

"AH, LADY FIA," the Duchess of Westfield said, an encouraging smile on her lovely face.

Fia came toward the group, avoiding looking at her cousin as she greeted the duchess and dowager duchess, dipping into a curtsey.

"It is good to you again so soon, Your Graces."

"May I present my husband?" the duchess continued.

Immediately, Fia realized what the duchess was doing and played along.

"This is His Grace, the Duke of Westfield, and his good friend, the Duke of Linberry."

"Your Graces," she said, sweeping again into a curtsey.

"I am glad to make your acquaintance, Lady Fia," Westfield said easily. "My wife was quite impressed with your playing yesterday."

At least from his remark, Fia understood now how she was supposed to have met the two women.

"Shall we sit?" Parkhurst said abruptly.

"That settee won't do for me," the dowager duchess remarked. "I like a stiff chair for my back." She took a seat in a chair next to where Parkhurst stood.

The duke and duchess sat on one settee, leaving Fia and Linberry to sit on the other. Her cousin took his seat and nodded to the butler, summoning the teacart.

"I was quite surprised to receive your note, Your Grace," Parkhurst said. He turned and looked to Fia. "And it seems my cousin has met your wife. How did this come about?"

"I was at Lord and Lady Capwells' townhouse yesterday, my lord, giving lessons to Lady Daisy and Lady Maisie."

"And I had come to visit there, along with my grandson's wife," the dowager duchess interjected. "Lady Capwell was most insistent that we hear her daughters play. Usually, I am not one to listen to children bang on the keys of a piano."

"I quite agree," Parkhurst said. "It can be most annoying."

"I was quite surprised at the Capwell girls' talent," the dowager duchess continued. "So much that Her Grace and I asked that they play another number on their stringed instruments. Lady Fia was accompanying her pupils." She smiled fondly at Fia. "You have a tremendous talent, my dear."

"Did you know Lady Capwell wishes for your cousin to play the harp at the ball she is giving to open the Season, my lord?" the duchess interjected.

Her cousin's eyes narrowed. "No." He looked to Fia. "Is this so?"

"Lady Capwell did mention it to me, my lord," Fia said, casting her gaze downward. "I played for her and Lord Capwell numerous times during my stay with them in Oxfordshire. I told her ladyship that I could not agree to such a request. That she would need to speak with you. I believe she was going to have Lord Capwell write to you regarding the matter."

"Out of the question," Parkhurst declared.

"And why is that, my lord?" the Duke of Westfield inquired politely. "My wife and grandmother had nothing but praise for your cousin's talent, as did Lady Capwell. Why, I think it would be a feather in your cap, my lord, if you allowed Lady Fia to play her harp. It would reflect well upon you, Parkhurst."

"Hmm."

She could see the wheels turning in her cousin's head, thinking that it might generate more interest—and income—if the entire *ton* heard her play. She even believed he would charge more for the lessons she gave.

"I will consider it," he said, stroking his chin thoughtfully.

The maids rolled in the teacart, with the butler hovering nearby to see that all was well.

"Aren't you going to pour out, Lady Fia?" the dowager duchess asked.

Fia froze. She had never poured out for any guests, much less two dukes and two duchesses. If she spilled any tea, Parkhurst would have her head.

Demurely, she smiled at the old woman. "It would be an honor if you or Her Grace poured out instead," she suggested.

"I can do so for us," the duchess said, taking the reins and making certain everyone had tea. "Manage your own plates," she suggested. "You will know what you like."

To her right, Linberry said, "It is your home, Lady Fia. You will be familiar with your Cook's treats. Would you make up a plate for me?"

"Certainly, Your Grace."

She placed several items on his plate, including two small sandwiches, a slice of strawberry cake, and a raisin scone. She herself never partook of tea and hoped her selection would measure up to His Grace's standards.

They ate and conversed for several minutes. Actually, Fia sipped her tea and only took two bites, nerves rippling through her so that she felt her hands shake. She set down her cup and saucer and listened to the conversation, holding her hands together in her lap.

"I hear you paint, Your Grace," Parkhurst said. "Portraits, is it?"

"Yes, I have painted several members of Polite Society," the duchess replied. "I recently gave birth to our daughter and only took up my brushes a few days ago. Sadly, I am out of practice." She turned and smiled at Fia. "You must know what that is like since you are also an artist in your own right, painting with music instead of colors."

Fia nodded in agreement. "If I do not get enough practice, I can feel myself slipping. That is why I try never to take a break."

"Alas, I was too large the last two months and couldn't even reach my canvas. The oil paints also bothered my sense of smell, which became quite acute while I increased. I need to get in that practice myself before I open up appointments to paint members of Polite Society again." She paused. "Hmm."

Dreading what was coming, Fia realized she was helpless to stop it. The Duchess of Westfield seemed a most determined person.

"I wonder . . . Lady Fia, you understand this need for practice. And you have such an interesting face, doesn't she, Your Grace?"

Westfield sat up and studied Fia. "Yes, you do, my lady. Most interesting."

"Your eye color is unusual. Quite a deep blue. And you have a plethora of golden shades running through your hair. Why, it would be a challenge to paint you. Yes, that is what I should do." The duchess turned to her husband. "I can practice and regain my skills by painting Lady Fia!" she declared enthusiastically.

Immediately, Parkhurst vetoed that notion. "That would be impossible, Your Grace. You see, my cousin delights in giving music lessons to young children. You yourself witnessed her doing so with Capwells' daughters. She would be unavailable to sit for you. I am sorry."

"I won't take no for an answer, my lord," the duchess said genially. "Why, I would be happy to work around Lady Fia's lessons."

"She is busy most days, throughout the entire day," the earl insisted.

The duchess touched her husband's sleeve. "I know. Lady Fia can come stay with us, darling. That would make things simple. She could go and teach her lessons and when she was done, she could spend time with me in my studio. Oh, please, Westfield.

Say Lady Fia might come and stay with us."

"Of course, my dear. I am certain the earl would be happy to grant such a small request." The duke turned to Parkhurst. "Anything to keep my duchess happy, you know."

"It is an excellent idea," the Duke of Linberry added. "I know how eager Her Grace is to regain her touch with her brush and how many members of Polite Society are clamoring for her to schedule their portrait sittings with her. If Lady Fia is willing to help Her Grace, why she would be helping *all* of Polite Society." He looked to her. "I hope you will agree with Her Grace's suggestion, my lady."

Linberry then looked to his host. "You would be making the duchess very happy, Parkhurst. We all know how important it is to keep a duchess happy. Why, I am ready to seek a bride this Season and Her Grace has vowed to help me find one. If you are also in Her Grace's good graces, so to speak, I am certain she would let all of Polite Society know of the favor you are doing her by loaning your cousin to her."

Parkhurst sat dumbfounded, not having a comeback.

"Then it's settled," the dowager duchess said. "Oh, it will be so good to have another young person in the house. You will have to play for me daily while you stay with us, Lady Fia. Music has always soothed me."

Beside her, the duke's posture changed. Fia wondered why.

"You must have your bags packed at once," the Duchess of Westfield declared. "Why, you can come home with us after tea, and we can go directly to my studio. Oh, this is going to be ever so much fun." She looked to her host, smiling sweetly. "Thank you, my lord, for allowing your cousin to come and stay with us. I promise you that Westfield and I will take excellent care of Lady Fia and make certain she gets to all her lessons."

Fia dared a quick glance at her cousin, seeing how he had been subtly nudged by the four visitors. He wore a perplexed expression, as if he were not quite certain how he had been talked into this.

"If you will excuse me, my lord, I will go pack now," she said.

"Oh, have your maid do that for you," the duchess told her. "And do bring your maid with you, Lady Fia."

She looked helplessly to Parkhurst. His face darkened, and she knew he would not wish it revealed that Fia had no lady's maid.

"Millie will be happy to accompany me," she said of her friend, knowing that Millie would be glad to leave the earl's house, if only for a short while.

The duchess rose, and everyone followed suit. "I can't thank you enough for having us to tea, Lord Parkhurst. You must let us return the favor and come to dinner one evening during the Season. Might you be looking for a bride?"

"Possibly," he said. "Of course, having your support in this endeavor would help, Your Grace."

"We will have to see which eligible ladies are available then. Perhaps it might also be time for Lady Fia to also think about taking a husband. I know you must enjoy giving your music lessons, my lady, but you cannot do that forever. You simply must wed and have children of your own so you may teach music to them." The duchess smiled brilliantly.

Parkhurst sputtered. "I really don't think—"

"What an excellent idea, my dear," the dowager duchess interjected, cutting off the earl. "A duchess playing matchmaker for two cousins. How delightful. It will be the talk of all Polite Society, how generous and giving you are of your time. But we must be on our way." She stepped to Fia and linked her arm through Fia's. "Help me down to the carriage if you would, my dear. Linberry, get on my other side."

Suddenly, Fia found herself leaving the drawing room—and house. The butler saw them out, assuring her that he would have Millie pack and to expect the maid within the hour at the Westfields' townhouse.

She thanked the servant and then was handed up into the ducal carriage, which was even grander on the inside than the outside. She took a seat next to the dowager duchess, and Linberry sat on her other side, while the Westfields sat opposite them. In the small space, Fia became aware of the warmth of the duke, since his side was resting against hers. She could also detect the tang of his cologne, a very pleasing scent.

The Duke of Westfield took his wife's hand and kissed it. "You, my love, should be a politician. You would dominate conferences where various representatives of different countries had gathered and have your way with them all. It was nothing less than brilliant how you handled Lord Parkhurst."

The duchess smiled up at her husband. "I did have a supporting cast helping me. You all played your parts to perfection, as if we had rehearsed numerous times. Especially you, Linberry. You claiming I could help the earl find a wife is what I think decided it for him." She sniffed. "Not that I would lift a finger to help that loathsome man. He'll find someone all on his own, a woman who wishes to be a countess and who does not care whom she weds to gain that title."

"Did you see the earl's eyes bulge when Gran tossed out about finding Lady Fia a husband, as well?" Westfield asked.

"It will allow Lady Fia to accompany us to social affairs this Season," the duchess said. "You must dance with her, Linberry. Everyone notices when a duke dances with someone. It will help draw the right attention to her."

Fia could not allow this talk to continue. "Your Grace," she said firmly, "I will not be attending any *ton* events. I am grateful to be out of my cousin's house for a bit and already am formulating a plan so I will not have to return. But I draw the line at the Season. I never made my come-out. I haven't a single gown in my possession that would be suitable."

The dowager duchess clucked her tongue. "You may not now, Lady Fia, but by the start of the Season you will."

She vigorously shook her head. "No, Your Grace. I mean it. I have but a few pounds to my name and have already earmarked how I am going to use those funds to make my escape. Besides, a few pounds wouldn't even buy the material for a single ballgown, much less have it made up."

The old woman took Fia's hand. "I have plenty of money, my dear, and I can spend it any way I choose. I have decided to sponsor you myself. You *will* make your come-out this Season— and I have a feeling that you will take the *ton* by storm."

CHAPTER EIGHT

THE CARRIAGE CAME to a halt in front of the Duke of West-field's residence. The duke climbed from the vehicle, followed by Henry. Westfield handed down the three ladies, with Lady Fia being last. Henry could not help but admire the woman. She had obviously loved her parents a great deal and suffered under her cousin's heavy hand. Henry had barely a passing acquaintance with Parkhurst and had nothing to do with the nefarious crowd the earl ran with.

He also admired how Lady Fia had stood up to the two duch-esses, not wanting to inconvenience them by attending the Season, and yet still glad the dowager duchess would help launch her into society. He studied the gown she now wore, noting it was serviceable as a servant's might be, and not something a lady of the *ton* would wear. The fact she had never made her come-out, much less had no appropriate gowns to wear to any social event, gnawed at him. Despite his better judgment, he was becoming more intrigued by Lady Fia.

"Come inside with me, Linberry," the duke said, clapping Henry on the back. "These ladies will be discussing fashion and gowns, things that make my head ache. I would appreciate your company so that I may excuse myself from theirs."

"Why don't you stay for dinner tonight, Your Grace?" asked the duchess. "We can have word sent that you will dine here instead."

"Thank you for your kind invitation, Your Grace," he told her.

Henry accompanied the group inside and, as the ladies went up the stairs, Westfield led Henry to a large, comfortable study.

"Have a seat, Linberry," the duke urged.

He did so, wondering if he had anything in common with this impressive man.

"Tell me about yourself, Linberry. I know little about you since you were several years behind me in school. What did you study at university?"

Henry spoke for a few minutes about his studies in history and geography, and the duke chimed in with interest, knowing quite a bit about both subjects. They discovered they each had a passion for the Middle Ages and Renaissance eras.

"Where does your ducal seat lie, Your Grace?" Henry asked.

Westfield shook his head. "I hate all this Your Grace-ing. Especially in private. If we are to be friends, you should call me Daniel."

He was taken aback by Westfield's request for such informality. Most dukes—even to their own families—were only addressed by their titles, even in private.

"Are you certain about that? It would be highly unusual."

Westfield grinned at him. "Well, we *are* dukes," he pointed out. "I say we write our own rules."

He found himself grinning at the man. "Very well then, Daniel. I am Henry to you in private. So, where is your ducal seat?"

"Westwood is located in northern Sussex." Daniel then elaborated on the size of the estate, including the number of tenants and horses.

"And you, Henry? Where is your ducal estate?"

"It is called Linfield, and is in southern Kent. We must be fairly close to one another. I am lacking in the intimate familiarity with it that you possess about your own estate. You see, I prefer town and only spent brief periods of time in the country. I do have an excellent steward, though, and receive a written monthly report from him."

Henry noticed a cart pull up in front of the duke's townhouse. It also drew Daniel's eyes.

"Hmm," his new friend said. "I believe we should go see what this is about."

The two men left the study and went outside, where the coachman was helping a servant from the bed of the cart.

"I am the Duke of Westfield. Are you Millie, by any chance?"

The maid's eyes widened. She dipped into a curtsey. "Yes, Your Grace," she said breathlessly. "I have packed Lady Fia's things and was told to bring them here and stay with her during her brief visit."

The duke smiled at the servant. "I rather think it will be an extended visit, Millie. Probably lasting the entire Season. My duchess and grandmother intend to launch Lady Fia into Polite Society so you might leave this household for one of her future husband's."

The servant burst into tears, surprising Henry. What surprised him more was Daniel handing over his own handkerchief to the maid.

"Dry your eyes, Millie," Daniel told her. "Was it so very bad at Parkhurst's place?"

Millie looked at the handkerchief in awe but chose to dab her eyes with it. "It was awful, Your Grace, and I am not one to gossip about my employer. Lord and Lady Parkhurst, Lady Fia's parents, were two of the kindest souls that walked the earth. If they knew how Parkhurst treats their daughter, they would be turning in their graves."

Two footmen had appeared, and Daniel said, "Let my people bring in Lady Fia's things, along with yours. I am certain my wife has let Mrs. Hampton, our housekeeper, know you are coming. A room should be waiting for you both."

The servant's mouth trembled as more tears ran down her cheeks. Millie wiped them away and said, "The instruments are what are most precious to Lady Fia."

She turned and pulled the tarp away, revealing several musical instruments. "His lordship said the harp would remain in his drawing room, but I brought the rest of her instruments, along with the sheet music. It's in the two pretty boxes."

Henry glanced into the bed of the cart and spied the boxes, along with two small valises. "Where are Lady Fia's trunks?" he asked.

The maid blushed. "Her clothes only filled one valise, my lord. Mine are in the other one."

"This is the Duke of Linberry, Millie," Daniel said. "So it is His Grace."

"Beg pardon, Your Grace," the servant said.

Henry pressed the issue. "I thought you were told to pack all of Lady Fia's things. Where are they?"

The servant looked up at him sadly. "This is all there is, Your Grace."

"All there is?" he echoed. "Why? That is impossible."

He thought about how extensive his own mother's wardrobe was. Why, her stockings alone would have filled a trunk.

Millie looked to Daniel. "May I speak frankly, Your Grace?"

"I expect honesty from my servants. You will be under my roof—and my protection. Be frank, Millie."

"I was lady's maid to Lady Parkhurst until her death and then served in that capacity to Lady Fia until the new Lord Parkhurst called her to town after her mourning period ended. I am now a parlor maid in his household, while Lady Fia is treated worse than some servants. She was given the worst room in the attic, living there in cramped conditions with all these musical instruments. Lord Parkhurst provides her a piddling sum. Lady Fia only has three gowns to her name. I did teach her how to sew. She tries to update these gowns each year by adding new cuffs or trim so that it appears she has a new wardrobe. The earl never provides her with much of anything. He has her working six days a week, giving music lessons to children. She barely has time to practice herself. She is isolated from those of her own class, beyond these lessons, and eats alone in her attic room. It is quite heartbreaking, Your Grace. I don't know what you and Her Grace did to remove my lady from Parkhurst's roof. I only pray you can keep her from returning there."

Rage filled Henry, learning how Lady Fia had been abused by her powerful cousin.

"Thank you for what you have shared with us, Millie," Daniel said. "Neither you nor Lady Fia will ever return and live with Lord Parkhurst," the duke assured the servant. "Go inside now and Mrs. Hampton will help you get Lady Fia and yourself settled. We have a music room, and I will instruct the footmen to take Lady Fia's instruments and cases to it."

"Thank you, Your Grace," the servant said, gratitude written on her face.

She left them, and Daniel instructed the footmen as to where to take the instruments and valises.

Once the servants left, Daniel said, "This troubles me a great deal. The situation is much more dire than what my duchess or I believed. Margaret is right. We need to help launch Lady Fia into society and help her make a brilliant match."

"She is attractive and of good temper," Henry assured him. "With your grandmother sponsoring her, she will be the talk of the *ton*. Do we know how old she is? If Parkhurst is still her guardian?"

"It is certainly something we need to find out. I had forgotten to ask that of Parkhurst when we were there earlier. If she is under legal age, the earl could demand she be removed from under my care. There would be nothing I could do to prevent him from doing so. Come, Henry. I think it is time that we joined the ladies."

They went inside and upstairs to the drawing room and joined the three women. Henry went and took a seat beside Lady Fia and said, "Your maid and instruments have arrived safely. His Grace had them taken to the music room. Millie said your harp was left behind, though."

"I suspected as much," she said. "It is quite large and difficult to move. Although I will miss playing it, at least I have my other instruments."

"There were several delivered. Do you play all of them?"

She nodded. "I do, Your Grace. I also take them to some of my lessons for my pupils to play."

"Tell us about those lessons," the dowager duchess urged.

"I start each student on the pianoforte," Lady Fia explained. "It is the foundation of all musical instruments. I teach them how to play it and how to read music. If I feel a student can learn to play adequately, I continue their lessons strictly on the pianoforte. If I believe they show promise and have talent and might enjoy a stringed instrument, I discuss this with them and their parents. Then I have the child pick up and become familiar with different instruments. I have a cello, violin, and viola. Most are drawn to the violin. If they become interested and show skill after a few lessons, then I suggest their parents purchase one for their use. That way, they may practice on their own since I must take the instruments with me to different households."

"How many lessons do you give in a day?" the Duchess of Westfield asked.

"It depends," Lady Fia said. "At the beginning of the Season, my cousin establishes who wishes to continue with their lessons from the previous year and has his secretary draw up a schedule. I can give three or four lessons each morning and definitely four in the afternoons. I also was asked by Lord and Lady Capwell to accompany them to their country estate after the Season ended last year. I was surprised Parkhurst granted me the privilege to do so, but Lady Capwell assured me that her husband was quite persuasive."

Henry noted the wistful smile on her face and asked, "Was it nice to leave town for the country?"

Her face lit with a radiant smile now, causing something to melt within him. "Oh, yes, Your Grace. I have always preferred country living to town. I enjoyed long walks, both by myself and with Lady Maisie and Lady Daisy. I was able to attend church and become active in their altar guild society. Why, I even was asked to dine with the earl and countess each evening."

He had never given a thought to where he dined because it had always been with his parents. He assumed from what Millie had said that a tray must have been delivered to Lady Fia's attic abode. Once again, anger filled him at how this delicate beauty had been treated by her own flesh and blood.

"You will dine with us every night," the duchess declared. "We will eat early because of the Season, though. In fact, dinner should be ready very soon. Though we are not in the Season just yet, my duke and I prefer to keep country hours when not attending a social affair."

The duchess looked to her husband. "Lady Fia has agreed, though reluctantly, to go for dress fittings tomorrow. I have sent word to Madame Planche, my modiste, that it will be quite a large order."

Henry looked to the woman beside him. "Are you comfortable with that, my lady?" he asked quietly.

"Frankly, no," she responded. "But Their Graces are most insistent, so I have agreed to have a few gowns made up to start. If I am to play at Lord and Lady Capwells' ball, then I would need something appropriate to wear."

"Oh, my dear, it will not be necessary for you to do so now," the dowager duchess remarked. "You will be dancing all night. Not playing."

Henry saw determination fill Lady Fia's eyes.

"I *will* play at this ball, Your Grace," she said firmly. "It has long been a dream of mine to play with an orchestra. I know the *ton* holds many balls throughout the Season. Perhaps I might attend one of those—but I will not be dancing."

"Why not?" the duchess asked.

"Because I do not know how to dance, Your Grace," Lady Fia revealed.

CHAPTER NINE

F IA SAW THE perplexed looks on the faces gathered around her. "You don't dance," the dowager duchess said. "But you must, my dear."

"I never learned, Your Grace," she said calmly. "Even if I had made my come-out, I would not have danced." Fia paused. "You see, I had an accident when I was quite young. I broke my left leg and the kneecap. It took months for them to heal. As I grew, I found if I spent too much time on my feet or overtire myself, I would begin to limp. Mama and I agreed that dancing all night at balls would be beyond me. I chose not to learn how so I would not be tempted to do so when that time came."

She looked at the group and saw their concern for her. "It is not so bad," she told them. "I do enjoy walking. I know my limits, though, and take care not to go too far or over challenging territory."

"You should see a specialist," the Duke of Linberry said. "There have been advances in medicine since you were a child. Something might—"

"Thank you, Your Grace, but no. It would most likely involve breaking the leg again." Fia shuddered. "I cannot go through that."

"But if you walk, surely you could dance a few numbers?" he insisted.

"Well, I have never had to worry about that," she said, her tone light despite her heavy heart. "Since I never made my come-out, there was no need to learn. Problem solved."

She smiled brightly, not wanting these perceptive people to see just how much she did care, both about having never been brought out in Polite Society, much less never learning how to dance.

"You will make your come-out soon, my lady," Westfield said. "I think you could be selective and dance a few numbers. You wouldn't have to do so all night. We can teach you."

"A duke—and duchess—giving dance lessons to me? I have already accepted your hospitability for a short while, Your Grace. I won't put you out and have you teaching me how to dance," Fia protested.

Linberry spoke up. "I quite enjoy dancing, Lady Fia. It would be no bother at all. I would be honored to teach you."

The duke's offer startled her. It took her a moment to find her voice. "No, Your Grace. You are a duke. A busy man."

"Not too busy to dance, Lady Fia." He smiled at her.

And Fia lost her heart to the Duke of Linberry in that moment.

"It is late in the day, but we could start tomorrow," he suggested. "When you are fresh after a good night's rest."

"No, I have lessons of my own to teach, Your Grace. Not to mention I must carve out time for Her Grace to paint me."

"Oh, that will not be necessary, Fia," the duchess said. "I never have my subjects sit for me as I paint."

The duchess explained how she used to practice by painting servants and how she sketched them and worked from those sketches.

"Besides, I haven't lost my talent. I just said so in order to have Parkhurst allow you to come and stay with us." The duchess smiled. "But don't worry. I will sketch you and show all those sketches to you. You can select the ones you like the best. I will work from those."

Fia frowned. "So, you *will* paint my portrait? You realize that Parkhurst will not compensate you for your efforts."

Margaret waved away Fia's concerns. "I'm a duchess. I don't need to be compensated. But I will produce a portrait of you because I want to do so. Do not worry. It won't go to Parkhurst." She smiled. "I am certain your future husband will be delighted to have it."

"About that," Fia began, only to be interrupted by the butler, who announced dinner was ready to be served.

"Take us into dinner, Linberry," the dowager duchess insisted.

The duke took the older woman's arm and offered Fia his other one. She took it, and a rush of warmth ran through her with the contact. She was aware of his scent. His heat. The hard muscles beneath her fingertips. Obviously, he did not do physical labor, being a duke, but he certainly did something to be in such wonderful shape.

The meal proved most enjoyable. Fia was so used to being alone and rarely in the company of adults. Their small party discussed a variety of topics. She found herself contributing some to the conversation but enjoyed listening even more.

Especially to the Duke of Linberry.

He seemed so lovely. He was solicitous to her, including her in the conversation, asking her about what she thought of everything from what they were being served to horses. When it came out that she enjoyed riding, Linberry insisted they ride together in Rotten Row.

"Oh, I am afraid that wouldn't be a good idea, Your Grace," Fia told him. "I have not been on a horse in almost a decade. I did love riding at one point and would ride around our estate with Papa to call upon tenants. I felt the equal of others when on the back of a horse," she explained. "I have always been conscious of the limp that comes out when I am tired."

"Why did you stop riding, my lady?" he asked.

"My parents both grew ill. I spent most of my days in their

sickrooms and when they passed, I did not have the inclination to ride again because it reminded me of happier times with my father. When I was summoned to town by my cousin, well . . . suffice it to say that I have not been in the saddle during my time here."

"Is your cousin your guardian?" her host asked.

"He was until I became of legal age. I am four and twenty years now." She hesitated. "I mentioned having a plan to leave Parkhurst's household. I know he would not legally be able to stop me from doing so."

"What is this plan of yours, my lady?" Linberry asked. "Do you plan to continue to teach music to students?"

"No, Your Grace. I fear Parkhurst will speak ill of me in Polite Society when I do leave his residence, which would cause me to fall out of favor with the *ton*. I have a few other ideas in mind." She fell silent.

"Ones you are not willing to share with us?" the duke pressed.

"No, Your Grace."

"It may not matter, Fia," the dowager duchess said. "You will make your come-out, and eligible bachelors will fall over themselves to get to know you."

"I cannot see why they would do so, Your Grace," she said. "In all honesty, I believe most men are looking for a woman with a dowry. The larger, the better. I have none."

She watched the two dukes exchange glances before Westfield said, "Are you certain of this, my lady?"

"My cousin informed me when I came to town several years ago. He gave that as the reason for me to start offering music lessons. Parkhurst said running a household could be quite expensive and that Papa had debts that my cousin would have to assume. He suggested I give lessons since I have some skill with several musical instruments."

Westfield frowned. "Even if your father were in debt, my lady—and I heard no rumors to that effect—he would have provided for children during his marriage settlements. Actually, some of your mother's dowry would have been earmarked for that very thing."

Fia thought over what the duke said before saying, "I did not know of any debts Papa accumulated. I was familiar with our estate and often examined the records with our steward. Even when we came to town for the Season, Mama was not overly extravagant with her wardrobe. And Papa was not a gambler or consumer of spirits." She paused. "I supposed he had made some bad investments. That must be what Parkhurst referred to."

"Or Parkhurst lied to you," said Linberry succinctly. "Do you think that is a possibility, my lady?"

Reluctantly, she said, "I came to that same conclusion long ago, Your Grace. However, as a woman, I could not question him or reason with him. He was my guardian for a few years and then after that, I was still dependent upon his goodwill to keep a roof over my head. Even if Papa had designated monies for my dowry—or it was part of his and Mama's marriage contracts—how could I access it?"

Again, she watched a look being exchanged by the two men.

"Do you give us permission to look into this for you, Lady Fia?" Linberry asked.

Hope sprang within her. "I would be happy for you to do so, Your Grace. Do I need to sign some type of papers allowing you to do so?"

"Usually, a duke's word is good enough for a solicitor," Westfield offered. "We would need the name of your father's solicitor, however."

"It is Mr. Bankston," she supplied. "I do not know his address, however."

"That will be easy to obtain," Linberry assured her.

"Oh, it would be wonderful if Papa had left me some money," she said, tamping down her hopes so that she wouldn't be disappointed if these men found nothing.

"If you do have a dowry, Parkhurst cannot keep it from you," the dowager duchess pointed out. "Perhaps that is why he put you to work and has never let you make your come-out," she surmised. "He was hoarding all funds for himself."

Fia sighed. "It would not surprise me if my cousin did that very thing. He was quite greedy as a child. He came to live with us when I was young, once it was determined that Mama would bear no more children and the possibility of producing an heir had passed. Theo—Parkhurst, that is—would steal food from the cupboards. He even took silver from the butler's pantry and sold it to have funds to gamble with while he was a student at university. Apparently, he was not very good at it."

Linberry looked at her, fire in his eyes. "We will look into this matter for you, my lady. I hope what we find will be pleasing to you."

"If for any reason there is no dowry, then I will provide one for you," the Duke of Westfield proclaimed.

Stunned, Fia sat in silence a moment before recovering. "I cannot allow such a thing, Your Grace. I am practically a stranger to you. Dowries are most expensive. I never would have you do this."

The duchess took Fia's hand. "My husband is mulish, Fia. If he is determined to do something, you had best go along with him."

"No," she said, her voice steady. "I will not accept His Grace's charity. I will stay in his house for a week or so. Then I will make my own way in the world, dowry or no dowry. There are people in London far more destitute than I. Help those in need, Your Grace. I can earn a living on my own."

A heavy silence hung in the air, and Fia knew she had overstepped her bounds.

She rose. "My apologies, Your Grace. I did not mean to offend you. I will pack my things and be gone within the hour."

Westfield stood. "You will do no such thing, Lady Fia. My duchess has requested your company. I aim to see she gets it. You must stay for as long as you feel comfortable doing so. I would ask a favor, however."

"What, Your Grace?" she asked, dreading his response.

"Would you play for us now that dinner is over?"

She almost went limp with relief. "I would be most happy to do so, Your Grace."

"Then we shall retire to the drawing room," the dowager duchess said. "The others are in for a treat, getting to hear you play. I, however, have done so and am tired. I will say goodnight to you all."

She left their company, and they moved from the dining room to the drawing room. Linberry again offered her his arm and Fia took it, delighted to be so close to him. He was a kind, decent man. She wished they had met under different circumstances. Mama and Papa would have liked him quite a bit. She had to remember that she was no longer of his world and only danced around its perimeter. Fia must guard her heart. She already knew he held a piece of it, which would only cause her heartbreak in the end.

They entered the drawing room, and she went to the pianoforte. "Do you have any requests?" she asked her small audience.

"Play whatever you would like," the duchess said.

Fia started with Mozart and moved to Bach before finishing up with Haydn.

"I hope that wasn't too much," she said.

"Not at all," Westfield assured her. "You play beautifully. Come join us, my lady."

She did so, and Linberry asked, "Have you ever taught adults the pianoforte, Lady Fia?"

"No, only children. Usually, adults, especially women, were introduced to the pianoforte in their childhood. Why do you ask, Your Grace?"

"I recall my mother playing some when I was a child. She stopped years ago." He hesitated. "My father died unexpectedly almost a year ago. It has upset Mama greatly. She has sunk into a lethargy which I and the doctors cannot seem to pull her from. I was hoping if she began to play once more, it might bring her solace. Would you consider taking her on as a pupil?"

She bit her lip, toying with the idea. "I would have to meet Her Grace and see if she truly would be amenable to doing so. If she agreed to lessons, I would be happy to attend to her."

Linberry smiled at her, causing Fia's heart to race. "Then you must meet Mama tomorrow." He looked to the duchess. "Would you be willing to act as Lady Fia's chaperone, Your Grace? Perhaps His Grace's grandmother might also be included in the visit."

The duchess smiled. "We would be happy to do this favor for you, Linberry." Turning to Fia, she asked, "What does your teaching schedule look like tomorrow?"

"People are only beginning to arrive in town. I was to meet with Mr. Bibby, Parkhurst's secretary, tomorrow morning. As of now, only the two Capwell girls are participating in lessons. I assume Mr. Bibby will send word to me as the schedule expands since I am here."

"When do you next see the girls?" Westfield asked.

"Not for another two days, Your Grace."

"Then you are free all day tomorrow?" Linberry asked.

"Yes, I am. That is, except for the morning. I am to see a modiste."

"Excellent." Linberry rubbed his hands together. "Come for luncheon tomorrow at one o'clock. I will make certain Mama is up and dressed. We can broach the idea with her. Afterward, you can come to our ballroom."

She frowned. "Whatever for, Your Grace?"

"We shall have our first dance lesson then, Lady Fia."

CHAPTER TEN

Henry had stopped in to see his mother when he returned from the Duke of Westfield's, having spent a good portion of his day with the duke.

And Lady Fia.

When he reached home, his mother's maid told him that Her Grace had retired for the evening. He told the maid he would be back at eleven tomorrow morning—and that he expected his mother to be awake in order to receive a visit from him.

He had risen early and ridden in Rotten Row again this morning, seeing Daniel there. They had ridden for half an hour and then walked their horses through Hyde Park in the early morning mist, the conversation easy between them.

Before they parted, Daniel had pointedly asked, "Are you interested in pursuing Lady Fia?"

Henry had no ready answer, being torn about her, and told the duke while he was considering taking a bride this Season, he would have to give it some thought.

Daniel had snorted. "Better not think for too long, Henry. Lady Fia might be a diamond in the rough now—but she is clever and kind and will be snatched up quickly."

He didn't want to admit that was a strong possibility because his feelings for Lady Fia were very mixed.

On one hand, he thought her cheerful and optimistic, if a bit on the quiet side. She had proven just how talented she was on the pianoforte last night in the Westfields' drawing room. And she was quite attractive. He had thought her merely pretty at first, but her looks were growing on him.

At the same time, he had never been one for controversy—and controversy would surround this woman. Already, she was known in the *ton* for giving music lessons to children. Ladies didn't simply have an occupation in Polite Society. Yet Henry understood that Lady Fia had not been given any choice in the matter. To keep a roof over her head and food in her belly, she had acquiesced to her cousin's wishes and gone out and taught a good number of pupils, not seeing a single farthing of the money she earned.

He was torn. His attraction to her was growing by the minute, but he didn't believe her to be suitable material as a duchess. Henry had always conducted himself as a gentleman, with none of the playing the rogue as so many men his age did. He didn't gamble. He drank in moderation. He was responsible and dependable. Moreover, he expected his choice in a bride to be a proper young lady, free of entanglements and scandals. He had told himself it would be best to look among the new girls making their come-outs this year. Choose one that was pliable and mold her into the type of duchess he wanted.

Yet all of a sudden, all he seemed to want was a golden-haired beauty with deep blue eyes and delicate features. One who'd had a difficult time for many years yet kept her chin up and did everything asked of her.

Could Lady Fia Sawyer make good duchess material?

Henry didn't know. He didn't want to ask Daniel because he thought his new friend would berate him for having to even ask that question. Already, Henry had learned that while Daniel was an example all dukes should aspire to be, he was a man in love with his wife and would do whatever necessary to please her. His duchess and grandmother had taken a shine to Lady Fia, so Daniel would support the woman in all things. Especially in helping her find a husband.

Perhaps he should merely do as the Duchess of Westfield asked. Dance once with Lady Fia and then let the other eligible suitors have at her. Of course, he must teach her to dance first before that occurred.

And that was something Henry was looking forward to.

After breakfasting and reading the newspapers, he retreated to his study to look over his correspondence. He had already received a mountain of invitations to the upcoming Season's events. Suddenly, they didn't seem to have much appeal to them. Unless Lady Fia might attend the same event.

"Balderdash!" he said aloud to the empty room.

He needed to stop thinking of the chit. Once more, he buried himself in his papers, including reviewing the last three months of reports sent to him by his Linfield steward, as well as the other reports submitted to him from his various holdings. This time, instead of skimming them as he usually did, Henry read them with a more critical eye. Daniel had talked so knowledgeably of his various estates yesterday. It had made Henry want to take a better interest in his own lands.

When the clock chimed eleven, he left his study and went upstairs to his mother's suite of rooms. He had offered her those of the duchess when they returned to town, but she had refused, wishing to remain in the rooms she always had stayed in when they had come to London from their country estate. On the other hand, Henry had moved into the duke's rooms. He recalled his daily visits to his grandfather in them, and though all his grandfather's things had been removed by Bosley, whom Henry had pensioned off, it still felt odd to him. Sleeping in the bed his grandfather had slept in. Sitting in the chair and having Ripley shave him, knowing Bosley had done the same for the old duke. Perhaps when he wed, he would allow his wife to redecorate these rooms. Of course, she would be installed in the suite of rooms belonging to the duchess.

Knocking upon his mother's door, her lady's maid answered.

"Her Grace is awake, Your Grace. She is still abed, however."

"I will see her now," he said.

Henry went through the sitting room and entered her bed-chamber, where his mother sat in bed, pillows fluffed behind her. A tray was in her lap, and she picked at the food there. She had lost weight during her year of mourning, another thing that concerned him, since she was almost too thin.

"So, you are now dictating when I have to awake and rise?" she asked, her displeasure with him clear.

"We are having guests for luncheon at one o'clock, Mama," he told her, perching on the side of the bed next to her and taking her hands in his. "Since we have returned to town, I have become friendly with the Duke of Westfield."

For the first time in a long time, her eyes lit with interest. "Westfield, you say? Oh, he is lovely. Your father had a slight acquaintance with Westfield and spoke well of him."

"I like His Grace quite a bit," Henry told her. "I have also met his wife and grandmother. They are calling on us today for luncheon, along with a friend of the duchess, Lady Fia."

"They are coming here? Today?" She nudged him from the bed and tossed back the bedclothes. Swinging her legs to the ground, she stood and looked to her maid. "What shall I wear? It will be two duchesses."

He did not remind her that she was a duchess herself. His father had held the title for a handful of hours before he died from the tragic fall. It still entitled his mother, though, to claim being the Duchess of Linberry. At least until Henry wed and his wife took that on, with his mother becoming the dowager duchess.

The maid stepped up. "The bottle green gown would be lovely, Your Grace."

Henry gave the servant a grateful smile. His mother had worn nothing but black and dark grays during the past year. It was time she came out of her mourning period and rejoined society.

"Yes, I think it will do. Press it now. And call for a bath for me."

"Yes, Your Grace." The maid left the room.

Henry smiled at Mama. "I have already informed Cook of our visitors today, but if you have any special requests, you can pass them along to her."

"Oh, I trust Cook completely. But a visit from *two* duchesses? This is wonderful news, Henry." She paused a moment and then added, "I know I have not been much company for you this past year. I miss your father terribly. Perhaps you are right, though, and I should take part in the upcoming Season. It would be good to see my friends again."

"That would entail a visit to your modiste," he told her. "While you are waiting for your bath, you could dash off a note to her."

She came and cupped his cheek. "You are a good son, Henry. I will do just that."

"Then I will leave you to it, Mama."

He left, returning to his study, hope filling him that today's visit would spark his mother's interest, and she truly would begin to live again. He thought he would share with her later that he was ready to take a bride. She might have some suggestions regarding his choice and help him narrow down the list of candidates.

Immediately, Lady Fia came to mind.

He knew her sweet nature would impress his mother, but Henry thought it best to step away from her. Yes, he had asked her to give Mama lessons on the pianoforte, and he had promised to teach her how to dance, but that was where those obligations ended. He still believed it best to choose a younger woman to become his duchess.

Just before one o'clock, the Westfield ducal carriage pulled up in front of the townhouse. He watched as the footman handed down the dowager duchess, then duchess, and finally Lady Fia. Though he had never really noticed what other women wore, he was aware of it now, especially because he knew how limited her wardrobe truly was. Today, she wore a gown of powder blue, very plain in design when compared to the day gowns worn by the other two women who accompanied her. He wondered if his mother would also notice and suspected she would.

Leaving his study, he went to the foyer, where Orville was greeting the party of three.

"Good afternoon, ladies," Henry said. "Let me take you to my mother."

He knew from past experience that his mother would be waiting in the drawing room. She was never one to keep visitors tapping their feet, and he led them upstairs. As they entered the room, his mother rose, looking lovely, a smile on her face for their guests.

Leading the party toward her, Henry said, "Your Grace, may I present to you my mother, the Duchess of Linberry."

His mother took the duchess' hand. "It is a delight to meet you, Your Grace."

He then introduced the dowager duchess and once more, his mother greeted the older woman warmly.

Then he said, "Finally, I present Lady Fia Sawyer."

Lady Fia dropped a curtsey and smiled up at his mother. "I am honored to meet you, Your Grace."

"Fia. What a lovely name."

"Actually, it is Sophia, Your Grace, but my father called me Fia from the cradle."

"And who might your parents be, Lady Fia?" his mother inquired.

Henry noted the shadow that crossed her face. "They were the Earl and Countess of Parkhurst, Your Grace. They have been gone for seven years now. I am an only child, and so my cousin inherited my father's title."

"Oh, I remember your mother clearly," Mama said brightly. "She was a lovely woman and always spoke so fondly of you, my lady."

Tears brimmed in Lady Fia's eyes. "Thank you for sharing

that with me. I miss both my parents a great deal."

Mama nodded. "I, too, have someone I miss dearly. My husband, Lord Strumbull, passed almost a year ago. Not a day goes by that I do not think of him." She took Lady Fia's hands in hers. "I am grateful for your visit today. It is the first time I have not dressed in mourning clothes."

"I know you must miss Lord Strumbull, but you have a fine son, Your Grace. The duke must be wonderful company to you."

"Alas," his mother said, "I have not been good company for Linberry. In my grief, I have locked myself away from the world and neglected him. My son is encouraging me to attend the upcoming Season."

"You should do so, Your Grace," Lady Fia encouraged. "While it will not bring your husband back, it would give you time to spend with friends." She looked to the Duchess of Westfield. "I am discovering just how important friendship can be."

The butler entered and announced luncheon was served.

Mama tucked her hand into Lady Fia's arm and said, "We should go and eat." Looking to Henry, she added, "Please escort the two duchesses in, Linberry."

As they left the drawing room, he said, "We are dining in the breakfast room. It is smaller and full of light. I thought it would be a more cheerful experience."

Henry was amazed at the change in his mother. She had barely put two sentences together for a year and had seemed interested in nothing. All of a sudden, she seemed to come to life again, thanks to the visit from these three women. He said very little during the meal, looking on approvingly as the women discussed everything from the latest fashions to the birth of the duchess' daughter two months ago.

"I had no siblings, and so I had not been around babes before," the duchess said. "But our Norrie has such a sunny nature for a child so young. Perhaps you might like to come to tea, Your Grace, and meet our daughter."

"I would very much like to do so," his mother replied. "I myself only had the one son and wished more babes could have come."

The meal was drawing to an end. Henry decided now was the time to approach his mother about lessons since she seemed to be in such a good mood.

"Mama, Lady Fia is a very talented musician. She plays numerous instruments." He looked at her and nodded encouragingly.

"Yes, Your Grace. I started on the pianoforte, and my music master discovered I had quite an affinity for it and music in general. He suggested I also take up the violin. I did so and then taught myself how to play the viola, cello, and harp."

"How remarkable," his mother commented. "Would you be willing to play some for us now?"

"I would like that very much."

"Then we should adjourn to the drawing room," he suggested.

Once more, his mother took Lady Fia's arm, so Henry escorted their other guests back upstairs.

"Come and sit with me, Your Grace," Lady Fia urged. "We can decide what I should play."

After huddling briefly, Lady Fia nodded and began to play. Henry watched her expression as she played, seeing a multitude of emotions revealed on it. When the last note sounded, she turned and smiled at his mother.

In that moment, Henry lost his heart to Fia Sawyer.

The two women rose and joined them.

"I so enjoy hearing you play, Lady Fia," the dowager duchess said. "I wish I had kept up with my own lessons and practice."

Lady Fia sprang from that remark and said, "I don't believe it is ever too late to continue playing." She turned to Henry's mother and asked, "Do you play, Your Grace?"

Sadness filled Mama's face. "I used to. A long time ago."

"Did it bring you pleasure?" Lady Fia asked.

"As a matter of fact, it did. I am not quite certain why I gave it up. I suppose my duties in running a household and raising my son became more important."

Lady Fia smiled warmly. "Well, His Grace is grown and certainly can take care of himself. As for his household, I am certain you have selected capable servants, and you could manage to steal an hour a day to play music strictly for yourself."

Doubt filled his mother's eyes. "Oh, my lady, I don't know about that."

Lady Fia took Henry's mother's hand in hers and said firmly, "Women do not do enough for themselves. They are always thinking of others. You have reached a time in your life, Your Grace, where it is time for *you*. If you enjoy playing, you should take up the instrument again."

"I don't think I could," his mother said. "The thought of sitting at the pianoforte again overwhelms me."

"Then I would be happy to step in and allay your fears. You see, I give music lessons to children of Polite Society. I teach the pianoforte and also the other instruments I play. I would not ask you to take up a new instrument, but I encourage you to play again for yourself. If you would like, I could spend a few hours with you and reintroduce you to playing. It would just be the two of us. No one else allowed in the room. You could discover if playing still brings you joy or not. What do you say, Your Grace?"

Henry held his breath as his mother hesitated. He couldn't tell her what to do. It was important that she come to this decision herself.

Finally, she smiled. "I would be happy to have you sit with me, Lady Fia, and see if you can teach this old dog some new tricks."

CHAPTER ELEVEN

F IA WAS PLEASED that the Duke of Linberry's mother had agreed to sit down at the keys of a pianoforte again.

"Do you remember some of the composers you were fond of?" she asked.

"Oh, I was particularly drawn to baroque. Scarlatti's sonatas and Bach's inventions, in particular," the duchess told her.

"Bach's inventions can become quite complicated. I think Number Eight would be a good one to start with, however. I will bring sheet music for it and anything of Scarlatti's that I can find." She hesitated and then said, "I will also bring some simpler songs, Your Grace. Bach's 'Minuet in G,' for instance. You must remember that it has been a good while since you touched a keyboard."

"I understand, my lady. When might you be free to instruct me?"

"Would tomorrow morning be good for you?" she asked, knowing that when she was in her deepest grief over her parents' deaths that she did better when she forced herself to rise and dress each morning.

"How about ten o'clock?" the duchess suggested.

"I will be here at ten," Fia promised.

"That reminds me of my promise," the Duke of Linberry said. "Mama, I am going to teach Lady Fia how to dance."

"How to dance?" his mother asked, clearly puzzled.

The Duchess of Westfield smiled. "Lady Fia spent a great deal of time in the country, Your Grace. After her parents' deaths, she wasn't ready to make her come-out. She has chosen to devote her time to her music and the pupils she instructs. I have convinced my friend that it is time for her to take her place in Polite Society."

The duke rose. "You know how I love to dance, Mama. After all, it is you who taught me how to do so. I offered to teach Lady Fia a few dances. I hope you can entertain our other guests for an hour or two while I make good on my promise."

His mother smiled approvingly. "Of course, Linberry." She turned to Fia. "If I may say so, my son is a most excellent dancer."

"I hope he will have patience with me," she said. "I have never attended a ball."

"Run along," the duchess encouraged. "You are in good hands with my son, my lady."

The thought of the duke's hands anywhere near her caused Fia to tremble.

They left the drawing room, and he said, "I thought we would go to the ballroom. That way, you will be familiar with one and not awed by it when you should be concentrating on your dancing."

"I did come to town with Mama and Papa each year, Your Grace, and we did have a ballroom. It is not as if I have never seen one."

"No," he said, a smile tugging at the corners of his mouth, "but you have never danced in one. There *is* a difference."

Fia knew there would be a difference. Because dancing involved touching your partner at certain times.

Touching *this* man was not a good idea. It would make her want things she couldn't have and show her how empty her life truly was. She had to find a way to put an end to this lesson.

They went to the ballroom. It was vast. Then again, this was the residence of a duke. Linberry pointed out where the musicians would sit and where his mother usually placed tables with beverages for their guests, as well as the area where the matrons sat to watch the dancers.

"I think I would be more comfortable with the matrons than out on the dance floor," she told him. "I have thought about this, Your Grace. I don't really think learning to dance is something I wish to pursue. I have observed a country ball my parents gave for their tenants. The English country dances were so lively. I fear my leg—actually, my knee—would never hold up to the strain."

His brow furrowed in thought. "You are right, my lady. Many of the dances are lively ones and would create a situation that might not suit your old injury. But," he added, "I believe there is one dance which would not be difficult for you to learn and would be much easier on your joints. The waltz."

Not the waltz . . .

Fia had never seen it danced before, but she certainly was aware of it. It was unlike reels or country dances, in that the entire waltz was performed with one partner. A partner who would hold her close the entire time the music played. She couldn't possibly allow the duke to teach her this dance.

"Come, let us go to the center of the room," he suggested.

Reluctantly, she followed him there.

"Let me show you the stance first."

"No."

His brows arched. "No? But how are you to learn the waltz if we do not practice it, my lady?"

"I cannot," she said, vigorously shaking her head. "I think it too . . . too . . ." Her voice trailed off.

"Too intimate?"

"Yes. I do not believe I should dance so closely to another, Your Grace. I have read Almack's does not even permit it to be danced there. Surely, the patronesses know better."

The duke stepped toward her, so close that she caught the tang of his cologne and felt the heat emanating from his body. "Yet the *ton* does dance the waltz in its ballrooms. It is not overly strenuous, Lady Fia. If you are to have one dance in your repertoire, it should be the waltz. Why don't we try it first before you make any decision?"

She gritted her teeth, knowing she couldn't speak the truth. It wasn't as if she could tell the duke that she was attracted to him and she felt it unwise to attempt learning to waltz with him.

"Perhaps a dance master would be better," she tossed out.

He shook his head. "They will all be booked with lessons for those girls making their come-outs. Besides, you heard my mother. I am an excellent dancer. The waltz is simple enough to dance. I hope I would be able to explain its steps and demonstrate them appropriately to you." His gaze burned into her. "Do you not believe I could be a teacher as you are?"

The hot blush scorched her cheeks. "I am implying nothing of the kind, Your Grace. I am certain you could do so. I just do not believe that I would be the best pupil. Despite my love of music, I am not graceful in the slightest. I fear I have two left feet and would make a fool of myself."

He smiled, warming her insides. "Then let me be the judge of that, Lady Fia. I am a patient man. If I cannot teach you the waltz, then I will admit defeat."

She knew further protests would land on deaf ears. "Then let us try. Be so good as to show me the steps."

Instead, he took her left hand and placed it on his shoulder, then sought her right hand and wrapped his left one around it. His right hand came to her shoulder blade. They stood so closely together that her breasts almost brushed his wide chest. Fia froze, a paralyzing bewilderment holding her in place.

"This is our stance," the duke said. "Be sure your feet are hip's distance apart."

She swallowed. "They are."

"We will keep our upper bodies straight and yet relaxed. All the movement will occur below our waists. You are going to start with your right foot. Bend your right leg slightly at the knee and step back so you land on the ball of your foot first."

He nudged her and she took a step backward.

"Have the left join it, staying parallel. Good. Now slide your right foot to your left, so they are barely touching. Nice. Again."

She repeated the steps and Linberry nodded. "You'll keep your feet low to the ground as we move from side to side. Now this time when we finish, move your left foot forward, landing on the ball first."

Fia did so stiffly.

"Relax your knees," he instructed. "And once the left foot has gone forward, bring the right foot up and parallel, then sweep the left to where it touches the right."

They tried the set of footsteps several times.

"It is a box," she realized. "Six steps and a box is formed."

"True. Now, we add a count. I don't know what this would be called formally in music, but the music goes in threes." Linberry held up his index finger. "Bum, bum-bum. Bum, bum-bum. Hear how I am emphasizing that first beat? That's the movement of stepping forward or backward. The other two beats are low to the ground and light. Let's put the steps together."

He began counting, and she followed his lead. Actually, the steps were quite simple as they moved back and forth.

"If you are moving well with your partner, he may guide you in circles. We should try that."

The duke had them make a quarter turn after the first two steps, so slight but very fluid.

"Do you always turn in the same direction?" she asked.

"Yes. The man always moves to his left and your right," he explained. "Are you ready to put everything together?"

"I think so," she said hesitantly.

He studied her. "There is nothing to fear. Your partner will take care of you. Let him guide you. Move on the second count of three."

He began counting again, and she followed instinctively. They danced back and forth several counts before he did a quarter-turn. Fia continued to land on the balls of her feet and moved when he did.

"I wish we had music," he told her. "Counting seems to take the romance from the waltz."

"I can help."

She began humming a tune in three-quarter time as they moved about the ballroom floor.

"Much better," he said, gazing down at her.

Fia could either stare at his chest or look into his eyes. She chose the latter, focusing on him as she hummed, moving with him as one. He began alternating their turns, sometimes only a quarter and sometimes a three-quarter turn. No matter which, she felt as if she was gliding across the ballroom.

"You are quite light on your feet, my lady."

"You are the light, graceful one, Your Grace," she praised. "Dancing with you is like dancing on a cloud."

He came to a halt and searched her face. Fia was aware how closely they stood. How her breasts now rested against his muscular chest. How his warm hand graced her back and his other one held hers lightly yet firmly. A deep longing filled her, unlike any she had ever known. She could not put words to it, only that she wanted him to never let her go.

"You know how to dance now, Fia," he told her, still holding her to him.

She should break away. Chide him for using her given name. But all Fia could do was stare up at him. She wet her lips nervously and saw his eyes drop to her mouth. Slowly, his head moved closer to her until his lips hovered just above hers. Still, he restrained himself.

"I want to kiss you," he said, his voice raw, full of emotion. "More than anything, I need to kiss you."

She made a decision. "Then do so, Your Grace. Because I want you to."

Fia couldn't believe she was being so brazen, especially since she had never been kissed. Her fear was if she passed up this moment, no other ones would follow. She was curious what a kiss was like.

Especially with the Duke of Linberry.

His lips touched hers, and she felt his smile against them. Then he softly brushed his lips against hers, over and over, the repeated action causing her belly to flutter. His hand tightened around hers, and his other nudged her until she was flush against him, able to feel his heart beating against her, its quick pace letting her know he was as moved as she was in this moment.

His mouth covered hers, harder this time, more demanding. She felt the place between her legs tighten. The kiss became intense, with all kinds of feelings rushing through, feelings she would deliberate on later because now—now—she only wanted to live in this moment.

Surprisingly, his tongue suddenly glided along her bottom lip, causing her to whimper. The duke's arm seemed to be the only thing holding her up as her knees grew weak, her limbs melting like snow on a sun-filled day. His tongue then moved along the seam of her lips, urging her to open to him. Fia had no idea what was going on, but answered by relaxing her jaw.

His tongue moved inside her mouth, shocking her. It stroked her tongue, causing shivers to run along her spine. Linberry leisurely explored every crevice he found, making her heart beat in double-time, sensations rippling through her like none she had ever known. His tongue grazed the roof of her mouth, causing her to giggle, something totally out of character, then he was drinking from her deeply, possessing her, making her feel as if she were one with him.

The kiss was reminiscent of the waltz as they moved to a music of their own making, intimate, passionate, and driving Fia to yearn for more.

But she was no typical member of the *ton*—and Linberry wasn't just a titled gentleman. He was a duke, someone totally beyond her reach. She had to stop this from going further.

Even as she relished the feel of him against her.

Fia turned her head, breaking the kiss, both of them panting from exertion. When she got up the courage to look him in the eyes, she saw the heat there and knew it was desire.

Desire for her.

Wriggling, she pulled her hand from his and stepped a few paces back, her breath still ragged.

"I am not sorry that I asked you to kiss me, Your Grace. I will say that it is unwise to ever repeat such an action."

Disappointment filled his face. "I asked to kiss you, Fia. Not the other way around. I am sorry the kiss went so far."

"I'm not," she said boldly. "I have never experienced a kiss before. I doubt I ever will again." She smiled wistfully. "You have given me a lovely memory, Your Grace."

He stepped toward her. "What if it did not remain a memory? What if it became a daily reality?"

She placed her palm against that rock-hard chest. "No. There will be no other kisses for us. You will wed a woman of wealth and intelligence, while I have no plans to wed at all. My desire is to continue to play my music. I have even begun writing compositions of my own. My goal is to play at *ton* events, Your Grace—not dance at them. I will humor the duchess and go to a few social affairs, but you and I both know my place is no longer in the glittering world of the *ton*."

Fia dropped her hand, feeling bereft as the contact between them ended. "I hope to play at balls and private events. Possibly even the opera. Your duchess may one day be gracious enough to hire me to play at a ball you hold in this very room. I might even teach the pianoforte to your children. But we will never speak of this kiss again, Your Grace. It is as if it never happened. Let us return to the others."

With regret, Fia turned away from the handsome Duke of Linberry and left the ballroom, her head held high.

CHAPTER TWELVE

FIA AWOKE AND rang for Millie. The maid arrived in an excellent mood.

"Oh, Lady Fia, isn't it simply wonderful here? The staff adores the duke and duchess. They all say it is the best household to work in."

"I am glad to see you so happy, Millie."

As the maid helped Fia into her undergarments, she said, "I would think you, too, would be happy to be here, my lady. Why, look at this lovely room you have been given."

"I am fortunate to have gained the friendship of Her Grace and the dowager duchess," she admitted.

Millie continued chattering away about various servants. Fia decided when the time came for her to leave the duke's household that she would ask Margaret to employ Millie. There was no way Fia could take the servant with her, and Millie seemed so happy now—as was Fia herself. Just being out from under Parkhurst's roof was not only like that first breath of fresh air on a cold winter's morning, but no longer living in his household had cleared Fia's mind, as well.

She chastised herself for being such a timid bird around Parkhurst. Now that she had physically escaped the man's control, thanks to her wonderful new friend's encouragement, Fia knew the next logical step was to rent those rooms and assert her independence from Parkhurst. After all, she was of legal age and had a means to support herself, unlike many women of the *ton*. By playing at the Capwells' ball, she truly believed it would lead to offers of teaching music lessons to other students. If she combined that with sewing, she could support herself and be free of the cage Parkhurst had imprisoned her in. Her wings would no longer be clipped, and she could soar to dizzying heights, courtesy of her music.

"When will you receive your new gowns, my lady?"

"The modiste has me coming back in three days' time."

"Tell me about them."

Fia described the five day gowns and two ball gowns she had allowed to be made up for her. She had explicitly asked the modiste for the gowns to be simple yet elegant because she planned to wear them when she played in the ballrooms of members of the *ton*. She hoped Lord Capwell had already approached Parkhurst and gained her cousin's approval so that she would be able to play at the opening ball. She knew of no woman who was a professional musician and while her presence might cause a stir, she believed her talent would win Polite Society over. It might be a novelty for her to play at balls, and she knew members of the *ton* enjoyed anything that brought them attention and made them stand above the crowd.

Fia went down to the large breakfast room, where she found the duke and duchess already seated. She had learned that the dowager duchess preferred taking her morning meal in her room.

"Good morning, Your Graces. I hope you slept well."

She allowed a footman to seat her, while another brought her a cup of tea, and a different one delivered a covered dish with her breakfast.

"Oh, Fia, please do call us by our given names," Margaret reminded her.

"It is hard to get into a habit such as that," she admitted. "However, I will try my best while I am here."

The butler brought the morning post to the duke, and he

thumbed through it.

"You have a few letters, Fia," he told her, giving them to a footman, who presented them to her.

"Ah, I recognize Bibby's handwriting. He must have placed some students on my new schedule for the spring."

She opened the letter and found that to be the case.

The next letter was from Lady Capwell, telling Fia that if she was still inclined to do so, she could play the harp at the opening ball of the Season since Lord Capwell had spoken to Lord Parkhurst and received his permission.

"Now, this is good news to share," she said. "I will be playing my harp at the Capwells' ball."

Disappointment crossed Margaret's face. "I know this is something you wish to achieve. I am only sorry that you will not be able to dance that night."

Talk of dancing brought back her lesson with Linberry yesterday, something Fia had deliberately not thought of. She could not afford to sit and dream about a life she was unsuited for.

Even though she was highly suited for kissing the duke.

"I only learned the waltz from His Grace," she told the pair. "Because of my delicate leg and knee, we agreed that lively reels and country dances would not be in my best interest. So if I do any dancing at a future ball, it must be the waltz."

The third letter awaiting her gave her pause. It was Parkhurst's handwriting. She swallowed and broke the seal.

Bibby will forward your teaching schedule to you, revising it as he arranges for new lessons to be given.

Lord Capwell spoke to me at White's yesterday, practically begging for you to play the harp at the ball he and his wife will host. That is something which I reluctantly granted my permission, though I now think it will be a good thing for you to play in public. That is, if you do an excellent job of it. If you stumble, you will embarrass not only yourself but me, as well.

For that reason alone, I will have the harp delivered to His Grace's residence later today. I urge you to practice every avail-

able moment when not sitting for Her Grace or teaching your pupils.

I hope by the time of the Capwells' ball that Her Grace will already have completed her portrait of you. When she does, have her paint over it. I have no need of your image in my household and would not pay for it.

Bibby reminded me your pin money will be due soon. I shall have him send it to you, as well. Do what you can with it to improve your wardrobe. We cannot have you looking shabby and reflecting poorly upon me.

Parkhurst

She closed her eyes a moment, calming herself. When she opened them, she saw Margaret looking at her in concern.

"Did you receive bad news, Fia?"

"It was a letter from my cousin. I shouldn't ever let what he says upset me."

"May I see it?" the duke asked.

Fia reluctantly handed it over. The duke's lips thinned as he read through it. He then passed it to his wife as Fia tried to eat some of her eggs.

"The man is outrageous," Margaret declared.

She shrugged. "What can I say? That is Parkhurst." She looked to the duke. "I have a favor to ask of you, Daniel," she said, deliberating using his Christian name in hopes of getting what she wanted. "My cousin lent me a horse and cart which I used to go to my lessons. I was hoping we might come to a similar arrangement."

"That's nonsense. You may have my carriage or my grandmother's to take you to and from your appointments."

Frowning, she said, "I am afraid that won't do. You see, by the time my teaching schedule fills, I am gone all day. I leave shortly after breakfast and usually do not return until five or six o'clock in the evening. I could not tie up your carriage that way."

"I have a barouche," he suggested. "I could have a footman

drive you in it."

"It might not be large enough for the two of us and my instruments, Daniel. Truly, if you will give me use of a horse and cart, I do not mind driving myself. After all, I am four and twenty and do not need a chaperone."

Fia hoped the duke would agree with her request because after her lesson this morning with the Duchess of Linberry, she had two different rooms she wanted to look at to see if either would be suitable for her to let once she ventured out on her own.

"If that is what you wish, Fia, I will arrange for it with my head groom."

"Thank you, Daniel. I hope it will not inconvenience you."

"Not in the slightest."

As they continued eating breakfast, she said, "I hope you don't mind my harp being delivered here."

"It can go in the music room with your other instruments," the duke said. "I hope you will play it for us. I have never heard a harpist play before. It is a most unusual instrument and never a part of the orchestra at balls."

"Give me half an hour to practice once it arrives, and then I would be delighted to play for you. The dowager duchess, as well."

Daniel rose. "I will go see the groom now about your transportation, Fia. When is your first lesson?"

"Not until ten o'clock. I am seeing the Duchess of Linberry."

"Would you mind coming to my sitting room now?" Margaret asked. "I would like to show you a couple of sketches I have done of you and perhaps do a few more while we are together."

They went to the sitting room, and Fia was amazed at the sketches shown to her.

"You have captured my likeness quite well. I don't often see myself. It is interesting to see how you view me."

"Don't tell me you did not even have a mirror at Parkhurst's," Margaret bemoaned.

She grinned mischievously. "Then I won't say another word."

Fia sat and talked with her friend for half an hour while Margaret sketched her numerous times.

"I like to draw my subjects as we talk. It helps me capture a variety of emotions." She put down her pencil. "I am sorry what Parkhurst said about painting over your portrait, Fia. I know that had to sting."

"Just when I think he cannot hurt me anymore, he does or says something that cuts me to the quick. He is right, though, Margaret. He will not pay for your work. I will have nowhere to display it. You might as well paint over it."

"Why do you say that? I have high hopes that as you make your come-out, you will draw the interest of eligible bachelors. Surely, one of them will offer for you." Margaret smiled, a twinkle in her eyes. "In fact, I have a suspicion that the Duke of Linberry might offer for you himself."

Heat rose in Fia's cheeks as she shook her head. "The duke is very nice and most handsome—but he *is* a duke. He would have no need to offer for me, a penniless music teacher. I know you and the dowager duchess want to launch me into Polite Society and hope that I make a match. Frankly, I don't believe it to be possible. I have skated on the edges of the *ton* for too long now. Besides, I would not feel comfortable being a full member. And we both know men wanting to wed are looking for ways to improve their social position and line their pockets. I may be the daughter of an earl, but I am more like an indentured servant. Despite what His Grace thinks, I doubt there is a dowry. If there had been, Parkhurst would have most certainly spent it on himself."

"He cannot do that legally," Margaret insisted. "I will tell you that Daniel has tracked down your solicitor. His office was closed, and Daniel spoke to the shopkeeper next door. It seems Mr. Bankston's brother up in Liverpool recently passed and that Mr. Bankston has gone north to settle the estate. Once he returns, however, Daniel will get to the bottom of this mystery."

She took Fia's hand. "And remember, Daniel himself said he would gift you a dowry."

Fia smiled sadly. "I know he offered to do so, but I cannot take his charity, Margaret. I don't have many things left to me—but one of them is my pride. I won't have the duke try to buy a husband for me. I know you mean well, but I must insist this not occur."

"Very well then. We will respect your wishes."

A knock sounded at the door, and the butler entered.

"Your Grace, Lady Fia's harp has arrived. I wanted to see if you wished for it to be placed in the music room."

"Yes, Hampton. It will allow Lady Fia privacy in which to practice it. Thank you."

"If you are finished sketching me, Margaret, I would like to go and supervise where the harp should sit."

"Of course. Go ahead. I will continue working on my sketches. When you come home later today, you can choose your favorites among them, and then I will begin your portrait."

"Even though no one will want it?"

"I will want it," her friend insisted. "You are becoming very dear to me, Fia." Margaret kissed Fia's cheek.

She left the sitting room and went to the foyer, recognizing several of her cousin's footmen. Following them to the music room, she had them set the harp near a window.

The footmen left, and the butler asked, "Will there be anything more, my lady?"

"No, thank you."

Fia warmed up her fingers with scales and then played two songs, the harp's tone soothing her. She then went to the two ornamental boxes in the corner of the room, selecting sheet music to bring with her to the Linberry townhouse.

Leaving the music room, she found the butler again and told him she needed the cart prepared for her.

"At once, my lady. It will be waiting outside the front door for you."

She went up to her bedchamber and retrieved her bonnet and shawl and slipped the newspaper page of advertisements inside her reticule. After meeting with the duchess, she would go and look at the two rooms, hoping one of them might become her new home.

Excitement filled her at the prospect of being mistress of her own place, even if it only entailed one very small room. No matter its size, it would be hers. All hers. Parkhurst would have no say in where she lived, or whether or not she could play her instruments at a ball, or write her own music. And for that matter, she was not the earl's chattel. Fia determined to put an end to Parkhurst collecting all the fees for the lessons *she* gave. She would speak to her clients' parents and set her own schedule from now on, arranging payment to come directly to her. She suspected by gaining those funds, she would have more than enough to live upon.

Returning downstairs, filled with exhilaration, she went outside and found a groom waiting beside the cart. He helped her into it, and she took up the reins. It only took her ten minutes to reach her destination. A footman greeted her and handed her down, saying he would stay with the horse and cart.

Fia thanked him and then went to the front door, praying she would not run into the Duke of Linberry.

CHAPTER THIRTEEN

Henry brooded in his study. He berated himself for having kissed Fia Sawyer. For offering for the chit.

Well, he hadn't *actually* offered for her. Not in so many words. After he had kissed her—the most magnificent kiss of his life—he had stupidly apologized for kissing her so thoroughly.

Even though he hadn't been sorry at all.

Then she had informed Henry she wasn't sorry about any of it, revealing she had never been kissed before, a fact that brought him immense satisfaction. That was, until she'd ruined it. She'd told him there would be no more kisses between them, informing him whom he should wed and making it perfectly clear that it would not be her. Lady Fia had no plans to wed. All she wanted to do was write music and perform it for others. She had predicted she might play for his guests in his ballroom one day and even give music lessons to his children.

She had left him speechless when she'd insisted they never mention the kiss again, breezily removing herself from the ballroom and having them join the others in the drawing room. The Duchess of Westfield and the dowager duchess then thanked him and his mother for a lovely afternoon, and Lady Fia left with them—leaving Henry shocked by her behavior.

And bedazzled.

He had never wanted a woman more than he had Lady Fia

Sawyer. Though he knew it foolish to try and pursue her, a part of him wanted to anyway. To somehow make her his.

Which was why he now brooded in his study, continually watching out the window for the ducal carriage to arrive, since he knew she was to give his mother a music lesson this morning.

"Bloody hell!" he roared, slamming a fist on his desk, his frustration growing by the minute.

Henry wanted to kiss her again. In fact, he wanted to do much more than kiss her. He wanted to possess her. Lady Fia had gotten under his skin. It was as if she were some addiction which he could not deny himself. That was utterly foolish. The *ton* would have a large group of women he could choose a bride from this coming Season. Newcomers making their come-outs. More seasoned girls who had a Season or two behind them. Even young widows rejoining Polite Society. A bevy of beauties that would be at his disposal, any one of them eager to wed a duke and become his duchess.

Then why on God's green earth was he only interested in the one woman who never wished to marry?

He blew out a long breath, crossing his hands behind his head and leaning back in his chair, placing booted feet atop his desk. The Season started in about ten days or so. It would be easy to avoid Lady Fia during that time. Once it began, he would honor his commitment and dance a single waltz with her—then move forward and find a wife who would appreciate him.

Yet like the siren's call from ancient Greek mythology, Henry found himself enthralled by Lady Fia. It was as if he were a sailor being lured by her enchanting music and voice. Those sailors in lore who listened to the siren's call wound up shipwrecked—or dead.

He couldn't understand why she drew him in the way she did. Maybe it was the thought of not being able to have her that whetted his appetite for her. If that were the case, then he would need to kiss her one more time to prove to himself that she wasn't any different than any other woman of the *ton*.

But his heart told him she was that rare gem among women, one who did not realize her own worth. Still, Henry had a reputation to maintain as a duke. He had always held himself to a higher standard and did not want the Vaughn name coupled with gossip or scandal of any kind. Lady Fia Sawyer was trouble. No good would come of yearning for her. He would put her from his mind and have his mother help him find a duchess.

Movement caught his eye, and he saw a horse and cart stop outside his townhouse.

Good God, Lady Fia was driving the vehicle!

Henry watched as a footman helped her down and retrieved a satchel for her. Ignoring everything he had just told himself, he hurried from his study to the foyer, arriving as Lady Fia entered, being greeted by Orville.

"Lady Fia," he said sternly, his voice expressing his disapproval.

She looked up, seeming so fragile, her blue eyes drawing him in. "Good morning, Your Grace. I am here to see your mother." She dipped a curtsey to him.

"Yes, I remember your appointment. May I take you to the drawing room?"

"Of course, Your Grace, but I was here only yesterday. I do believe I can find the drawing room on my own. I have always been good with directions."

He merely frowned at her and offered his arm to her. She took it—and a ripple of need burst inside him at the touch. Henry swallowed, drowning in desire for her. He tightened his jaw and led her up the stairs to the drawing room.

His mother sat at the pianoforte and rose when they entered the room. "Ah, Lady Fia. It is so good to see you again. Hello, Linberry."

"I am happy you wished to visit again, Your Grace. With me and your pianoforte."

Mama beamed. "Why, aren't you a clever girl?" She looked to Henry. "You may leave now. Lady Fia and I are going to have our lesson."

"I wouldn't call it a lesson," Lady Fia said. "More a reintroduction to the instrument and music. Shall we look through the sheet music I brought? I think you might be familiar with some of my selections."

The two women went to a settee, and Lady Fia opened the satchel, withdrawing pages of music.

He stood a moment and then moved the length of the drawing room, fully intending to leave, yet finding he couldn't do so. Instead, he took a seat in a grouping of chairs on the far side of the room. He faced away from the pair, toward the door, and slumped a bit. A bit of guilt ran through him, knowing he was eavesdropping, yet he couldn't seem to help from doing so.

They spoke for a few minutes. While he could not hear their exact words at such a great distance, he heard the enthusiasm in their tones.

They must have sat on the bench together. He heard keys being struck, some with ease, others with hesitancy. Then he could hear the tone shift to encouragement.

For a good hour, Henry listened to the two women play. He could definitely tell when Lady Fia was playing because his mother's playing had a hesitancy about it. At least it did at first. By the end of the hour, he noted the increased level of confidence.

Quietly, he rose, seeing they sat close together, both concentrating on the music before them. He slipped from the room and paced the corridor outside, waiting a bit before making his entrance. When he did so, he cleared his throat to make them aware of his presence.

"Oh, Linberry, you must come here," Mama said.

Striding the length of the room, he arrived at the pianoforte. "Yes, Mama?"

"I have found joy again in playing," she told him, color in her cheeks for the first time in a year. "Oh, I am not very good yet, but Lady Fia believes I can be with practice."

Lady Fia looked up at him. "Her Grace is being modest. She recalled quite a bit from her youth. I told her much of playing is muscle memory. It is locked within her, and she has the key to open to the music itself. I think in a very short time Her Grace will be playing for guests."

His mother pinkened at the suggestion. "I will have to think on that, my lady. But would you play for us again? I so enjoyed hearing you do so yesterday."

"I would be happy to, Your Grace."

Mama rose from the bench and sat in a nearby chair, but Henry took her place on the bench. "I shall turn the pages for you, my lady."

She studied him. "Do you read music, Your Grace?"

"I do not. I do take instruction quite well, though. Ask Mama."

"He has always been a good boy," Mama praised.

"All you have to do is nod or give me a word, and I will turn the page for you."

"If you insist."

Reaching for the satchel, she flipped through several pages before bringing a handful to the instrument.

"This is Beethoven. Are you familiar with his work, Your Grace?"

"I may be. Play it for me, and we shall see."

He could have listened to Lady Fia play all day and night, especially since they were sitting so close to one another. Their upper bodies brushed against one another as she played, while from their hips to their legs were firmly beside each other. It only made him want more of her. The taste of her was already in his mind.

Now he wanted more.

He wanted all of her.

She finished the piece, which had been rather emotional, and Mama clapped enthusiastically.

"You are a marvel, my lady. So very talented," Henry told her quietly.

Lady Fia stood and gathered her music, placing it in the satchel once more. "Thank you, Your Grace," she said formally.

"Will you come and give me another lesson?" Mama asked.

"I don't think you need my guidance, Your Grace," Lady Fia replied, crossing to stand before his mother as Henry remained on the bench. "I can see how quickly everything came back to you. You merely need help in selecting what to play. I will give it some thought and have a good number of pieces delivered to you. Some will be simple, as the minuet you played, while others will be more challenging."

She paused and opened the satchel, removing some sheet music. "I will leave these with you so you will have something to work on until I am able to send other compositions to you."

"Are you certain I don't need your help?" Mama asked.

Lady Fia smiled. "What you *will* need is an abundance of practice, Your Grace. Having played before, you understand in order to become proficient, you must practice. I can tell how happy you are seated at the pianoforte. Practice will not seem as drudgery to you, as it sometimes does to others. The hours at your instrument will be ones which bring you comfort and joy."

"Thank you for helping me be brave enough to try and play again, my lady. Without your encouragement, I doubted I ever would have touched the keys."

Henry rose and came toward them. "I can tell my mother is eager to get back to the pianoforte. Mama, stay and play. I will see Lady Fia out."

"Oh, thank you, my dear." She clutched the sheet music in her hands, her cheeks full of color.

"My lady?"

Lady Fia nodded at him and exited the drawing room, Henry right behind her. They went down the stairs and to the foyer.

"I must thank you for sparking Mama's interest in something. Ever since my father's death a year ago, she has been morose, keeping to her rooms. It is wonderful to see her happy again."

"I have found great solace in music myself, Your Grace. Especially after the deaths of my parents. I hope reintroducing your mother to something she once loved will help her move forward."

"Do you think we should have another dance lesson before the Capwells' ball?"

He watched the blush tinge her cheeks and knew she was not unaffected by him.

"No, that will not be necessary. I won't even be dancing. My cousin has granted permission for me to play my harp at the ball. I will be focusing on my music, Your Grace. Speaking of that, I should go and practice myself. I did not play it all those months I was with the Capwells and their daughters. This opportunity is too important to me. I want to play my best."

Disappointed that there would be no further dance lessons, Henry took her hand and kissed it, her cheeks now reddening and the blush traveling down to her throat.

"Then I look forward to hearing you and your harp, Lady Fia. Since we won't have an opportunity to dance, I would request that you dine with me when supper is held."

Her eyes widened. "I don't think it appropriate, Your Grace. After all, I will be a musician. Not a guest. And surely you will dance the supper dance and be obliged to sup with your partner."

Henry squeezed her fingers slightly since he still held her hand. "I will sup with you, Lady Fia. I won't take no for an answer."

She bit her lip, causing desire to flare within him. "If you insist."

"I do," he said firmly, finally releasing her hand.

"Then I am off to practice my harp," she said, the tremor in her voice apparent.

"I hope to see you soon, my lady."

As Henry watched her leave, he plotted a way to do so, admitting to himself that he could never be interested in another woman as his duchess. Something had changed within him. It was no longer lust that he felt for this woman. No, it was much, much stronger.

Lady Fia Sawyer was the one for him.

He started to return to his study and then decided he would worry about Lady Fia returning safely home. He went out the front door, knowing his long strides would allow him to keep her in sight. Westfield's townhouse was only a short distance away, and he would go to the corner of the square before returning home.

It surprised him, however, when she turned in the opposite direction of her supposed destination. Perhaps she had one more lesson to give before heading back to practice her harp. Still, he felt uneasy and decided to follow her, not liking that she was a woman alone in a large city. Looking about, he spied a hansom cab and signaled for it.

The driver came toward him. "Where to, my lord?"

"Follow that golden-haired woman in the cart," he said as he climbed into the vehicle. "But not too closely."

He watched as they left Mayfair and went through other neighborhoods close by, though he was not familiar with them.

When Lady Fia brought her horse to a halt, Henry told the driver to move toward the pavement and remain there. She climbed from the driver's seat, her satchel in hand. Surely, she was not giving a music lesson here. It was a working-class neighborhood, and he doubted any parent could afford lessons for a child, much less have a pianoforte inside their abode.

She stopped a young boy who had been playing with a friend and now parted from him. After a moment, the boy nodded eagerly and went to the cart. Lady Fia lifted him into it, and the boy took the reins. Puzzled at her giving the child access to the horse and cart, Henry continued watching the scene unfold. As Lady Fia entered a building, he realized she had asked the boy to stay with the horse and watch it for her.

"You want to stay or go, my lord?" his driver asked.

"Stay until the woman comes out. We will continue to follow

her."

"Right you are, my lord."

Henry sat for a quarter-hour until Lady Fia emerged from the building, a smile on her face. She set her satchel at the boy's feet and then opened her reticule, passing a coin to him. Then she swung him down and he ran off, a gleeful expression on his face.

Once more, she climbed into the cart and took up the reins, blending into the moving vehicles on the road. The hansom cab driver pulled back into traffic in order to follow her. Henry knew she couldn't have given a music lesson in so short a time, but was curious what she had been doing inside the building.

This time, she went in a direction he was totally unfamiliar with, further east. The traffic grew heavy. Twice, she brought the horse to a stop, calling down to someone for what he supposed might be directions to her next stop. They arrived in a seedy part of London, where she brought the horse to a halt. His driver did the same, pulling in half a block behind her.

The driver spoke up. "This isn't a good neighborhood for you to be in, my lord. Same for that young lady. I don't even like to come here myself."

"I will make it well worth your time," Henry said, pulling out a guinea and giving it to the driver, who quickly looked around as he pocketed it.

He hoped Lady Fia would not exit her vehicle. He was fearful for what might happen to her if she did. Then he saw two men coming down the pavement toward her, a predatory air about the pair. One of them grabbed the horse's bridle, and the other stepped up and began speaking to her.

"Stay here," he ordered. "I think the lady is going to need my assistance."

CHAPTER FOURTEEN

FIA DROVE TO the address of the first room in the advertisements she had scoured. When she arrived at her destination, she didn't want to leave Daniel's horse and cart unattended. Usually, a footman or even groom watched over her transportation during her lessons. But no footman would greet her in this working-class neighborhood.

Then she spied two boys playing in the street. Fia waved to one of them, moving away. Though she hated to part with any of her precious coins, she could not lose the duke's horse and cart after he was so generous to provide it for her. She called out to the boy as she exited the driver's seat, taking up her satchel. He must have been eight or nine years of age and gave her a happy smile.

"Yes, Miss?"

She shook her head, realizing he did not mistake her for a lady in the plain gown she wore.

"I have a favor to ask of you. I have an appointment within this building."

He glanced over her shoulder. "Oh, you know Mrs. Kent?"

"I have not had the privilege of meeting Mrs. Kent, but I am going to look at a room that is coming available soon. If I promise to pay you a ha'penny, would you watch my horse and cart?"

The boy's eyes lit up. "Yes, Miss! Do I stand beside it, or can I sit and hold the reins?"

She knew he would prefer holding the reins and said, "Oh, you must sit in the driver's seat of the cart. I wouldn't have it any other way."

She lifted the boy, and he sat proudly on the bench, taking up the reins.

"I'll stay right here, Miss. You can count on me."

"I won't be long," she told him and then moved to the front door of the boardinghouse.

Knocking, she waited patiently until a gray-haired woman with light blue eyes opened the door.

"May I help you, Miss?"

Not wanting to be known as Lady Fia, she said, "I am Miss Sawyer. I saw your advertisement in the newspaper and wish to look at the room that is coming available. Is now a convenient time, Mrs. Kent?"

The woman looked over her shoulder. "I see you have Hal watching your horse. Well, come inside and see what I have."

Fia entered, and they went up a flight of stairs and down a long corridor to a room at the end. She noticed a door at the end of the hallway.

"Is this another entrance?" she asked.

"Yes. There is a staircase beyond that door. It is another way to enter the boardinghouse, but I keep that door locked. I prefer for my tenants to come and go through the front door only."

The landlady reached into her apron pocket and withdrew a set of keys, searching through them until she found the one that unlocked the door.

Opening it, Mrs. Kent turned the knob and pushed the door open, indicating for Fia to enter first.

She stepped inside and saw the room, while small, was twice the size of the attic one she slept in at her cousin's townhouse. This one even had a window. The room contained a bed, a washbasin stand, and a small wardrobe, a pleasant surprise. She moved about the room and went to the window, looking out and seeing all was well with the horse and boy.

Turning to Mrs. Kent, Fia asked, "How much does the room let for, and when might I be able to move in?"

"It will be available Saturday next, Miss Sawyer."

The landlady named her weekly price, which was a little more than what Fia wished to pay. Mrs. Kent added that if Fia let it by the month instead of by the week, she would receive a small discount.

"I have one other room I would like to view before I make my decision, Mrs. Kent."

Impatience crossed the older woman's face. "Well, I can't go holding it for you. I'll need either a yes or a no."

Fia wanted to tell this woman that she wanted the room, but she owed it to herself to at least see the other one first.

"I feel the need to visit the other property, as well. I hope you can understand that I wish to be careful with my funds."

The gray-haired woman nodded, her face changing to one of sympathy. "I do understand, Miss. I have been a widow nigh on twenty years. If it makes any difference to you, the price includes breakfast in the mornings."

Fia had not realized a meal would be included. If she could eat a hearty breakfast each morning, she might get by with something from a street vendor in the evening.

"That is good to know, Mrs. Kent. I will stop by personally tomorrow morning and let you know of my decision."

"You seem to be a sensible woman, Miss Sawyer, not the kind who would cause me any trouble. Tell you what I'll do. I won't let the room until noon tomorrow."

"Oh, thank you, Mrs. Kent. That is most kind of you. I appreciate your consideration."

The landlady accompanied Fia downstairs and showed her a dining room where the tenants gathered for breakfast each morning.

"It's not bragging to say that I'm a good cook," Mrs. Kent told her matter-of-factly. "I offer a hearty breakfast. Meat. Potatoes.

Eggs. Bread. It should fill your belly."

"That sounds ideal, Mrs. Kent. I look forward to visiting with you tomorrow morning."

The landlady escorted Fia to the front door, and she returned to the horse and cart, opening her reticule and giving Hal his ha'penny.

She helped the boy to the ground, and he thanked her profusely, beaming at her.

"You gonna stay at Mrs. Kent's?" he asked.

"It is a strong possibility. I have one other place to look before I commit to Mrs. Kent."

"I wish you well, Miss."

Fia climbed into the cart and took up the reins again, clicking her tongue to start the horse. She had a vague idea where to go next but stopped twice, asking directions of others. When she arrived at the street on which the boardinghouse was located, she looked about the neighborhood, seeing it was shabby. Stopping the horse at the address, she wasn't certain if she wanted to go in and look at the room. It was one thing to live somewhere rundown and quite another to live in a place where she might fear being robbed each time she stepped outside. Mrs. Kent's room was only slightly more in price than the one here. Especially if she rented from Mrs. Kent by the month, she would save a small amount of money—and have a meal a day included in the price.

Deciding to leave and return to the Westfields' townhouse, she saw two men hurrying toward her. One gripped the bridle of her horse. The other came to stand beside her.

"Good day," the stranger said.

"Good morning," she replied stiffly. "Would you mind asking your friend to step aside? I am leaving."

"Got the wrong neighborhood, did you?" the man next to her said. He had greasy hair and dark eyes that darted about.

"Yes," she said. "I just stopped a moment to get my bearings, but I'm ready to be on my way now."

"A fancy piece like you should know how to have a good time," he told her, reaching up and seizing her wrist.

"Take your hands from me at once, sir!"

The man only laughed, turning and grinning at his friend. "Hey, you hear that? She called me *sir*. I like that." He turned to her again. "I like you. Now, come on down without a fuss."

Fia tried to jerk away from him. "Let go," she said.

He only tightened his grasp. In a swift movement, she grabbed the satchel at her feet and swung it, hitting the stranger in the side of the head, hard enough to have him release her. He stumbled back, cursing, as his friend who held the horse dashed toward her and latched on to her forearm, tugging on it to try and force her from the bench to the pavement. Since the horse was now free, Fia thought to drive away.

And then the man released her.

It was all a blur. One moment, he gripped her arm. The next, a fist came flying out of nowhere. Blood spurted from his nose, one which Fia knew had to be broken now. The first man stepped up and swung wildly, but his face met her savior's fist. Once more, blood gushed from a nose.

Then she turned to thank her rescuer—and was stunned when she recognized him.

It was the Duke of Linberry.

"Your Grace," she managed to say as he doffed his coat and handed it up to her.

"Please hold this, my lady. I still have work to do."

By now, both men who had threatened her were snarling as if they were rabid dogs. One still cradled his nose, while the other glared daggers at the duke, balling his hands into fists.

"You'll wish you didn't butt into other people's business," the man told Linberry.

"Saving the lady from the likes of you *is* my business."

One advanced toward the duke menacingly, but Linberry threw the first punch. Then another and another.

"Watch out!" Fia cried as the other man rushed toward the

fighting pair.

But the duke had already made quick work of his opponent, as his final punch caused the attacker to fall to the ground. Linberry then let loose a string of vicious blows that was almost a thing of beauty if not for the violence created.

Moments later, both men lay on the ground, one unconscious and one moaning.

Linberry removed a handkerchief and dabbed his bloodied knuckles.

"Oh!" she cried, setting aside his coat and scrambling from the bench, jumping to the ground.

She captured his wrist and raised his hand, seeing the injured knuckles.

"You're hurt. Because of me."

He shrugged, pulling away from her and wiping blood from his other hand before wrapping the handkerchief about it. "I usually box at Gentleman Jackson's gymnasium. He insists that we wrap our hands before sparring. Now, I see why."

Tears filled her eyes. "I am sorry you are injured."

"It's nothing. Just a few scrapes. Now, those two?" Linberry glanced at the men who were both stirring. "They are missing a few teeth and sport broken noses. Excuse me a moment, Lady Fia."

The duke stepped toward the men. Both cringed.

"I want you to pick yourselves up and leave as quickly as possible. Else I will thrash you again."

"Yes, my lord," one of them mumbled, pushing himself to his feet and grabbing the elbow of his companion.

"If I even hear of you approaching another female with the intention of harming her, you will answer to me," Linberry called out as they hurried away.

He turned to her. "No need for tears, my lady." He glanced at his hand, bound with the handkerchief. "I would offer you my handkerchief, but it is already in use."

She laughed, tears spilling down her cheeks. "I have my own,

Your Grace."

Going to the cart, she picked up her reticule and removed a handkerchief from it. Fia wiped away her tears.

"Exactly *what* are you doing here?" she asked.

The duke smiled at her, a smile that took her breath away.

"I was about to ask you the very same thing, Lady Fia."

CHAPTER FIFTEEN

HENRY WAITED FOR Lady Fia's reply, his knuckles aching terribly, but she seemed speechless. Then he saw determination fill her eyes, and she looked at him in defiance.

"Frankly, Your Grace, it is none of your business. We are not friends—barely acquaintances—and I don't think—"

"We have *kissed*, Fia," he reminded her. "I would say we are certainly more than acquaintances."

His comment caused color to flood her face.

"Then I will say it again, Your Grace," she said stiffly. "It is none of your business why I am here. Just as it is none of my business to know your movements either."

He smiled easily at her. "Oh, I do not mind telling you why I am here. I was looking out for *you*. And it is a good thing I came along when I did, else you would have found yourself in quite a pickle."

Her jaw dropped, and Henry took that opportunity to turn to signal his hansom cab driver. He saw the man had already pulled his vehicle close to them.

The cabbie jumped from his bench and came toward them. "Everything looks right as rain, my lord. Thanks to you, this young lady is fine." He glanced to Fia. "I hope you have thanked his lordship properly. It wouldn't have gone well for you, Miss." Looking back to Henry, he asked, "Are you ready for me to take you home, my lord?"

Henry said, "No, I will see the lady home myself."

He tried to hand over another coin, but the driver shook his head. "You have already compensated me amply, my lord. Why, it was worth the cost of a fare itself to watch the show you put on as you handled those two ruffians with ease. Your right hook is a thing of wonder to behold. I suppose you have taken a few boxing lessons in your time."

"I frequent Gentleman Jackson's gymnasium. I have learned quite a bit during my bouts there."

"You have the instincts of a street fighter, my lord," the cabbie praised. "Too bad you're a toff, because you could make a pile of money as a boxer."

"I will take that as a compliment."

"Then I will say good day to you, my lord. Miss. My advice is not to tarry."

The driver left them, and Henry turned back to Fia. "I will take you home now."

For a moment, he saw the fear which sprang into her eyes and knew she believed he would return her to her cousin's house. Anger rippled through him, knowing how afraid she was of the earl.

"I meant return you to the Duke of Westfield's, Fia," he said gently. "I would not take you to Parkhurst under any circumstances."

Her eyes filled with tears. "Thank you," she said quietly.

He turned and reached for his coat, slipping back into it and then took her by the waist, lifting her to the driver's bench.

Henry climbed up after her and said, "I will take the reins if you don't mind."

She nodded meekly, and he urged the horse on, turning it around at the next corner and heading in the direction from which they'd come. He recognized the fine lines of the horse and knew Daniel must have given permission for the horse and cart to be lent to her. He doubted, though, that his friend knew that Fia had driven alone all about London in it.

They rode in silence for several minutes before he hesitated, not certain which way to turn.

"I am excellent at directions, Your Grace. Once I have been somewhere, I never forget how to return to my starting point."

Now that she was speaking to him again, Henry was desperate for conversation with her. He knew she would clam up again if he asked her why she had traveled to such a terrible neighborhood. Instead, he thought his mother was a safe topic between them.

"I must thank you again on the changes you have wrought in Mama. We have always been close. It has been awful to witness her wither and die on the vine this past year. My father's untimely death affected her tremendously. I have had several physicians examine her. They have tried all manner of cures."

He gazed into her eyes. "Only you have gotten through to her."

"It wasn't me. It was music that reached her soul. Her Grace truly enjoyed playing as a girl and young woman but let her responsibilities overshadow any pleasure for herself once she wed." Quickly, Fia amended her statement. "That is not to say she wasn't happy in her marriage or having you as her son. Women do sacrifice a lot of themselves for others, though. She is at a point in her life where she should take a little pleasure in activities she enjoys."

She paused. "In fact, while we are out, I have one stop for us to make."

He agreed to do so, merely to remain in her company longer and Fia instructed him where to go.

They arrived at their destination, and he did as she had done previously, stop a boy and give him a coin to watch the horse and cart, promising another one when they returned.

"Where are we?" he asked.

She smiled. "This is where I purchase sheet music for my pupils. I had promised Her Grace that I would select several pieces for her. This way, you may take them home to her, and she can begin practicing them."

Henry escorted her inside the shop and a man in his early sixties with a headful of snow-white hair beamed and came toward them.

"Ah, Lady Fia," he greeted warmly. "It is so good to have you back in town. How did you enjoy your time in the country with Lord and Lady Capwell?"

"It was divine, Mr. Dutton. My two pupils' talent is immense. Working with them on a daily basis only allowed it to flourish even more. Both girls are playing at a remarkable level. I enjoyed being in the country after so many years of being trapped in the city. It was nice to be out and about, breathing in the clean country air."

She paused. "Oh, I have forgotten my manners." Fia turned to Henry. "Your Grace, this is Mr. Dutton." Looking back to the shop owner, she said, "This is the Duke of Linberry, Mr. Dutton. I have reintroduced his mother to the pianoforte. She played when she was younger and stepped away from it for many years. Her Grace recently lost her husband, and I thought music might bring her comfort, as it did to me when I lost my parents. I sat with her today, and she was a bit rusty. Her talent began to blossom the longer we were at it. I would like to pick out a good deal of music for her."

He chuckled. "You know my shop as well as I do, my lady. Feel free to browse and select what you wish. I will leave you to it."

Henry accompanied Fia around the store as she thumbed through different pages, handing the ones she wanted to him. Soon, he held quite a stack.

They went to the counter, where Fia spread out everything. She placed each number in the order she wished, telling Henry, "Please keep them arranged this way when you present them to Her Grace. I have placed them by the level of difficulty required to play them, with the easier pieces on top, moving to more complicated ones. I would like Her Grace to master them in this order. I do not want her attempting something too difficult and becoming frustrated."

She handed the stack to Mr. Dutton, who had joined them. He took a pencil and began marking the prices on his pad, adding up the figures.

"Mr. Dutton creates an account for each of my pupils and sends the bill directly to their parents. He will establish one for you, Your Grace. I would be happy, though, to come in anytime and choose more for your mother. Why, Her Grace could even join me if she wished."

The shop owner gave Henry the total cost. Henry provided his address and the name of his secretary.

"I send a monthly bill if that suits you, Your Grace."

"Unlike many of my peers, I see my bills paid regularly and on time, Mr. Dutton."

A sigh of relief escaped the man's lips. "Thank you, Your Grace," Mr. Dutton said. "Lady Fia, it is always a pleasure to see you. I assume your schedule will be filling up soon, and you'll be back soon to choose more sheet music for your students."

"Mr. Bibby is working on it as we speak. I will be frequenting your shop, as always, Mr. Dutton. A good day to you."

"And to you, my lady. Your Grace."

"Good day, Mr. Dutton," Henry said and escorted Fia from the shop, where they reclaimed the horse and cart.

"Mama is going to be quite pleased to have all this sheet music in hand so soon. Once more, I express my gratitude, Fia."

Her nose wrinkled. "You must not address me in such a causal manner, Your Grace. I may have kissed you—and given you the wrong idea about me—but I have told you we cannot become familiar with one another. Your place is among the *ton*. Mine is skating on the edges of it."

"That is not right, and you know it," he said harshly. "Parkhurst has done you a disservice by keeping you from the company of your peers. You are an earl's daughter and should be treated as one."

"I believe that ship has sailed, as they say," she said lightly, but Henry suspected Fia was more upset by her exclusion from Polite Society than she let on. "I have told you that I have begun to write my own music. I do not think God would have given me such a great talent if it was not to be used to benefit others. Truly, I enjoy teaching young people how to play an instrument. I also find playing myself quite liberating. Perhaps Parkhurst has actually done me a favor. Otherwise, I would have been as other girls of my age and class, making my come-out and a marriage. This way, I can be my own person."

Henry suspected what Fia had done today, thinking back to the building she had entered. He supposed it to be a boardinghouse. The way she spoke now, along with knowing she was of legal age, she must be planning to leave the earl's household and try living on her own. He wanted to chide her for thinking to do so but knew that would alienate him from her. That was the last thing he wanted to do. He didn't quite know how he would accomplish his goal—but he knew it now.

To woo Fia Sawyer and make her his duchess.

Yes, it seemed she did not want to be bound by the conventions placed upon one of her class. He had hoped to avoid scandal, which would attach to her because of her goals. Then he recalled how Daniel had wed a woman who was a portrait artist. Margaret made for a remarkable duchess and yet still continued painting, even though she had now given birth to their child. Henry supposed if one duke could wed a woman who had an occupation, another one could do so, as well. He hoped once they did wed that Fia would not spend her entire day giving music lessons. He could see her writing and performing, however. He wanted her to be happy. If music made her so, he would not keep her from it.

The question now was how to court her—and convince her to wed him.

They arrived at the Westfields' townhouse, where a footman

greeted them. He helped to hand down Lady Fia and told Henry, "I'll take the cart around to the mews, Your Grace."

Henry looked to her. "I know you are a guest and don't believe you should invite me in." He grinned. "I am finding there are some advantages to being a duke. I suppose one of them is inviting myself in. After all, who is going to show a duke the door?"

They were greeted by Hampton, who said, "Their Graces are in the drawing room. May I take you to them?"

"Thank you, Hampton," he said. "We would appreciate that."

The butler announced them, and as they entered the drawing room, Henry saw the duke and duchess sitting together, holding hands and talking. He felt a stab of jealousy at such closeness, wanting the same for himself.

For him and Fia.

They crossed the room and the duchess said, "How delightful to have you call, Your Grace." Looking to Fia, she added, "How was your lesson with Her Grace?"

As they took their seats, Fia elaborated on his mother's talent and enthusiasm. "I believe Her Grace will be playing beautifully in a short time. I emphasized to her how important practice is—and I should do so now myself. I only touched the harp for the first time this morning after it was delivered. If I am going to play in a little more than a week for Polite Society, I should put in practice time of my own."

"Might we listen to you play a few songs?" Henry asked, loath to part from her.

"I have never heard a harpist," Daniel said. "Would you mind, Fia?"

Immediately, Henry noticed the use of her Christian name and guessed the couple had asked her to use it.

"Oh, yes," said the duchess enthusiastically. "Just a couple of numbers, Fia. Then we will leave you to your practice."

"As long as you realize I am more than a bit rusty and may

make a few mistakes."

They adjourned to the music room, full of her instruments, and Fia took her seat at the harp. She ran her fingers up and down the strings several times in what he supposed was a type of warmup, similar to the scales she had asked his mother to play during their lesson this morning. Then she settled into a song, plucking the strings as if magic were present in her fingers. Fia played her instrument with an intensity and reverence, moving Henry more than he could say.

She played three songs before rising and coming toward them. He knew now not only did he want her as his wife, but he also wanted her to share her talent with others. He had said so himself. A duke usually made his own rules. Henry believed he and Fia would write their own rules and the *ton* would accept them. If they didn't?

Who really needed the *ton*?

"Thank you for playing for us, Fia," the duchess said. "If you made any mistakes, I would never have guessed."

"I'll admit to two," she said. "It was easy to cover them." She smiled. "Besides, I knew I had a forgiving audience."

Not wanting their time to end with her, Henry said, "What of the portrait that Her Grace is painting of you?"

Margaret smiled. "Oh, I am glad you brought that up, Your Grace. Fia, darling, I would like you to look at all the sketches I've completed now. It will only take a few minutes and then you can return to your practice. If you choose the ones you like best, then I can start on your portrait tomorrow morning."

"I would be happy to do so, Margaret."

The duchess rang for a servant and told the maid where the sketches were. They chatted amiably for a few minutes before the maid returned with a stack of sketches.

"Give them to Lady Fia," the duchess instructed.

And since Henry sat next to her, he was able to see them as she went through the large pile.

He was taken aback by the duchess' talent. Margaret had

captured Lady Fia from various directions and with a variety of emotions.

"How can I choose?" Fia asked. "They all are so good." She paused. "I still think you draw me as prettier than I truly am."

"You are not pretty," he said, feeling her stiffen beside him. "You are quite beautiful, Lady Fia."

She took in a quick breath, her eyes widening, then she said, "Thank you, Your Grace." Looking to the duchess, she added, "I am not sure I can choose, Margaret. Would you do so for me?" She returned the sketches to the duchess.

"Of course. Some of my clients do have trouble making a decision." The duchess rose. "Shall we leave Fia to her practice, Your Graces?"

The three left the music room and once in the corridor, the duchess fretted. "I simply do not know which ones to choose. I do find Fia's face quite interesting."

"Then allow me to select the ones for you to work from," Henry said boldly.

"Why would you wish to do so?" Daniel asked, a knowing look in his eyes.

"I believe you have already guessed at my answer," he said cryptically.

"Well, *I* would like to know why," the duchess complained.

"What if I told you Lord Parkhurst told Fia that he would not pay for the portrait?" Daniel said to Henry. "He instructed Fia to tell my duchess to paint over it once the portrait was completed."

Rage boiled within him. "Then I would say I believe I would enjoy using Parkhurst's face for my punching bag." He looked to the duchess. "Under no circumstances are you to let that happen."

"Why is that, You Grace?" she asked, biting back a smile.

"Because not only do I want every sketch you have drawn of Fia once you are done, but I also want that painting to hang in my drawing room," he shared. "I have decided that Lady Fia is my choice. I need her as my duchess. No other woman holds a candle to her." He sighed. "How I will convince her to speak her vows with me, though, is a conundrum."

The duchess slipped her hand through the crook of his arm. "Then we will have to put our heads together to make that happen, Your Grace," she purred.

"Henry. Please, call me Henry."

She smiled. "Henry it is. Henry and Fia. I rather like the sound of those names linked together, don't you, darling?"

The duke grinned shamelessly. "I agree, my love. And if Henry and Fia can be half as happy as we are, then they will be very happy indeed."

Henry now had powerful allies on his side. He asked to see the drawings again and selected three.

"Use these in creating your portrait of Fia. I will pay your usual commission."

"Oh, that won't be necessary, Henry. I am painting the portrait as a wedding present, it seems." She smiled. "The first time I have done so. This is quite exciting. Especially since it will be a surprise."

"We will do everything we can to help you make your case to Fia," Daniel said.

"The most important thing is not to see Fia strictly as duchess material," Her Grace pointed out. "Yes, I do understand you want her as your duchess—and she will make for a magnificent one— but Fia is also a woman in her own right. Acknowledge that she has feelings. Thoughts. Opinions."

"I agree," Daniel added. "As much as Margaret made my head swim with desire and I wanted her as my wife, for a while I clung to the notion of what Polite Society would think of me if I allowed unconventionality in my duchess."

The duchess sniffed. "Allowed. Do you hear that, Your Grace? His Grace thought he would *allow* me to be me." She touched her husband's face lightly with her fingers in a sweet caress.

"Exactly my point," his friend said. "Don't give a damn about the *ton* and their thoughts. I have learned they are quite forgiving of dukes and the various choices we make. Instead, focus on getting to know the woman Fia is. Her likes and dislikes. Her interests. Her passions." The duke paused. "And most of all, after you have come to know her as a trusted friend?

"I suggest kissing her," the duke concluded. "As much as possible."

The duchess smiled, her face lighting up. "I couldn't agree more."

He grinned. "Well, we have already done that once. Shall I say we are most compatible in that area?"

The duke and duchess laughed in delight.

"Then if she is still digging in her heels, you must convince her with more kisses," the duchess said matter-of-factly. "And perhaps even more."

"You think I should seduce her?" he asked. "No, I cannot force her or trick her. Fia must want to wed me."

"Then I think more kisses are called for," Daniel said. "We will help you create an opportunity to do so. Stay for tea, Henry. Then perhaps you and Fia can stroll our gardens afterward. You and Fia can become better acquainted. And if good conversation leads to even better kisses?" She grinned shamelessly. "Then I see no harm, Linberry."

Henry liked that idea. Very much.

CHAPTER SIXTEEN

F IA PRACTICED ANOTHER two songs, satisfied with her level of play. The harp had always been an innate part of her. Plucking its strings seemed second nature to her. Playing the pianoforte was slightly different. While she had hundreds of songs in her head that she could play on it from memory, practicing the instrument was something she knew she must keep up. It was too easy for her fingers to become tangled otherwise on complicated runs. She did not think Margaret or Daniel would mind her practicing in this music room, which also contained a pianoforte, as did their drawing room.

What she struggled with now was whether or not she should let the room at Mrs. Kent's boardinghouse. The place was far from her Mayfair students. She would not have extra coins to be taking hansom cabs to and from the lessons. In fact, once Parkhurst realized she was no longer under his roof and thumb, she did not know if those lessons would even continue. She knew he could be vindictive and since he had never liked her, Fia believed he would spread vicious rumors about her, causing her to lose her pupils. Even if she were allowed to continue teaching a handful, she would have to discuss with those parents about changing the financial arrangement in order for her to be compensated and not her cousin.

It might be best to merely cut ties with her students and take up dressmaking as she pursued a musical career of her own. Fia hoped that Margaret would allow her to keep the musical instruments she had brought with her to the duke's townhouse in this music room after she left. Since practicing in the boardinghouse would not be practical, as she couldn't disturb the other boarders, she would ask her friend if she could stop by daily to practice here. In the quiet of this music room, Fia also hoped to continue writing her own music, something she had only begun during the months she lived in the country with Lord and Lady Capwell.

A knock sounded at the door, and she rose to answer it, finding Hampton on the other side.

"It is teatime, my lady. Her Grace is requesting your presence in the drawing room."

"Thank you," she said to the butler. "I will go immediately."

When Fia entered the room, it did not surprise her to see the Duke of Linberry still there. It seemed as if he had formed a friendship with Daniel, and Fia supposed Linberry would be a frequent visitor to the house. She would need to avoid him as much as possible.

Even though she longed for his kiss.

"Ah, there you are, Fia," Margaret said. "Come join us. His Grace was kind enough to stay for tea. Gran is out visiting with friends."

Fia took a seat on the settee beside the duke, again catching a whiff of his tantalizing cologne.

"Did you have a good practice with your harp?" he asked her.

"Yes, Your Grace. I will need to meet with Lady Capwell, however, and see what I am to play at her ball. I am not certain if she wishes me to play along with the other musicians or if I am to play a few numbers on my own. I will be at her townhouse tomorrow morning, though, for a lesson with her daughters. I can speak with her then about her expectations for the evening."

Margaret began talking about the upcoming opening ball and reminiscing about her first Season last year, one in which she had met and wed her duke.

"I hope you will enjoy this Season yourself, Fia," she said.

"I assume you will be staying with us the entire time," Daniel said.

"My cousin has other ideas about that," she said. "He will expect me to return home once Margaret finishes my portrait."

The duke looked to his wife and then said, "Leave Parkhurst to me. Once Margaret finishes your portrait, I will merely tell him you have become a beloved companion to my duchess and that you will reside with us the reminder of the Season."

"You are opening a world of trouble for yourself, Daniel," Fia warned. "I do not think it wise for you to rile him."

Daniel's brows rose. "You do not believe I can go toe to toe with the earl?"

"He is a nuisance. You will not want to put up with him. I do appreciate your efforts on my behalf, though. It has been a long time since someone cared about me."

Linberry held up fisted hands, revealing his bruised knuckles. "If Parkhurst needs to be put in his place, then I can do so."

Margaret gasped. "Good God, Linberry! What have you been up to? I thought those who boxed at Gentleman Jackson's protected their hands."

Fia held her breath, hoping the duke would not reveal where he had been injured.

"I merely tried something new today, something I will definitely keep from doing in the future," he said breezily. "Any boxing on my part will see my hands properly wrapped in the future."

"I am sorry I did not notice before now," Margaret apologized. "They don't look as if they have been attended to. Should we send for a doctor?"

Her husband laughed. "My dear, a few bruised knuckles are nothing for a doctor to tend. Every man I know has been in a scrape or two and seen his knuckles in the same condition. Henry will survive—as long as he doesn't go punching out his sparring partner again without protection."

Fia breathed a sigh of relief, knowing Linberry would keep her secret since he had not corrected either the duke or duchess. But she knew now that placed her in his debt, a place she did not wish to be.

Teatime drew to a close, and Margaret said, "I thought Nanny would bring Norrie down to see us. We must go to the nursery and visit her instead," she told her husband.

"You are right, my love, though I had promised Henry to show him our gardens once tea ended." Daniel turned to Fia. "Would you mind strolling through the gardens with His Grace? The duke and I have been discussing some changes he wishes to make in his landscaping, both here in town and at his ducal seat."

It would be churlish for Fia to turn down the duke's simple request, and so she said, "I would be happy to do so."

"Then it is settled," Margaret said. "I hope we will see you again soon, Your Grace. Come along, Daniel. Our daughter awaits us."

The couple left the drawing room, and Fia glanced to the duke. "I have never seen the duke's gardens myself, Your Grace. I doubt I will be much of a guide."

"If I become lost, I will rely on your keen sense of direction to find our way out."

Fia hesitated a moment and then said, "Thank you for keeping my secret. I do not know what I would have done if you had not come along and rescued the horse and me. His Grace would have been down a fine horse and cart, because I believe those men would have taken and sold them."

He took her hands in his, gazing intently at her. "Do you not realize, Fia, they would not have only sold the horse? They would have sold *you*. You were in far more danger than you know."

"Sold *me*?"

She recalled bits and pieces of what the stranger had said to her, and an icy fear struck her. She knew, despite her age, that she was an innocent in many ways.

"Then I owe you my life, Your Grace. I do not know how I will be able to repay you."

He raised a hand to her cheek and cradled it, flooding her with warmth. "There is no debt to honor, Fia. But you must promise me never to go back to that neighborhood again. It is not safe for a lady to roam about London without a companion. In fact, I think I should speak to Daniel regarding this. You should not be driving yourself to lessons. You should always be accompanied by your maid, at the very least. It would be even better if a groom or footman went with you."

"I have gone about town on my own these past six years, Your Grace," she said sternly. "Mayfair is quite safe during the day. I travel in a small area of it and always have a servant available to watch my horse and cart, unlike today. There is no need for a maid to accompany me."

She rose. "Are you ready to take a turn through the gardens?"

Linberry stood. "Yes. I would like that very much."

They went to the rear of the house and exited, finding the gardens' entrance in front of them. The duke took her hand and placed it through the crook of his arm. She liked the feeling of being close to him more than she should.

They strolled at a leisurely pace. She pointed out the various flowers which were beginning to bloom.

"What are your favorite flowers?" he asked.

She considered it a moment and then replied, "In spring, I love jonquils best. Summer lends itself to a larger variety. I would have to say my favorites are irises and dahlias during those warmer months. I do, however, like anemones, which grow in the autumn."

"You seem quite knowledgeable about flowers," he noted.

"I grew up in the country. Our gardens became a home away from home for me. I followed our gardener about. He allowed me to help with the planting."

"You miss the country."

"Desperately," she admitted. "Once Parkhurst sent for me, I

have remained in town all these years until Lady Capwell asked me to travel to Oxfordshire with them. I enjoyed that respite in the country."

"Do you believe Lady Capwell will ask you to travel with them again once the Season ends?"

"I am not sure what my future holds, Your Grace. Whether I am meant to continue with my pupils and their music lessons, or if I could earn a living being a musician myself. I will have to see how the next few weeks unfold."

"I thought the dowager duchess was sponsoring you in your come-out."

She smiled ruefully. "I have allowed Her Grace to purchase a handful of gowns for me. She is also making certain that I am included in a few invitations issued to her. That means I will attend a few events. As I told you before, I do not see myself ever becoming a part of the *ton*, much less wedding a gentleman."

He halted, his hands going to her waist, moving her so that her back rested against a large oak tree.

"I think you should reconsider your plans, Fia. What if you could have music—and marriage?"

Her heart beat wildly. She knew he was going to kiss her.

And she wanted him to. Desperately.

His lips touched hers, and the gentle kiss caused a deep yearning within her. For marriage. For children. For a stable life.

For love . . .

She turned her head away from him, and his lips grazed her cheek, moving to her ear. It shocked her when his tongue ran along the shell of it, sending a frisson of pleasure through her. Then his teeth captured her earlobe, and the place between her legs tightened in response.

His lips glided back to her mouth, which became a willing participant in the kiss, much to her dismay. He eased open her mouth and once more, he drank from her. Without meaning to, she mimicked his actions, hearing a low groan come from him. He pressed his body against hers, pinning her to the tree.

Time ceased as they explored one another with deep kisses. When he broke their kiss, she whimpered in protest, seeing a knowing look appear in his eyes. He kissed her nose lightly and then her chin. He found her pulse point and flicked his tongue against it, causing shivers of delight to run through her. Then he nipped at her throat, soothing the love bites with his tongue.

One hand left her waist and cupped her breast. He kneaded it, and she gasped. Slowly, he rubbed the pad of his thumb back and forth against the nipple, which had sprung to life at his touch. He lightly tweaked it, causing the place between her legs to grow heavy with need. Fia knew her breathing was erratic, and she wanted to explore more of what this man's touch could offer. She raised a hand and brushed the backs of her fingers along his cheek. His eyes closed, a satisfied smile appearing on his handsome face. She looked at him longingly, knowing how much she wanted him.

And how she was wrong for him in every way possible.

Still, she brought her other hand up to frame his face, pulling him down for what she promised herself would be one last kiss between them.

The kiss went on and on, making her aware of feelings she had never known before. She relished it and then broke the kiss.

"Though I thought I would never kiss anyone again—least of all you—I appreciate what you have shown me."

"There is a world of touch to be explored, Fia," he said, his voice low and rough. "I would like to do so with you."

He moved to kiss her again, but she placed the tips of her fingers against his lips.

"No, Your Grace. No more kisses. No more temptation. If I am to stay my course, we must not be alone again. You are a gentleman. I know you will respect my wishes in this matter."

Fia lowered her hands, his gaze burning into her.

"I will honor my promise of supping with you at the first ball. In the future, however, we are to remain distant acquaintances."

He stepped away from her, allowing her to pass by him. She

started up the walkway in the direction they had come from. He did catch up with her, taking her hand and slipping it through his arm.

"I am a gentleman, Fia. I would never betray your trust in me. Nor would I touch you if you did not want me to."

Oh, but how she *did* want him to. Still, she knew any further encounters between them would only lead to heartbreak if she continued to go down this path.

"I appreciate that, Henry," she said softly, using his Christian name for the first time. "Most men of the *ton* would not be nearly as respectful. That is why you will make for a fine husband when you do decide to wed."

They returned to the house, and she went with him to the foyer. He took her hand and raised it to his lips, pressing a hot kiss upon her fingers.

"Go and take care of your knuckles, Your Grace," she told him, blinking rapidly to keep her tears from falling.

"Take care of yourself, Lady Fia."

She noticed he used her title once again, feeling the intimacy between them slipping away. It was what she wanted even as her throat grew thick with emotion.

"Tell Her Grace hello for me," she said, wanting to prolong this last time together.

His gaze met hers. "I will."

The duke released her hand. Still, they continued to stare at one another a long moment.

Then Fia smiled brightly, knowing it was the right thing to push him away. "Good day, Your Grace."

"Good day, my lady."

She watched him leave and then went upstairs to her bedchamber. Tears were a luxury which she had not partaken in for many years, knowing they were of no use. They never changed a situation and usually made her feel worse.

This time, though, Fia collapsed onto the bed and let them come, weeping for things—and the man—she could never have.

CHAPTER SEVENTEEN

F IA BREAKFASTED WITH the duke and duchess the next morning, receiving a note from Mr. Bibby while she ate. He had added three pupils to this afternoon's schedule.

"What correspondence did you receive?" Margaret asked.

"It is from Parkhurst's secretary. Mr. Bibby keeps my teaching schedule. I am to add three students this afternoon, two I have taught in the past and one new pupil."

"Will you be back in time for tea?" her friend asked.

"No, I am afraid I will have to miss it today. Actually, I will miss it most if not all days, with more of the *ton* returning to town and lessons being scheduled. I did put my foot down with Parkhurst, though, after I returned from the country. He had me teaching six days a week in the past. I said I would only do five so that I had time myself to practice." She hesitated and then added, "And write."

The duke looked at her thoughtfully. "You are writing music?"

"I started doing so during the last few months," she confided. "I had much more time on my hands after I gave Lady Maisie and Lady Daisy their music lesson of the day. They would go off to practice. While I did some of that on my own, I also found a growing need to express my creativity."

"What have you written? Compositions for the pianoforte?"

the duke asked.

"Yes, for the most part, but I also have written a few pieces for the violin."

"I think Parkhurst making you work six days a week was outrageous," Margaret said. "Even five is too much. You shouldn't be working at all."

"I will keep to the schedule for now," she said, knowing it might be taken from her, and she should savor the time she had left with her students. "It still leaves me Saturdays for my own use and after attending church on Sunday, most of that day, as well."

"I don't know how you will keep up these lessons and attend the Season," Margaret said. "The late nights are frequent, especially the night when a ball is held."

"I won't go to events every night," she reminded her friend. "Just a few. Her Grace knows of my wishes and says she is being circumspect with the social affairs she will take me to."

Margaret started to protest, but Daniel held up a hand. "Some is better than none, my sweet. Let Fia go to the events she wishes to attend."

"Very well." Margaret sighed. "I am off to paint." She left the room.

"Thank you for your intervention," Fia said to the duke. "I know Margaret has my best interests at heart, but I don't wish to marry."

"You don't think you could keep up with your music and a husband?"

She sighed. "Frankly, I don't think I will be comfortable at these *ton* events, Daniel. I won't know anyone, beyond the two of you."

"You know Linberry."

Fia frowned. "You know what I mean."

"My grandmother is a formidable woman. She will make certain you are introduced to many others."

"Having an introduction and making true friends are two

different things, and you know it. I don't see myself being comfortable around members of Polite Society. I have been on my own for a long time, Daniel. I spent several years nursing my parents before their deaths, then spent a year of mourning alone in the country. Once I was summoned to town by Parkhurst, I spent years without the company of adults. Only when I went with the Capwells to their country estate did I even dine with adults. Of course, I have made friends with Margaret. She is a true champion for me. I hope we will continue our friendship no matter what comes."

He frowned. "You seem to believe there is some impending doom hanging over you."

"I don't wish to return to my cousin's household. When he understands that, I look for him to blacken my name. It may cost me pupils. Even the chance to play at *ton* gatherings. If that is the case, I do not expect you or Margaret to remain friendly with me. There is no need for you to associate yourself with scandal. If—or when—that occurs, I would beg for you to step away."

He looked at her sternly. "We will not abandon you, Fia. Do not ask that of us."

"You are most kind, Daniel. You and Margaret. And your grandmother. I say we should not borrow trouble. We can make informed decisions once I see how Parkhurst reacts."

"No matter what your hateful cousin does or says, you will always have our friendship and a place to stay."

"I thank you for that. Now, I must be off for my lessons."

Fia returned to her room, tamping down the strong emotions running through her. It was hard after so many years of being alone to have someone in her corner. She treasured Margaret's friendship. Daniel's, too. She refused to allow their names to be tarnished along with hers, though.

She placed her bonnet upon her head and tied its ribbons and collected her shawl before going to the music room for some sheet music to share with the girls. Hampton called for her horse and cart and soon Fia was on her way to the Capwells' townhouse.

When she pulled up, she saw the girls standing at the window. They waved at her, and she returned the wave. By the time she had been helped from the cart, both girls had run from the house and awaited her on the pavement.

"Good morning, Lady Fia!" they proclaimed in unison.

"Good morning, my ladies. Are you ready for your lesson?"

"Yes!" they cried.

She accompanied them to the drawing room, where she had them both play a different piece individually, and then a third one together. She talked with them about ways to improve and then had them each play another two songs separately. After that, they moved to the pianoforte. Although both girls spent much more time on their violin and viola, Fia thought it important for them to keep up with the pianoforte since they wouldn't cart about their stringed instruments. As they grew older, she knew they would not only entertain guests at their parents' gatherings, but they would also be asked to play in others' homes.

As the lesson drew to a close, Lady Capwell appeared. Fia had the girls play a song together that they had already performed for her earlier in the lesson. She noted how each had already taken her advice and made adjustments, which improved their playing.

Lady Capwell told the girls their governess was waiting for them. They told Fia goodbye, and then Lady Capwell asked if she had a few minutes to talk.

"I was hoping for that very thing, my lady."

"First, tell me about the girls' progress," the countess urged.

She did so, noting how Lady Capwell seemed pleased.

"I would also like to discuss with you your playing at our ball. I have spoken to the conductor of the orchestra. He and many members of the orchestra play at numerous balls throughout the Season. He was delighted to have you come and play with them."

Fia thought the conductor delighted merely because it would please the countess if he were. She doubted he wanted a stranger playing with his group, much less a member of Polite Society.

Lady Capwell picked up a piece of parchment on the table beside her. "These are the numbers they are to play. I assured Mr. Johnson, the conductor, that you would already know each tune or be able to pick them up quickly. I also told him I wished for you to play a few selections on your harp without the orchestra. He discouraged that idea, though, saying it would simply be too hard to hear the harp with so many others. Do you have an idea what you might wish to play for our guests alone? Because I have an idea I am toying with."

"I will think on it, especially now that I have a list of the other numbers to be played that evening."

The countess said, "I would like you to play in the background as our guests eat. Supper usually runs for about three-quarters of an hour or so."

For a moment, disappointment filled her, with Fia knowing she would not be able to dine with the Duke of Linberry now. This was too great an opportunity to pass up, however. The supper room would be filled with members of the *ton*. If the opening ball had entertainment during supper, it might become *de rigueur*, with other hostesses eagerly wishing for music in the background to entertain guests as they supped. A harp was a quiet, elegant instrument and would be perfectly suited for this purpose. It might be the impetus she needed to persuade others to have her play for them.

"That would be wonderful, my lady," Fia said with enthusiasm. "I will work on creating a list of pieces to play, both during the ball and while supper takes place. Thank you again for this opportunity."

"You are the one I should thank, Lady Fia. You have brought out such a talent in our daughters and are much beloved by them. I believe our guests will be enchanted with your playing." Lady Capwell smiled. "Would it be possible for you to come two hours before our ball begins? Mr. Johnson wants to make certain your harp is in tune and would like to hear you play and then rehearse with his musicians before our guests arrive."

She hated to inconvenience the Westfields but supposed there was nothing she could do about it. She supposed the duke would allow her to use his carriage, which she would then send back for them.

Bidding the countess goodbye, she settled herself in the cart, taking up the reins and making her way to Mrs. Kent's boardinghouse. On the way, she decided to take the room. Fia believed she would make a favorable impression on Mr. Johnson. If she did, he might ask her to play with his orchestra at future balls. Even if he didn't, instinct told her that Lady Capwell having Fia play at supper would inspire others to do the same and that she would be able to earn a living doing so, at least being able to pay for her room during the Season. Once it ended, though, she might have to try dressmaking. She would see Madame Planche tomorrow for her fitting and might take the modiste aside and sound her out regarding a position at her shop.

Her spirits high, Fia drove to the boardinghouse, seeing the same two boys playing in the street. Hal tossed a ball to his friend and ran toward her as she climbed from the bench.

"You're back! Are you going to let a room at Mrs. Kent's?"

"I am and have come to tell Mrs. Kent of my decision in person."

"Do you need me to watch your horse and cart again?" he asked hopefully.

Though she knew it meant parting with another precious coin, Fia nodded. "I was about to ask that very thing, Hal."

He smiled brightly. "I gave my mum the ha'penny. She bought some yeast with it. She makes good bread. I will bring you a slice after you move in."

"That is very thoughtful of you. Shall I help you up?"

She helped him up to the bench, where he lifted the reins. "I'll be here when you get back, Miss."

"It's Miss Sawyer," she told him.

"Miss Sawyer," he said with a nod.

Fia went to knock at the door of the boardinghouse. Mrs.

Kent opened it immediately.

"Been watching for you, Miss Sawyer," the older lady said. "I hope it is good news you bring me. I have learned that my tenant needs the room until Sunday next, though. I know I had promised you could have it sooner. I will clean and thoroughly air it on Monday. You could move in on Tuesday."

"I am here to tell you that I will take the room, Mrs. Kent. Waiting a few more days will not be a problem. In fact, I would prefer to move in on Tuesday."

This way, she could perform at the opening ball on Monday night and return home with the Westfields.

"May I give you the first month's rent when I move in?" she asked the landlady, knowing she would receive her pin money soon. After paying for her room, though, Fia would be left with very little. The good thing was she would have adequate gowns to wear, thanks to the Dowager Duchess of Westfield, and would not have to spend a farthing on updating the gowns she currently possessed.

"That will be acceptable, Miss Sawyer. I know you are going to be an excellent tenant, and we will get along famously."

"How many other boarders currently say here?" she asked.

"I have six. One is leaving. You'll take his place. I have another coming to rent in two weeks' time so I will be up to seven." Mrs. Kent smiled. "I knew you would be back, Miss Sawyer. My rates are reasonable. I keep things clean and tidy."

"I agree on both accounts. That—and the fact you include breakfast in your rate—made my decision."

"Then I will look for you in two Tuesdays, Miss Sawyer."

Fia returned to the horse and cart, seeing Hal sitting proudly in the seat, a petite woman talking to the boy.

"Miss Sawyer, this is Mum. Mum, this is the nice lady I told you about."

Hal's mother smiled at her. "All my boy did was talk about how he got to sit and watch over your horse, Miss Sawyer. Thank you for allowing him to do so and for the ha'penny you gave him."

"I owe him another one."

"No, you don't. You paid him plenty yesterday. We look out for one another in this neighborhood. Will you be joining us?"

"I will. Mrs. Kent has let a room to me. I will move in not this coming Tuesday, but the next one."

"Then I look forward to getting to know you. We live across the street." She pointed to a large house. "It's me and the mister and our five children, along with my sister's family. They number eight. I am Mrs. Harper, by the way."

"A pleasure to make your acquaintance, Mrs. Harper."

"I hope you will stop by for a visit once you are settled in, Miss Sawyer. I know Mrs. Kent does not provide an evening meal. You are welcome to join us any time. One more face won't be a problem."

"That is very generous of you, Mrs. Harper. I would love to come and meet the rest of your family. I will do so soon," she promised.

Fia left and drove to her next lesson and the two after. Her new pupil, a girl of seven, proved to be most eager. She looked forward to working with the girl for as long as she could.

Returning to the Westfields' townhouse, she dropped off the horse and cart and entered the foyer, where Hampton told her the dowager duchess wanted to see Fia in her sitting room. The butler took her to the room and announced her.

"You are coming home late, Fia," the dowager duchess said. "You missed tea. Margaret said that is not an uncommon occurrence."

"I rarely have time for tea, Your Grace."

"Gran," the old woman prompted.

"Gran," she said wistfully. "I never knew any of my grand-parents. I thank you for looking out for me."

"Here are a stack of invitations I have received. I wanted to go through them with you and see which ones appealed to you the most. I can tell you about each hostess and the ones I would choose to attend."

Though Fia now believed she would be busy being paid to play at social affairs and not attend them as a guest, she did not want to disappoint the old woman.

"Then we shall go through each one." Fia lifted the first. "Tell me about this one." She handed it to the dowager duchess.

As they sifted through the invitations, Fia tried to commit names to memory and the events associated with each host. Of course, she recognized many of the names from having read the gossip columns for years. It would be interesting to put names to faces.

"I believe we have been selective in our choices," the old woman told her. "It is time to dress for dinner. Would you ring for my maid?"

She did so and then went to her room, where Millie helped her out of her gown and into a fresh one.

"It will be ever so nice when you have something new to wear, my lady," the maid said.

"I go to Madame Planche's shop tomorrow."

Fia dined with the Westfield family and offered to play her harp for them after dinner. Once she had played three numbers, she excused herself, telling them she had to compose a list of the works she would perform at the Capwells' ball.

She did just that in her bedchamber, trying to strike a good balance between composers and musical periods, making certain she did not repeat a number being performed by the orchestra. When she had what she deemed to be the perfect list, she placed it aside and rang for Millie to help her prepare for bed.

Once she was tucked beneath the bedclothes, Fia realized she was tired after such a busy day. She was proud that it had been so busy that she had not thought of the Duke of Linberry a single time. She quickly fell asleep.

And dreamed of him instead.

CHAPTER EIGHTEEN

F IA LOOKED OUT the carriage window as they headed to Madame Planche's dress shop. The streets were crowded with both vehicles and pedestrians crossing. She was grateful not to be driving her horse and cart in such heavy traffic, as it was Saturday, and she had no lessons to give.

She had received another note from Mr. Bibby this morning. While her cousin had honored her request not to have her teach on Saturdays, he must have told his secretary to keep the same number of pupils on the schedule. Mr. Bibby's letter had promised Fia this would be the final schedule, simply because she had no more room on her calendar. He had grouped the students who lived close to one another so her travel time between lessons was cut to the bone. Still, she was seeing forty-four students throughout the week, starting on Monday. By next Saturday, she would be exhausted. Instead of practicing, she would probably need to sleep.

It bothered her that even with time off from teaching, she would not have enough time to compose and practice as much as she would like. Besides doing those tasks, she would also, as always, jot down notes on each pupil's progress and send these notes to their parents, as well as think about the next sheet music to order. She feared she would not have the time to stop by Mr. Dutton's shop and do this in person. Instead, she would have to send her requests by post and have the sheet music delivered to her, where she would then distribute it to her students.

"You are quiet, Fia," Margaret said, drawing Fia's attention from her thoughts.

"I have much to think about."

"Are you composing a new song in your head?" her friend asked.

"No. Actually, I am thinking about my students and their lessons. Mr. Bibby has sent me my final calendar. Thankfully, he has organized it so that lessons are grouped by areas. That will be most convenient."

"How many lessons will you teach each week, my dear?" asked the dowager duchess.

Taking a deep breath, Fia expelled it. "Forty-four, Your Grace."

The old woman looked taken aback. "Wait. My hearing is not always the best these days. Did I mistakenly hear you say forty-four?"

"You heard me correctly, Your Grace," Fia confirmed.

"No, that cannot be," Margaret said. "Why, you will be gone literally all day at that rate."

She shrugged. "It cannot be helped. Parkhurst speaks to the parents and gives the names of those he has approved to Mr. Bibby. Mr. Bibby merely makes up the schedule."

"No, no, no," the dowager duchess protested. "How can you see so many children during the week and still attend social affairs of the Season?"

"That is one of the reasons I thought we should be selective in the events I participate in, Your Grace."

"You cannot stay out until near dawn and get only an hour or two of sleep before rising and putting in a full day," Margaret said. "You will collapse. Not every event is in the evening. There are garden parties, for instance. Those are wonderful to attend."

"I will have to miss those. Even though I do enjoy looking at flowers."

Margaret cocked her head. "Did you enjoy showing His Grace our gardens?"

Fia felt the blush spill across her cheeks. "His Grace knows very little about flowers. I was able to point out numerous examples to him and recommended a few of them to him."

"I rather like that young man," the dowager duchess said. "I liked his mother and father, as well. Lord and Lady Strumbull were very warm, kindhearted people. Now, the Duke of Linberry, the present duke's grandfather?" She sniffed. "He was arrogant and unkind. Very unpleasant to be around. His grandson is certainly an improvement." She paused, a twinkle in her eyes. "I think he might be a good match for you, Fia."

She shook her head. "No, Your Grace. I am not duchess material. The *ton* has their idea of what a duchess should be—and it certainly isn't a music teacher who is a pauper."

"And you think they believed a portrait painter would make for a good duchess?" Margaret demanded. "I am certain there are still whispers behind my back because I choose to continue to paint." She took Fia's hand. "Be yourself, my dearest friend. The right man will find you, be it Linberry or another gentleman."

She wanted to counter with the fact she did not want any man to find her. She wanted to find herself and believed she would be happiest in the midst of the musicians who played for the *ton*. Fia kept silent, though, not wanting to ruin their outing.

They arrived at the dress shop and were greeted by Madame Planche herself. The shop was crowded, with it being a little over a week before the Season began.

"I have three of Lady Fia's day gowns and one ballgown close to completion," the modiste told them. "The other gowns are far enough along for her to try them on, as well. We will make the necessary adjustments, and she should have them by next Wednesday. Come with me, my lady. My assistant has your gowns ready for your fitting."

"I will come with you," the dowager duchess said.

"Well, you aren't going to leave me waiting here," Margaret

complained good-naturedly.

All three women trekked through a doorway. Madame led them to where one of her assistants waited.

"See to the day gowns," the modiste said. "When Lady Fia is ready to try on her ballgown, call for me."

"Yes, Madame," said the assistant.

Over the next half hour, Fia tried on all five of the day gowns. The assistant pinned her here and there, and the dowager duchess had her turn several times, viewing Fia from different angles.

"You look good in a variety of colors," Margaret complimented. "Not many women do."

As Fia studied her image in the full-length mirror and saw how she looked in these new gowns, she realized how pathetic her current wardrobe had become. No wonder even a child such as Hal Harper had not thought her to be a lady.

"I think Fia should have some of that watered silk made up," the dowager duchess said. "Do you know what I refer to, Margaret?"

"No, I don't, Gran."

"Come with me, and let me show you," the old woman insisted. "We will bring back a few bolts of it. I want to have it here and get Madame's opinion when she returns."

Her friends left, and Fia knew she needed to make the most of her time alone.

"Do you enjoy working for Madame Planche?" she asked.

"Very much so," the assistant said carefully, pins in her mouth. She removed them. "We are very busy this time of year, but Madame is more patient than other modistes I have worked for."

Madame entered at that moment, looking at Fia with a critical eye. "I like it. Sky blue is an excellent color for you." She looked at her assistant. "Fetch the other ballgown if you would. It is closer to being finished than I thought."

As the assistant left, Madame said, "I hope you are pleased, my lady. I tried to keep your gowns timeless and elegant as you requested, especially your ballgowns."

"I appreciate your efforts on my behalf, Madame. I also have something to ask you."

The dressmaker cocked an eyebrow. "Yes?"

"I teach pianoforte to children of the *ton*. I am also going to play my harp at the opening ball of the Season. My circumstances might be changing, however."

"They should. You are quite pretty, my lady, and you will be beautiful in my creations. I would assume you will be receiving offers of marriage."

Fia shook her head. "I have no dowry and no plans to wed. There is a possibility that I may soon lose the opportunity to teach music. If so, I will need to find a way to earn an income. My maid has taught me to sew. I wondered if you might have any openings at your dress shop."

"Hmm." The woman studied her. "I am always looking for women who have a talent with their needles."

She stepped from the small box she stood upon and retrieved her dress. "I embroidered the cuffs on this gown. It is but one example of my work."

"Why must you work, my lady? I would think even without a dowry, you could make a marriage. Those two duchesses seem to think so, else they wouldn't be paying for these gowns."

"I have some things I wish to keep private, Madame. Only know that I have a vengeful, spiteful cousin who would love to see me tossed from Polite Society altogether. If he manages to do so, I will need to seek a way to support myself."

The modiste nodded. "If that happens, my lady, come to me. I can always make a place for a skilled seamstress. You might have to work outside the shop, however."

"Oh, I have already let a room. It has a large window with good light. I would not mind coming here to collect materials and sewing from the boardinghouse."

Madame sighed. "I hope it does not come to that, my lady. I hope some gentleman will take one look at you in one of my gowns and sweep you off your feet." She paused. "I am a practical woman, however, and understand better than most how a living must be earned. If you find yourself in need of a position, please return to my shop, and we can discuss the matter further."

The assistant returned with the second ballgown at the same time the two duchesses brought the bolts of material they had found. A lengthy discussion ensued, ending with Madame agreeing to make up another two gowns for Fia, one a day gown in soft yellow and a ballgown in rose. Madame herself supervised the fitting of the two almost-completed ballgowns, and Fia knew they would fit her to perfection when finished.

Margaret asked for the gowns to be sent to her residence when Madame tried to arrange a time for Fia to return for her final fittings.

Rather than go into why Fia would not be available to come to the modiste's shop, Margaret said it would be more convenient if the modiste or one of her assistants came to them.

"I will do so simply because it is you, Your Grace," Madame Planche said. "For no other. I can have all the gowns completed by Wednesday as a favor to you."

Margaret looked pleased and said, "Thank you for your efforts, Madame. Might you call at five o'clock?"

The dressmaker nodded. "Of course, Your Grace."

They said their goodbyes and returned to the carriage.

"I think your wardrobe is a good start," the dowager duchess said. "If you are pleased with Madame Planche's work, we can arrange for more gowns to be made up."

"That won't be necessary, Your Grace," Fia said. "What Madame is making for me is more than enough."

The old woman frowned. "You do realize in Polite Society that once a gown has been worn to an event of the Season, it is never repeated."

She hadn't—and the news shocked her. "But . . . I wear the gowns I possess over and over and have for several years."

Margaret winced and then gently said, "It might be time to

retire those gowns, Fia, dear. They have seen better days."

She had thought she had been clever in trying to make them over and change things about them so that they seemed brand-new. What a fool she had been. Fortunately, she usually saw only servants and children when she called upon her students. It was rare when she spoke to a parent, Lady Capwell being an exception. The other parents preferred her written, weekly progress reports. She wondered now if they were too embarrassed to meet with her in person and see her in her shabby clothing.

Making light of things, Fia said, "Then I will see if Millie or one of your servants might be able to use them once I have my new gowns on Wednesday. As to more gowns, Your Grace? I think six day dresses and the three ball gowns are more than plenty. If I must repeat wearing one, I will. There is no shame in appearing in a dress a second time in my eyes."

The dowager duchess merely shook her head. Fortunately, the old woman held her tongue, though. Fia knew both women disagreed with her, but she was not going to take advantage of the largesse she was being shown. In her opinion, it was ridiculous for women of Polite Society to wear a gown once and discard it. What a waste, when so many went hungry and needed clothing.

They returned to the townhouse, and the butler said that His Grace was in the library waiting for them.

"My grandson doesn't need my company. I am off to take a nap," the dowager duchess declared.

Fia accompanied Margaret to the library, a room she had yet to visit in the grand townhouse. When they entered, she stopped in her tracks.

"I feel as if I have entered a bookstore," she proclaimed. "I have never seen so many books in one place. Neither Mama nor Papa were great readers. Our libraries both in the country and town were quite small."

Daniel rose and greeted them. "I have always enjoyed books.

Please take advantage of what you see here, Fia, while you are staying with us. And if you don't finish a book before you leave, feel free to take it with you."

"You are very generous, Daniel. I will try to finish what I start. Although I don't know if I will have much time to read. Between lessons and my own practice—and going to a few society events—I am going to be quite busy."

"It's because of your heavy schedule that I suggest we go for a ride now in Hyde Park. Do you ride, Fia?" the duke asked.

"I did many years ago. I would be woefully out of practice, though."

"How about a carriage ride then?" Margaret suggested. "Surprisingly, the day has grown warm, and there is no wind to speak of. We could take the barouche."

"Oh, that would be wonderful," Fia said.

Hampton entered the room. "His Grace, the Duke of Linberry, is here, Your Graces."

Daniel looked surprised. Or he did a good job of pretending to be surprised. She wasn't sure which.

"Show him in, Hampton. Thank you."

Moments later, her heart pounding, the duke stepped into the library. His eyes went straight to her and held her gaze before he came toward them, greeting each of them. Margaret insisted they sit. Fia, who was closest to a chair, plopped into it, glad she would have some distance between her and this man she so wished to avoid.

"I did not know if you would be home or not, Daniel. I looked for you at White's earlier and when I did not see you there, I hoped you might be at home."

"I had several documents to go through. Estate business."

"You will be happy to know I am reading my estate reports with a more careful eye these days, thanks to your good influence," Linberry said. "Once the Season ends, I plan to take a tour of my various estates and get to know each steward better. The tenants, as well."

"You won't regret it," Fia said, unable to keep quiet about a topic she felt passionate about. "Papa and I used to make the rounds of our estate at least once a week. He believed it was good for his tenants to see him out and about on the land. He knew each of them by name. All of their wives and children, too. They appreciated him for doing so."

"I will wager they also worked harder because of his interest in them," Linberry said.

"I believe you are correct, Your Grace," she said. "Of course, as a duke you will have many more estates than Papa had. It will take you much longer to become familiar with all who live on your various lands."

"I think it is important for me to build a relationship with my tenants," the duke said. "My father left that kind of thing to his estate manager. My grandfather, the duke, preferred town life and rarely, if ever, went to his country lands."

"My cousin is much the same," Fia said. "Once my parents realized Cousin Theo would become the heir, he spent all his school holidays with us. He took no interest in the land, though. I don't think he has visited Parkwood once since my parents' deaths. He is one for town life."

She saw the flush rising on the duke's cheeks. "I fear I have been guilty of the same behavior, my lady. Taken with town life and all the opportunities to be had. The company. The events. The outings." Linberry paused. "Upon becoming the new duke, though, I should have taken a stronger interest in my country estates and the tenants residing there. Daniel has convinced me how important it is. I see your father also believed the same."

Nodding, she said, "Papa knew he held the earldom—but it was really in trust for all who depended upon him."

"I now understand that, and I agree." He smiled. "I hope you approve."

Nerves flitted through her as he gazed at her. "It is not for me to approve or disapprove of your actions, Your Grace. You alone are accountable to yourself. What the *ton* thinks of you does not matter. What you know—in your heart—*that* is what counts."

"You are wise, Lady Fia," Linberry praised. "I wish I had your wisdom."

Silence hung in the air before Margaret said, "We were about to take our barouche to the park, Linberry. Would you care to join us?"

The duke smiled. "I would be happy to come along for the outing."

Despite knowing she should avoid him, Fia was pleased he would join their party for the drive through Hyde Park.

CHAPTER NINETEEN

Henry had been miserable ever since he had left Fia two days ago. He forced himself to stay away yesterday—and found he couldn't today.

He had tried. He had dealt with correspondence. Given his secretary a handful of invitations, telling the man to send word that he would attend these events. Went to White's and talked with a few acquaintances before having a cup of coffee and reading the newspapers.

It had not been enough. He felt the burning need to see Fia. To talk with her. He had never felt so comfortable in a woman's company. She was much more than her good looks. Lady Fia Sawyer was a woman with depth.

He had found himself on the Westfields' doorstep, asking if Their Graces were in. The butler had taken him to the library and to his joy, Fia was with the pair.

Then the duchess issued an invitation for him to accompany them to the park.

"I would be happy to come with you, Your Grace," he said easily, keeping his eyes on the duchess and not Fia. "It is a fine day to go for a leisurely drive." He paused, knowing he might be pushing things, but added, "Perhaps we might stop and have a sweet treat at Gunter's once we are done."

Henry dared to glance in Fia's direction and saw happiness

light her face. "Have you ever been to Gunter's, my lady?"

"Not for many years, Your Grace. Not since Mama and Papa were alive. We would go several times while the Season was in progress. Mama was particularly fond of the sorbets."

"And you?" he prodded.

"Oh, I like everything they serve." Her smile was contagious. "But I have a fondness for the maple."

"Ah, that is one of my favorites, as well," he told her. Looking to the duke and duchess, he said, "Would you be agreeable to stopping at Gunter's after our drive?"

"I think it's a grand idea," the duchess said. "I am so glad you suggested it, Linberry. Hopefully, it will not be too crowded. It becomes so once the Season begins."

"Well, that is a week away," the duke said. "We should take advantage of going while we can. Let me ring for the barouche to be readied."

A quarter-hour later, the two couples headed out the front door and climbed into the duke's barouche. Daniel handed both women up, taking a seat next to his wife.

Leaving Henry to sit beside Fia.

He had noticed she did not wear any type of perfume and supposed her miserly cousin did not provide her with the means to have such small luxuries. Still, Henry was more than ready to bury his nose in the clean scent of soap coming from her skin. He didn't see how that would be possible, though. She had put a halt to their kisses, emphasizing once more how she had no plans to wed and wished to pursue her music. If the Duchess of Westfield could be a duchess and paint, surely Fia could be a duchess and play her music.

Somehow, he would have to get her alone again and have a private conversation that would tell her that very thing. Henry simply needed to work on the when and the where. He might have to wait until he had her to himself at supper on the night of the Capwells' ball. There were always a few tables for two scattered about a supper room. He would speak to one of the earl's footmen so that one of those tables could be reserved.

Then he would speak his heart to this woman.

The drive through Hyde Park was enjoyable. The springtime weather was absolutely perfect, sunny with a hint of cool in the air and absolutely no wind. They passed a few other carriages, stopping to talk to the occupants. Fia, who did not know anyone in Polite Society since she had never made her come-out, had to be introduced to everyone. Two people had known her parents and conveyed their sympathies to her for losing them so closely together. One viscountess bluntly asked why she had never made her come-out.

A brief, awkward silence followed the question, with the duchess quickly saying, "Lady Fia will make her come-out this year. The Dowager Duchess of Westfield is sponsoring her."

"Oh, I see," the viscountess said, nodding approvingly.

They drove on, and Fia said, "I suppose I will get a lot of that. People questioning why I have never made my come-out. I suppose I should come up with a ready answer or deflect as you did, Margaret."

"That viscountess is a terrible gossip," the duchess said. "That actually will go in your favor. By this time tomorrow, half of London will know Daniel's grandmother is sponsoring your come-out. It isn't often a duchess lends her hand and name to a girl. That alone will quiet most of the gossip."

"Shall we head to Gunter's?" Daniel asked. "It is warm enough that I have worked up an appetite for one of their ices."

The duke told the driver, "Head to Berkeley Square. Gunter's Tea Shop."

"Aye, Your Grace."

When they arrived, the customary group of coaches packed around the shop was absent.

"Shall we go inside?" Henry asked.

"No, it is such a pretty day," Fia said. "It would be lovely to have the sun on my face and dip my spoon into an ice."

Daniel signaled to a waiter standing at the doorway. He

dodged across the road to take their order.

"What might I get for you?" he asked their group.

The two women settled on maple, while Daniel asked for bergamot and Henry decided upon chocolate. Within a few minutes, the same waiter weaved his way through traffic, bringing their ices on a tray and distributing them. They took up their spoons.

Henry took a bite of the chocolate and almost groaned aloud. It had been some time since he had come to the shop, and he had missed the sweet treat.

"How is your maple, Lady Fia?" he asked.

"Very good." She grinned. "Almost too good. And your chocolate?"

"Sinfully delicious." He paused. "Here. Why don't you try a bite of it?"

Before she could protest, he dipped his spoon into the cup and brought it to her lips. She opened and he slipped the spoon inside, much as he wished he could slip his tongue inside her mouth and taste the maple within.

"Mmm. Very good," she said as he lifted the spoon from her mouth. "If I ever have an opportunity to return, I will certainly order the chocolate."

He knew he had been forward in pressing the taste on her and looked at her hungrily.

She must have thought he eyed her maple ice, though, because she said, "Would you care for a taste of the maple, Your Grace?"

"I would."

Leaning toward her, Henry opened his mouth slowly. Fia brought up the spoon. His eyes never left hers as he sampled the ice. She slowly pulled her spoon from his mouth, nervously wetting her lips as she did.

If they had not been in public, he would have pulled her onto his lap and drunk his fill of her. Heat rolled through him, stirring his blood. He took another bite of his ice, hoping it would help to cool him.

"What in tarnation is this?" an angry voice said.

Henry knew by the blood draining from Fia's face who it was even before he turned.

Parkhurst.

He glanced to his left and saw the earl, who was perched on the seat of a phaeton, his face reddening in anger. Parkhurst had pulled next to their barouche, and the two men were close together.

But Parkhurst's focus was on Fia. Or rather, his wrath.

"I demand to know the meaning of this," Parkhurst spat out.

"We are merely having an ice, Lord Parkhurst," Henry said, trying to draw his attention from Fia.

The earl glared at him. "I wasn't talking to you, Linberry. I was talking to *her.*"

He felt Fia trembling next to him. She said, "We are—"

"You should be at one of your lessons. Not gallivanting about town." Parkhurst's look would cause even the strongest of men to wilt.

Before Henry could come to Fia's defense, though, he sensed a change in her. She sat taller. Her trembling ceased.

"I have no lessons today, my lord," she said evenly. "If you will recall, you allowed me to take Saturdays off."

"For you to practice. Not frolic."

"Their Graces were going for a quick drive in the park, along with Linberry. I had practiced quite a bit already and decided a brief respite would suit me. We stopped for an ice."

"You should not be out in public," Parkhurst said, his eyes narrowing.

"And why is that, Parkhurst?" Daniel asked, inserting himself into the conversation. "I have seen the long hours Lady Fia puts in with her pupils, as well as heard her practicing. She is devoted to both, but even those with a great devotion could stand to pause and enjoy life a bit. I believe that to be reasonable."

"What you believe is none of my concern, Your Grace,"

Parkhurst said, turning his glare from Fia to the duke now. "I am the one who cares for my cousin. I can see you and your wife's influence has not been a good one on her."

Henry saw cold fury turn his friend's eyes wintry as Daniel said evenly, "My wife and I are among the elite of Polite Society, Parkhurst. We are a duke and duchess who have befriended Lady Fia and enjoy her company tremendously. Be careful what you say."

The warning hung in the air.

He watched a flicker of doubt enter the earl's eyes as Parkhurst stood without speaking.

It was Fia herself who broke the silence. "I have done all you have asked, my lord. I teach a large number of pupils at your request. I am practicing my harp and will do our family name proud come the Capwells' ball. But I intend to stay with Their Graces through that ball."

A burst of pride ran through him, seeing how Fia bravely stood up to this bully.

"I have heard Lady Fia play," he chimed in, "and her talent will be the talk of the *ton*, Parkhurst. You should be immensely proud of her and her dedication to her music."

His gaze held that of the earl's in a standoff until Parkhurst was the first to look away.

"Then I will expect you home the following day," Parkhurst told her.

"I find Lady Fia's company most enlightening," the duchess said. "I would prefer that she stay with us during the Season."

"And I say finish up your portrait of her and then send the chit home to me," Parkhurst said, drawing a gasp from the duchess.

"You go too far, Parkhurst," Daniel said, his tone now deadly.

"And you do not go far enough in reining in your wife, Your Grace," snapped the earl. "A woman should be seen and not heard. Any man worth his salt should be able to control his wife."

Daniel quickly stood, his eyes narrowing as he glared at the earl. "You have insulted my wife, Parkhurst, not to mention how you have shown your petty nature. In truth, you have no legal control over Lady Fia since she is of age."

"I don't care if she's of age, Your Grace. She is of my household. My responsibility. I know of no women in Polite Society who do not acknowledge they are under the protection of the head of their family. I merely take my duties to my family seriously."

Henry rose to his feet now. "Then perhaps you should have treated Lady Fia as family, my lord, and not a servant to rent out to teach musical lessons to others."

Daniel now took up the banner, adding, "You are using horrendous judgment, Parkhurst, if you think to challenge two dukes *and my duchess*. If the *ton* senses blood in the water, they will know which side to take."

Henry nodded in agreement. "The repercussions of you daring to cross Their Graces or me will prove disastrous to you, my lord. I can guarantee you that."

Henry's words lingered in the air, his gaze locked with Parkhurst's.

Quietly, Fia said, "Let it go, Your Graces."

They looked to her questioningly and then Daniel said, "If you insist, my lady." He sat.

Henry commanded the earl, "Leave, Parkhurst. I am certain you have somewhere to be."

The way the man looked at him, Henry knew he had made an enemy. He had to remember that he was now a duke. His title alone gave him power far beyond that of an earl. If he had to use it against Parkhurst—especially in defending Fia—he would.

Parkhurst flicked his wrists, taking off. The occupants in the barouche sighed collectively.

"If a more vile man walks the face of the earth, it would surprise me," the duchess said. "I have never been one to think to use my position in Polite Society to hurt another, but I am more than ready to give that man the cut direct when I next see him."

"I want to wipe him from the face of the earth," Daniel growled. "He insulted you, my love. The both of us."

"He is not worth it," Fia said, taking her friend's hand. "Promise me, Margaret, that you will merely have nothing to do with him."

"I cannot allow you to return to his household, Fia," the duchess said. "I fear you would be a prisoner there if you did. You already were before you came to us."

Fia kissed the duchess' hand. "And you and Her Grace rescued me. You have offered me your friendship. I am blessed to know you. I will not have you getting into confrontations with Parkhurst. I would not wish to see him drag you down in the eyes of the *ton*."

"That will not happen," Daniel assured her.

Henry wanted to take Fia's hand and reassure her that everything would be all right. He couldn't do that, however, and so he said, "You are a shining light, Lady Fia. Parkhurst may hold your father's title, but he is a boor."

The smile she bestowed upon him made his heart sing.

"Thank you, Your Grace. That is a lovely compliment."

"I believe our ices have melted," the duchess said. "Shall we order more?"

"Why don't we go inside this time?" he suggested. "That way, we will have no more interruptions."

"A splendid idea," agreed Daniel.

They left the barouche and crossed Berkeley Square, entering the tea shop and quickly being seated. He asked the waitress for the exact same order, and it was quickly brought to them. He had feared Fia would grow quiet after the encounter with Parkhurst. Instead, she seemed in good spirits.

As they ate, she told them of a few of the selections she would play with the orchestra and on her own, her cheeks growing pink and her face animated as she did so. Looking at her, Henry couldn't think of a more beautiful woman than Fia Sawyer. His eyes were drawn to her mouth every time she slipped the spoon into it and the urge to kiss her grew stronger with each bite.

Once they had finished, they returned to the barouche and the Westfields' townhouse.

"I must return to my own home," Henry told them. "Even though I felt like a bit of an intruder, I thank you for inviting me to accompany you."

"It is always a pleasure to see you, Your Grace," the duchess said. "Come back anytime. Friends need no invitation."

He warmed at her words—and knew they might give him a chance to see Fia again. Somehow, Henry needed to subtly press his suit.

Because the golden-haired beauty had laid full claim to his heart.

CHAPTER TWENTY

FIA TOLD HER last student of the day to continue to practice the piece they had worked on this afternoon. She also left another number for the girl to begin to learn for her next lesson.

"You did very well today," she praised. "Keep up the good work. I will see you at this time next week."

As she went to claim her horse and cart which a footman held for her, she wondered if there *would* be a lesson with this child next week. Fia had written what she thought was a very nice note, canceling her lesson with her final student today because she had to get home and dress and be at Lord and Lady Capwell's no later than seven o'clock tonight. Although the ball did not commence until nine, Lady Capwell said that Mr. Johnson, the conductor of the orchestra and a man who conducted many of the orchestras at *ton* balls, wanted to meet her and have her practice a few numbers with his members before he gave final approval for her to play with them this evening.

She had explained this in her note to the viscountess, even offering to give the woman's daughter a makeup lesson this coming Saturday if the viscountess was agreeable. Fia proposed that she extend the lesson to double the usual length to make up for the cancellation. Instead, she had received a blistering reply in return, telling her it was unthinkable for her to cancel and that they would be finding another instructor for the daughter's pianoforte lessons.

She knew after her debut as a musician in Polite Society tonight that this might happen with other clients. She had taken the time to write notes which she would deliver at each of the lessons this week and had already done so with her students today. In it, Fia asked for the funds for the lesson to no longer be directed to Lord Parkhurst but rather they be sent to Mr. Bankston, her father's solicitor, whom her cousin had chosen not to use. Fia had written to Mr. Bankston, knowing from Daniel that the solicitor was not in town at the moment, telling him of how she had asked the parents to direct funds for their children's musical lessons to him and pleading with him to hold them in reserve for her. Eventually, she supposed she might open some kind of account with a bank, if that was even possible. Women had few legal rights, and Fia did not know if opening an account and holding funds at a bank would be one of them. If not, she trusted Mr. Bankston to keep the monies for her.

That is, *if* her pupils' parents sent it to him.

She knew they would see her tonight, either playing with the orchestra or during the supper hour. They might not want their children taking lessons from her if she were a working musician. They might also object to sending money not to her cousin, but to someone else instead. She would have to wait and see if—or how many—canceled lessons with her as the viscountess already had.

Pulling up in front of Daniel and Margaret's townhouse, she saw the groom awaiting her. He handed her down before climbing onto the bench and taking up the reins in order to return the horse and cart to the duke's mews.

The moment Fia was admitted to the foyer, Hampton came toward her.

"Her Grace would like to see you, my lady. She is in her studio. It is on the top floor."

"I can find it myself, Hampton. Thank you."

Fia started up the stairs, not taking time to drop off her satchel of sheet music or the violin case she carried. Only one pupil had attempted the violin today and she knew she would not be bringing it back to his next lesson. She had briefly discussed with his mother that while he had a talent for the pianoforte, the boy seemed uncomfortable with the violin.

Reaching the top floor, she went past the nursery and to the end of the hall, where Margaret had said her studio was located. Upon entering it, she saw her friend seated upon a stool, a paintbrush in her hand.

"Ah, Fia. You are home."

Margaret rose to greet her, taking the violin case and satchel from her and setting them down before giving Fia a warm embrace.

"I suppose you are wondering why I asked for you to come here."

"You have finished my portrait and wish to show it to me. That would be my guess."

"You are exactly right. Come."

Margaret led them to a corner of the room, and they stood in front of the easel which held Fia's portrait.

It was breathtaking.

Margaret had painted her in the rose-colored ballgown, which Madame Planche had delivered this past week. Fia had tried on all the day gowns first, Madame and Margaret fussing over her, and then put on the ballgowns. She had never worn such finery in her life. And now, she was pictured in that finery for all time, unless the canvas was painted over as Parkhurst wished.

Margaret had placed Fia on the ducal staircase, which Fia thought was an unusual setting for a portrait. The gown floated around her and complimented her skin, bringing a warmth to her cheeks. Her friend had captured Fia with a dreamy expression on her face, a half-smile playing about her lips.

"I look . . . beautiful."

"Of course you do," Margaret declared. "Because you are."

"I would not have thought to paint me sitting on the stairs."

"I did not want the usual staid portrait of you sitting in a chair in a drawing room or library. I thought this would be a place to paint you where you came to life."

She blinked back tears. "It is hard to believe that I look like this. I know you are my friend, though, and you see me in a different light than most."

"I am always true to my subject, Fia. This is how I do see you. I believe the rest of Polite Society will share my vision of you with you making your come-out."

"I don't know if they will pay much attention to someone sitting in an orchestra while they dance and chat," she said drily.

"But you won't always be in the orchestra. You will move among the *ton*."

"I still don't believe that is possible, Margaret," she admitted. "Despite being sponsored by the Dowager Duchess of Westfield. I have already lost one pupil today and think other parents might make the same decision. I also need to impress Mr. Johnson, the conductor, tonight if I am to be asked to play at other *ton* affairs. It is how I will earn my living because I will be leaving your household early tomorrow morning."

Margaret frowned. "You are still thinking of what your odious cousin said, aren't you?"

Fia nodded. "He ordered me to return after this ball tonight. When I do not do so tomorrow, he will no doubt come looking for me himself. I will not be here—and you will not know where I have gone."

She had arranged with Hampton to have her transported to the boardinghouse, along with her trunk.

"But where will you go, Fia?"

"As I said, you need not have access to that information, so it will be impossible to divulge it to Parkhurst. I will ask two favors of you, however. One, I wish to leave my instruments here and practice in your music room on Saturdays if you will allow it. Where I am living will not be conducive to my practicing there."

"You are welcome here day or night, and you know it, my

sweet friend. What else?"

"I cannot afford to take Millie with me. You know I have very limited funds. My pin money did arrive this week. I will be using a good portion of it to travel to and from lessons and any *ton* events that I am asked to play at."

"I am happy to keep Millie in waiting for you, Fia," Margaret told her. "I still believe that you will make a match this Season. Then once you have, you can reclaim Millie as your lady's maid and your portrait to hang in your new home. As far as you traveling, I assume you are talking about paying for hansom cabs to take you various places."

Fia thought Margaret a bit mad to think a match might be made under the current circumstances. No, that was too harsh. Perhaps her sweet friend was merely an optimist. But Fia knew how vicious the *ton*—and her own flesh and blood—could be. No match would ever be made, at least with a gentleman from Polite Society.

She pushed those thoughts aside and said, "I am. It would be too far for me to walk with my bad leg. I certainly cannot take one of Daniel's horses and carts for my own use. I would have nowhere to house them, much less afford the horse's feed."

"On the night of any engagement you have, you are welcome to take the dowager duchess' carriage. Since I assume you have arranged with Hampton to deliver your things wherever you are going, he will be able to instruct a coachman where to pick you up."

"That is most generous of you, Margaret."

Her friend hugged her tightly. "I don't want to see you go. I do not like this idea of you living on your own without being under Daniel's protection. You should not have to face Parkhurst alone."

"I doubt he will even notice if I am in an orchestra, especially since he rarely attends balls and when he does, he makes for the card room. If he does see me? He would not dare to cause a public scene in front of all of Polite Society."

Her friend frowned "I am not certain of that, Fia. He was quite rude to us at Gunter's. If he could be that disrespectful to two dukes and a duchess, he would think nothing of belittling you in front of the *ton*."

"I won't let him," she told Margaret. "I am moving on, creating a new life for myself. I am old enough to do so and do not want him in my life."

She excused herself, knowing she needed to dress for the ball. She rang for Millie and asked the servant to bring her a small plate of something to eat. Fia had not eaten since breakfast early that morning. She also told the maid to have hot water for a bath brought up.

While she waited for Millie to return, Fia laid out all her new gowns on the bed, along with the various new undergarments and slippers. When the maid returned, she looked about the room, confused.

"Set the tray here," Fia instructed and then had Millie come sit in the chair opposite her while she ate.

"What is going on, my lady?"

"I am moving somewhere else for a short while," she revealed.

"It's Lord Parkhurst, isn't it?" Millie asked.

"Yes. He has demanded that I return to his residence tomorrow. I do not wish to do so."

The maid shivered. "Neither do I, my lady. Where are we going?"

"Only I am moving to another location. I have arranged with Her Grace for you to stay here. Do whatever Hampton and Mrs. Hampton ask of you. Her Grace has promised not to send you back to Parkhurst."

"How long will you be gone, my lady?" Millie asked, tears forming in her eyes.

She decided to tell a small, white lie. "I am not certain, but you will be cared for here. The dowager duchess and Her Grace are trying to bring me out into Polite Society. If I make a match, I will send for you."

The maid beamed at her. "Oh, that would be wonderful, my lady."

"In the meantime, please pack my things, all but something for me to wear tomorrow. I will leave the house quite early. No one will know where I am going, so Parkhurst won't be able to get that information from you or anyone else."

"What about dressing for events, my lady? How will you do so without my help?"

"I will dress myself as I did when we were living with the earl. I have mastered a simple chignon and that will do for my hair. I believe I can find someone to help lace any undergarments. I can take care of the rest of my toilette."

Fia pushed the tray aside, having only taken a few bites. The thought of what she was doing overwhelmed her. Nerves were also beginning to gather as far as her playing went tonight and she did not think she could take another bite.

The bathwater arrived and Millie bathed her, pouring in bath oil that smelled like roses.

"Where did this oil come from?" Fia asked, not used to such luxuries.

"The old Her Grace sent it to me today, my lady. She favors you quite a bit."

Millie toweled off Fia and then dressed her in the layers of clothing. She hoped Mrs. Kent would be willing to help in the future, supposing she would have to offer the landlady a coin or two in order to do so.

When she was ready, Fia looked to Millie, whose gaze moved up and down her mistress.

"You look lovely, my lady. No one will be able to take their eyes off you in this gown."

She did not want to draw unwanted attention. Yet at the same time, she hoped her talent would have others taking notice of her. Now, all she had to do was pass muster with Mr. Johnson.

Going downstairs to the foyer, Hampton met her.

"Your harp was delivered to Lord Capwell's, my lady," he informed her. "The carriage is waiting to take you to the ball." The butler paused. "As for the other business we discussed?"

"Millie is packing for me as we speak, Hampton. I will be downstairs at seven tomorrow morning and accompany my things to my new lodgings. Only the coachman will know where I am going, so if Lord Parkhurst comes looking for me, you may look him in the eyes and truthfully say you have no idea where I have gone."

Sympathy filled the butler's eyes. "I understand, my lady. On behalf of the household, we want to wish you the best of luck. It has been our pleasure to serve you while you have been a guest of Their Graces."

"Thank you for everything, Hampton."

Fia left the house and went to the grand carriage awaiting her and was handed up by a footman. Since it was two and a half hours before the ball even began, the streets were fairly empty. They made good time, arriving at the Capwells' townhouse ten minutes later.

The Westfield footman handed her down and grinned. "Play your best tonight, my lady."

"Thank you," she said, nerves sweeping through her.

She turned and headed toward the door, knowing tonight would be one which decided her future.

CHAPTER TWENTY-ONE

O NCE INSIDE, FIA was taken to the ballroom, now filled with massive bouquets of flowers, its floor gleaming from all the polish applied to it. She gripped the handle of her viola case and headed toward the group of musicians that she saw on the opposite side of the room. As she reached them, she heard one grumbling.

"I cannot believe Johnson made us come an hour earlier than we normally arrive. All for some high and mighty lady who thinks she can play with the likes of *us*." The man sniffed haughtily.

His companion, though, had spotted her and said, "My lady, are you looking for Mr. Johnson? He is there, talking to the fair-haired gentleman holding the violin."

"I am, sir. I am Lady Fia Sawyer and look forward to playing with the both of you this evening."

The first man snorted. "If you think you can play with professionals, lady or no lady, you are sadly mistaken."

He turned away from her as the other one gave her an apologetic smile.

Fia had known there would be resistance to her playing with the orchestra, but now knew just how deeply the resentment must run. And if the players felt that way, then how would their conductor treat her?

She swallowed, gathering her courage, and headed toward the man who had been pointed out. Mr. Johnson had tufts of white hair on the sides and back of his head, while his bald pate shone atop his head. She waited for him to finish speaking to the musician, then approached.

"Good evening, Mr. Johnson. I am Lady Fia Sawyer, come to play with you and your group of musicians this evening."

She saw the skepticism in the man's eyes. Whirling, he commanded, "Take your places."

Immediately, the numerous conversations ceased as the black-clad musicians took their seats and eyed her with interest. She could see curiosity on the faces of some, while others looked as if they hoped she would fall flat on her face.

The conductor turned back to her. "I have already spoken with Lady Capwell. There will be no harp solos during the ball. *If* I allow you to play with us, my lady. The harp is a quiet instrument and alone, it would not be heard over the din of conversation, much less be conducive to the dancers having to strain to hear it, as I am sure you are aware of."

She heard the sarcasm in his tone and raised her chin a notch. "Actually, I would not know this, Mr. Johnson, for I have never attended a *ton* ball."

He frowned. "You have never been to a ball?" he asked.

"No, sir. My parents passed before I was to make my come-out. My guardian became my cousin, Lord Parkhurst, who assumed my father's title. I remained in the country and then came to town at Parkhurst's behest, where I have devoted my time to teaching music lessons to children of the *ton* the past six years."

Fia paused, her gaze penetrating the man. "That has been my life, Mr. Johnson. Music. I live for it. Teaching and playing. Now, you asked me to come early to hear me play. I shall do so for you."

She marched toward her harp, sitting at the edge of where the musicians were gathered, and set down her viola case. She had brought it in case the conductor would allow her to also play it with the orchestra.

Looking to him, she asked, "What is it you wish for me to play?"

"Anything, my lady," he said, his tone dismissive.

Steadying her harp, she brought her fingers to its strings. She took a deep breath and began to play. She went on for a full minute before Mr. Johnson called out, "Halt!"

She paused, her fingers lingering at the strings.

"Play Mozart," the conductor commanded.

Fia did so for a good half minute until Mr. Johnson interrupted again. "Haydn," he said, his face showing interest now.

The game went on another five minutes, with him calling out a different composer's name, and Fia playing a selection from that composer.

Mr. Johnson raised a hand, and she once more stopped playing. "I see you have brought another instrument, Lady Fia. Why?"

"Because my goal is to become a member of your orchestra, Mr. Johnson. I know the harp can be impractical, especially at a ball, and so I thought I would bring my viola and let you hear me play it so you can see I am worthy to play with your musicians tonight—and other nights, as well."

His gaze bored into her. "You think I would offer you a position in *my* orchestra?"

"That is my hope, sir."

She heard the murmurs of the musicians, knowing every eye was on her now.

"What shall I play for you, Mr. Johnson?"

He named a difficult Lucia Bova piece.

Fia opened the case and removed her viola and bow. She settled it on her shoulder and tucked her chin onto it, taking up her bow and beginning to play. Once again, the conductor let her play for a good half minute before he called for another piece, and then another and another.

Finally, Fia saw his expression change and knew she had won him over with her playing. He turned his attention to the orchestra members.

"We shall rehearse together now. Lady Fia, you will join us on your viola."

The conductor named a selection, and the musicians played it in its entirety. Mr. Johnson had them play two more pieces before asking her to move to her harp. They played another three before the conductor nodded with satisfaction.

"I find it highly unusual for a woman to have a talent for music, but you have proven to be the exception, my lady. You are welcome to play with us this evening—and in the future."

A buzz broke out among the musicians as they gossiped about her. For her part, she was filled with elation, seeing a long-held dream would become a reality.

Mr. Johnson came toward her. "You feel the music, don't you, my lady?"

Fia nodded. "It is in my soul, Mr. Johnson. An innate part of me that always seemed to exist. I love playing and have recently begun composing music of my own."

She could tell she had sparked his interest, and he asked, "Would you play one of your original pieces for me?"

"With pleasure."

Securing her viola against her once more, Fia moved her bow to the strings and began to play. The piece was one she had composed in Oxfordshire, one she was particularly fond of. She realized the talk had died among the musicians as they all listened to her play now. When she finished and lowered her bow, Fia was thrilled when the group applauded her.

"You wrote that yourself," Mr. Johnson stated.

"Yes, sir. I would like to compose more, but I am busy five days of the week giving lessons."

"A talent such as yours should not bother with lessons, Lady Fia. You should be writing and performing music."

"I am humbled by such praise," she told him, gratitude filling her as she saw the attitude of the other musicians had now changed regarding her. Even the first man who had spoken ill of her met her gaze, a genuine smile on his lips as he nodded respectfully to her.

"I do not believe there will be an objection if we add you to our orchestra, my lady," the conductor said. "I will discuss the details with you if you are interested in my offer."

"Very much so, Mr. Johnson. I also play the violin and cello if you find that helpful."

He dismissed the group and told them to report back at a quarter 'til nine. He then told Fia about some of the upcoming engagements.

"We play at many of the balls during the Season, as well as garden parties. Sometimes, a hostess will hire a string quartet from within our group for a smaller affair. Lady Capwell told me you would be playing your harp during tonight's supper hour."

"Yes, that is correct. I am hoping it will draw enough interest so that others might engage my services." She paused and then added. "I fear I may lose some—if not many—of my pupils after tonight, though. It is one thing to have me come to a client's house and teach their child pianoforte in private. It is quite another for a lady of Polite Society to try and earn a living by playing at *ton* events."

"Aren't you paid for the lessons you give?" he asked, obviously perplexed by their conversation.

Fia shook her head sadly. "No, my cousin takes the fees I earn. I wish to be on my own and make my way by playing and hopefully writing music."

"You may play at any event we are engaged to do so, Lady Fia."

"I am thrilled to accept your offer, Mr. Johnson. However, the Dowager Duchess of Westfield has a mind to try and launch me into society this year, despite my advanced age. Would it be possible every now and then to exit quietly and dance a number before returning to the fold? Her Grace is a dear soul and has been very good to me. It would please her if I did dance once or twice during an evening."

"Your talent is immense, my lady. You may play as little or as often as you choose. I believe you will be a wonderful addition to our group."

She beamed at him. "I will certainly play each song with you this evening. Thank you for allowing me to play with your musicians. I am most grateful."

"I would like to meet with you and hear more of your original compositions."

"I will let you know when I can do so, Mr. Johnson. Right now, I spend every morning and afternoon giving lessons, so there is no time during the day. If I lose any of those clients, I will let you know what has opened up in my schedule. Then we might meet."

"Call me selfish, but I hope you do lose those students," he declared. "I can pay you enough to earn a decent living. That would leave your days free so that you might write then."

"If that is the case, it may not be such a bad thing if I do lose my entire roster of clients."

"You have a gift, Lady Fia. It should be shared with others. I fear it is wasted by you teaching children to bang on the ivories."

She chuckled. "Then let us see how this next week plays out, Mr. Johnson."

⟫⟫⟫⟪⟪⟪

HENRY GLANCED INTO the mirror, excited for the first time in a long time about attending a ball.

Because Lady Fia Sawyer would be there.

He went downstairs, where Orville informed him that the Duke of Westfield's carriage had just arrived. He thanked his butler and went outside, climbing into the vehicle and greeting his friends.

At first, he had turned down Daniel's offer to ride together to the Capwells' ball, thinking it would be too difficult to sit in close proximity with Fia without kissing her in front of the other couple. Daniel must have had an inkling of Henry's thoughts because he told Henry that Lady Fia would be going to the ball separately in order to practice with the hired orchestra. Once he knew that, he told his friend he would be happy to accompany them.

"You look quite lovely, Your Grace," Henry complimented the dowager duchess. "As do you, Your Grace," he said to the duchess.

"Remember, you must call me Margaret. I thought we had already decided you would do so." She laughed merrily. "After all, I am a duchess and get what I want."

He joined in her laughter. "Very well, Margaret. I will remember to do so in the future."

"Do you think you have made any progress with Fia?" she asked.

"I still hope to make Lady Fia my duchess." It felt good admitting that aloud.

A satisfied smile turned up the corners of her mouth. "I think you would be well matched, Henry. I know I had asked you to dance with Fia to bring attention to her. Instead of one dance, you should ask for two this evening. That way, your intentions will be clear to everyone present."

"I wish I could, but Lady Fia has already informed me she will not be dancing at all this evening. I had engaged her for the supper dance, but she said she would need to be playing with the other musicians during that number. However, I told her to reserve supper for me. We shall dine together, either with you and Daniel, or hopefully at a table for two."

"I suggest a table for two in the corner," Daniel said. "It will make quite a statement. You can speak to a footman of Capwell's. It is easy to arrange."

"I will do so once the ball commences. Thank you for your advice."

"We want the best for Fia," Margaret said. "She has led quite a difficult life since the death of her beloved parents. It would be wonderful if you brought happiness into her life." She paused. "And perhaps, love."

Henry did believe he was in love with Fia, but couldn't say the same for her, especially after she had told him to keep away from her. He would do his best to woo her, though. Break through her reservations.

"I will make my intentions known tonight. I will call on Lady Fia every afternoon." He paused. "Oh, no. I won't be able to do so if she is teaching lessons."

"Fia is worried after tonight that there will be no lessons given," Margaret revealed. "She thinks those of the *ton* will not want her in their homes once she is working as a musician."

"That is preposterous!" he proclaimed.

The dowager duchess met his eyes. "And yet we all know just how judgmental Polite Society can be. Especially in regard to a woman."

"I must tell you that Fia will no longer be living with us after tonight," Margaret said.

"Don't tell me she is moving back to Parkhurst's townhouse."

"No, she is moving *because* of Parkhurst. I do not have any idea where she is going. She fears the earl will come to us and demand that Fia return to his residence. She told me if we had no idea where she had gone, we would not have to lie to him."

But Henry did have a good idea where Fia might go. He now understood where she had gone the day he had followed her and assumed she would move to the building she had first called at, especially since she had only entered the one place that day. He could not imagine her living there when she deserved so much more. When she became his duchess, he would shower her with gifts. Clothing. Jewels. Whatever she desired.

Determination filled him as they reached Lord and Lady Capwell's townhouse and entered it, joining the receiving line. Once they had greeted their hosts, Henry accompanied his friends into the ballroom, gazing about and immediately spotting Fia.

"I will see you later," he told the couple, making his way along the outskirts of the room, saying hello to a few friends, and then reaching the orchestra.

Fia sat beside her harp. Henry also noticed a case sitting next to her, the instrument sitting atop it. He supposed she would play both tonight.

She looked up and blushed.

"Good evening, Lady Fia. I see you are ready to perform with the orchestra."

She rose and curtseyed. "Good evening, Your Grace. Yes, Mr. Johnson, the conductor, has graciously allowed me to play with his musicians tonight. He even listened to me play one of my own compositions."

"You write music?" he asked, intrigued by the idea.

Her blush deepened. "I do, Your Grace. I have only recently begun this endeavor, but I believe I have a talent for it."

"You are a woman of many talents, my lady," he told her, causing her face to turn bright red. "I came to wish you well in your playing tonight—and to remind you that we will sup together."

She bit her bottom lip, causing desire to pour through him.

"I am sorry, Your Grace, but I will not be able to honor that promise to you. Lady Capwell has asked me to play my harp during the supper hour so I will not be available to dine with you." She paused. "This way, you will be able to ask someone to dance and enjoy her company at supper. I had felt guilty about keeping you from the dance floor, especially since you have remarked how you enjoy dancing so very much."

He bowed to her. "Good evening, my lady."

Moving away, Henry knew this wouldn't do. He wanted— no, needed—to spend time privately with her.

Returning to the hallway leading into the ballroom, he saw the receiving line had almost ended and waited for the last of the guests to come through it. Then he moved to the Capwells, smiling the smile that he knew usually got him whatever he wanted.

"Lady Capwell, I have a request of you."

The countess looked bedazzled. "Anything, Your Grace."

"I wish to sup with Lady Fia Sawyer tonight, but she told me she was engaged to play during the supper hour."

Lady Capwell nodded. "Yes, I have asked her to play for my guests as a special treat."

Henry's gaze pinned that of the countess. "And I am requesting that you free her up in order for me to dine with her." His tone made it obvious that this was no request but rather a command.

"Of course, Your Grace. I will inform Lady Fia of the change in our arrangements."

He thought a moment. "Please wait to do so. Playing for your guests as a member of the orchestra tonight means a great deal to her. I wish for her to focus on that task without distraction."

The countess said, "I understand, Your Grace. I will speak to Lady Fia before the supper dance begins."

"Thank you for such consideration, my lady," Henry said with warm approval. "I appreciate your desire to accommodate my wishes."

With that, he bid his hosts farewell and returned to the ballroom, where he signed a few programmes. Although he did not want to dance with anyone but Fia, he did enjoy dancing. By signing some dance cards, he also hoped to prevent pushy mamas forcing their daughters upon him. He would also dance enough to please Lady Capwell. He wished that her ball would be a successful one, since she was doing him a favor.

The musicians began tuning their instruments, and Henry went to claim his first partner for the opening dance, knowing his eyes would constantly stray to Lady Fia Sawyer.

CHAPTER TWENTY-TWO

Fia MOVED FROM the harp to the viola at Mr. Johnson's direction. She had known every song being performed this evening and had played from memory, not needing to share music with a fellow musician.

The waltz would be the next number. A part of her wished she could dance the tune with the Duke of Linberry. Oh, how she had enjoyed twirling about his empty ballroom as he taught her the simple steps. It was better, though, that she remain playing on the musicians' platform while he socialized with all the women of marriageable age. She had seen him dancing a few times tonight, watching him move effortlessly no matter what the dance. He was a man in the prime of his life, one in need of a duchess in order to secure an heir and continue the family line. He would have no trouble finding a woman of worth.

Still, she would have liked to have had one dance with him this evening.

She had tried to avoid looking at others as the ball progressed, knowing she had to be a topic of conversation. Or gossip, if the truth be told. With all the other musicians in black and white, she certainly stood out in her rose-colored gown. She had thought to dress according to her station as she played but realized that would only make her stick out as a sore thumb. She would take this gown and the periwinkle one, since she liked the cut of them the best, and see if Madame Planche might be able to dye them a darker color. Black would be too severe and seem as if she were in mourning. Hopefully, a darker color would help her blend in more with the group of musicians.

A gentle touch on her shoulder alerted her someone was nearby. Fia glanced up to see Lady Capwell standing there.

"Good evening, my lady. I hope you are pleased with my playing so far. I look forward to entertaining your guests on my harp shortly."

"That will not be necessary, Lady Fia," the countess told her. "I know I had arranged for you to play during the supper hour, but you will now be free to spend that time with the Duke of Linberry."

"What?" she said, a little too sharply.

"His Grace requested your company at supper. Naturally, I could not afford to tell a duke no. Linberry is well thought of by the *ton*. I was happy to honor his request."

Anger seethed within her, and Fia tried to temper it. "I thought we had decided my playing at supper would make your ball stand out."

Disappointment filled the countess' face. "Yes, I know we did. Perhaps another time."

"Have two of your footmen carry my harp to the supper room," she instructed.

"But . . . what of His Grace?"

"I will see to His Grace." She glanced over and saw Mr. Johnson awaiting her attention. Turning to the countess, she said, "I must now play with the others. Do not worry, my lady. His Grace will be most understanding. I guarantee it."

The countess looked doubtful but moved away, her husband coming to claim her and leading her onto the dance floor. Mr. Johnson counted them down, and the strains of the waltz began. As Fia played, her anger grew. She spied the duke standing to one side of the ballroom. He wasn't watching the dancers.

He was watching her.

Quickly, she averted her eyes and focused on her viola. She allowed the music to wash over her, soothing her. By the end of the song, she had firm control over her temper.

But she was going to give a certain duke a piece of her mind.

Lord Capwell invited his guests into the supper room and couples retreated there, joined by the matrons who watched the dancing and gentlemen streaming from the card room. The musicians began dispersing, heading to a separate room, where a supper had been set up for them.

Fia waited in place, watching as Linberry made his way toward her. By the time he reached her, the ballroom was almost empty. She stood, placing her instrument and bow on the chair she vacated.

"How dare you?" she asked, her voice low and controlled.

"How dare I?" he asked. "What are you referring to, Fia?"

Through gritted teeth, she said, "I am Lady Fia to you. I do not appreciate your familiarity. And I certainly despise how you went behind my back and arranged with Lady Capwell what I would be doing for the next hour. I told you I could not sup with you. That I was to play for the guests."

"You have played enough already," he chided. "You must be tired. You will still play after supper."

He smiled, one which practically made her bones melt. She hardened herself to it.

"I never tire of playing," she told him. "And I simply must play at supper. I want to draw the attention of those hosting future balls. If they see Lady Capwell has entertainment at supper, they also will want to do the same—hopefully with *me* as that entertainment, playing my harp. You have robbed me of that opportunity, Your Grace. Simply because you are a duke does not mean you are not insufferable. I do not wish for you to meddle in my life. Do you understand that?"

"I understand that you were to sup with me. That playing your harp would prevent that. So I took action to correct it."

"Have you not been listening to a word I say, Your Grace?

Get it through your thick skull as I speak plainly. I must play for the Capwells' guests now. It is important to me that I do. I am not going to dine with you. Not now. Not ever. I do not wish for your company. I do not want to be alone with you. I do not want to converse with you. Do I make myself clear?"

"Perfectly," he said.

She thought he would be put out. Instead, he looked rather amused. Smug, almost.

"Why don't you sup with me and then play?" he suggested.

"No," she said stubbornly. "I will not."

Fia marched past him and left the ballroom, following the noise of the guests and finding the supper room. Her harp sat waiting for her.

She moved to it, breathing slowly and deeply, calming herself. She could not afford to be upset or distracted by anything.

Especially a tall, handsome duke.

Slipping into the chair beside it, she brought her fingers to the strings and began to play softly. At first, no one seemed to notice, all attention turned toward the buffet and where to sit. Gradually, though, the guests began to realize she played and turn in her direction. She continued to play and after a few moments, the members of Polite Society returned to their plates and conversations. Still, she provided an ambiance that added to their dining experience.

Fia deliberately did not look about the room and focused on her instrument. She had always enjoyed the harp and never more so than this night, in this moment, playing for the *ton*.

Guests began finishing their meals and drifting back to the ballroom. She could tell several stared at her as they passed. She kept up her playing, losing herself in the music, until Lord and Lady Capwell approached her.

Ending the song, Fia glanced up at them. "Was it as you wished, my lady?"

The countess smiled gently. "Most definitely, Lady Fia. I have received nothing but compliments on my idea of having a musician play in the background while supper commenced. I do believe I may have started a trend, all thanks to you. Why don't you take a few moments to yourself before you return to the ballroom?"

"Thank you. I will do so."

Though she was now hungry, she was too nervous to eat. Instead, Fia went to the retiring room, which was beginning to empty. Slipping behind one of the curtains, she relieved herself.

Then she heard two women gossiping.

"What is she thinking, playing with those men?" the first said.

"She is rather good, though. Did you hear her on her harp as we ate?"

"A lady simply would not do so in public. At least one properly brought up, that is. Lord Parkhurst must be quite embarrassed by his cousin's outlandish behavior."

The second chuckled. "And yet I would wager that many hostesses of upcoming balls or events will wish Lady Fia to play at their affairs."

"I am certain they will. But she will be ostracized from Polite Society now. Why, I heard she is being *paid* to play tonight. How gauche."

The voices faded and Fia finally parted the curtain. She washed her hands and took the towel offered by the attendant.

"You shouldn't care what they say, my lady," the servant said. "I heard a bit of your playing earlier. You are as talented as any man."

"Thank you," she said, blinking back tears.

Fia had expected this, and yet it still stung hearing it spoken aloud. She returned to the ballroom and seated herself at the harp again, which had been brought back to the ballroom.

The rest of the evening went by in a blur. While she enjoyed playing in public, it saddened her that the very thing she loved doing would cut her off from the *ton*. Of course, she had never truly been a part of them. Now, she would hover around the edges.

The musicians finished a lively reel and prepared for the final dance. Once again, it would be a waltz.

Suddenly, the Dowager Duchess of Westfield was at Mr. Johnson's elbow. The old woman spoke to the conductor a moment and then nodded, moving away, and returning to the area where the matrons sat and watched the dancing.

Mr. Johnson came to her. "You may take one of your respites, my lady, and dance this final number."

Puzzled, she told him, "I have no partner, Mr. Johnson."

"Yes, you do."

Fia glanced over her shoulder and saw the Duke of Linberry.

"Her Grace arranged for us to waltz together," he said apologetically.

She didn't think he was sorry at all.

But she would never cause a fuss in public and rose. "Thank you, Mr. Johnson, for excusing me. I will see you at tomorrow night's ball."

It was one of three being held this week that the conductor had asked her to play at. She had agreed to do so, knowing more events would come.

The duke offered her his arm. "Shall we?"

Placing her fingertips atop it, she allowed him to guide her to the dance floor. A sudden attack of nerves struck her. "Might we move away from the center, Your Grace? I believe I have drawn enough attention for one night."

"As you wish."

He led her to the edge, and they took up their positions. Warmth flooded her at his touch, causing her cheeks to burn. He held her hand lightly yet firmly. Her insides flipped and flopped, making her feel excited and slightly nauseous at the same time.

The music began for the first time without her being a part of it tonight. Linberry eased her back as she focused on the steps. They came to her easily, however, and she felt light as air as he guided her around, incorporating the slight turns which made the waltz come to life.

"You had the dowager duchess intervene for you, I suppose."

"No. Though I wish I would have thought to do so. She came up with the idea all on her own and found me, asking if I had a partner for this dance."

Fia frowned. "Why didn't you?"

His gaze held hers. "Because I decided I wanted to watch you play."

His eyes darkened, and Fia guessed they burned with desire. She swallowed, trying to think of some witty retort. None came. She found herself happy to be in his arms, moving to the music in three-quarter time, finally a part of the crowd at a ball.

"You recalled our dance lesson," he noted. "You are moving with ease."

"It is all your doing, Your Grace," she admitted. "You are guiding me about, almost as if I don't have any will of my own."

He searched her face. "I would never want that, Fia. You have a strong will. You are a determined woman with lofty goals. I can see the conductor has been pleased with your playing tonight."

"He has asked me to play at two other balls this week. And possibly a garden party." She frowned. "I cannot play at it unless I am let go from my teaching."

"It will be hard for you to burn the candle at both ends. Playing nights at balls. Teaching all day. You won't get much rest."

"How can I even think to rest when I am finally getting to do what I have dreamed of?" she asked.

"It really means that much to you, doesn't it?"

"It does," she said fervently. "I want to play and compose music. I want to be able to take care of myself."

"I think you are more than capable of doing so. But what if I wished to take care of you?"

His words caused her to stumble. Linberry paused a moment, allowing her to get her bearings, bringing her a bit closer to him. The spice of his cologne made her long for him to kiss her again. Now that would be the Kiss of Death, having a gentleman kiss her in a crowded ballroom. She would never teach a pupil again and would never be allowed to perform with an orchestra.

"I think you feel pity for me, Your Grace," she told him. "I have said this before. You need to find a bride acceptable to Polite Society. You are a good man who will do great things with the right woman by your side. I can never be that woman."

"Can never be—or would never *want* to be? There is a difference, Fia."

Oh, he was far too clever and observant for his own good.

"I have shared with you that I will not wed. You are the opposite—you must wed in order to provide an heir and continue your line. I have seen a good number of very pretty girls tonight, Your Grace. Any one of them would be delighted to become your duchess."

"What if I don't want a pretty featherhead as my wife, Fia? What if I want you?"

She swallowed, hurting as she said, "Then you will come to know that even a duke doesn't always get what he wants."

The music ended, and they stopped moving. For a moment, Fia relished the feel of him against her, wishing life had been different. That her parents had not died. That she had made her come-out as she should have. That she would have met this man under different circumstances.

Pushing away from him, she curtseyed. "Thank you for the dance, Your Grace."

He stepped toward her, invading her space. "Collect your viola, Fia. We must be on our way."

"What do you mean?" she asked.

"I suppose you are riding home with the Westfields." He paused, a slow smile spreading across his face. "Well, so am I."

CHAPTER TWENTY-THREE

FIA DECIDED NOT to lie down after returning from the ball at five o'clock that morning. She was afraid if she did, she would fall into a deep slumber. She needed to collect her things and go to Mrs. Kent's boardinghouse and then have breakfast before her first lesson of the day.

Millie had helped her to undress, and Fia insisted the maid help her into her everyday corset before slipping into a dressing gown. She dismissed the servant and sat, thinking of the night that had just passed. The highlights included playing alongside the orchestra members and even playing her harp during the supper hour for the guests.

She would not think about the duke.

She would not.

Yet Fia couldn't help herself. She could still smell the tang of his cologne on her from not only their dance but sitting too close to him on the carriage ride home. The man stirred feelings in her which she refused to recognize, knowing she lied to herself.

The sudden urge to capture those feelings overwhelmed her, and she quickly dressed, placing her dressing gown in the open trunk, and closing and latching it. She went to the music room, where she had left her viola, and sat at the piano. No one would hear her now with the door closed.

And so Fia began to play, tinkering with a melody running

through her head. The song came to her quickly, in a rush of emotions, being expressed through the music she created. Within three-quarters of an hour, the piece was completed. She tinkered with it a few minutes longer, knowing at some point she would commit it to paper when she had more time. For now, though, it was burned into her heart and her memory. Every note, every chord, every beat reminded her of the duke.

She left the music room with her satchel of sheet music and violin. Mr. Johnson had requested she play the violin at the next ball. Going to the foyer, she told the footman on duty that her trunk needed to be carried down. He looked surprised not only to see her dressed at this hour but by her request.

"Mr. Hampton knows of this," she explained.

Off he went, returning with a second footman and climbing the staircase. Minutes later, they returned with her trunk. The clock chimed and a knock sounded at the door. The first footman answered it.

"I am here for Lady Fia," the coachman said. "Bring her trunk to the cart."

She had asked the butler to arrange for a cart and not the ducal carriage. She did not want to be seen descending from it. Though the neighborhood was a working-class one and not unsavory as her second stop had been, she did not want to give any bystander the idea that she came from money. Most of her savings had gone toward renting the room from Mrs. Kent. She would have to be very careful in her use of hansom cabs in order to make her funds stretch as far as possible.

Hampton appeared. "I wanted to tell you goodbye, my lady," the butler said. "Is there anything you need?"

The Duke of Linberry came to mind. She quickly banished that thought.

"No, thank you, Hampton. Millie packed my things. I am ready to leave. I will see you weekly, though. Her Grace has given me permission to come and practice in the music room each Saturday."

The butler smiled. "Then we will look forward to seeing you and hearing you play. I quite liked the song from this morning."

She was taken aback by his comment. "I am sorry. I did not think I would be bothering anyone."

"Oh, I am always up early, my lady. I enjoyed hearing it very much. I even paused outside the door and listened a bit. The melody is quite haunting."

Hampton walked her outside and helped hand her into the cart, where she was seated next to the driver. She waited until the butler left before giving the coachman the address. He flicked his wrists, and the horse started up.

The streets of London were coming alive at this time of the morning. Fia watched with interest as they made their way to the boardinghouse.

Once there, she told the coachman, "Her Grace will send a carriage for me some nights. You will be the one who drives me to those *ton* events. I must ask you not to divulge my whereabouts and prefer that you pick me up at the corner we just passed, where the apothecary's shop is. Tonight, I would ask you to come at seven o'clock."

"I can do that, my lady," he said.

"Thank you. You see, my cousin will most likely come calling today and demand to know where I am. He must not learn where I am."

The driver nodded knowingly. "I will keep your secret, my lady. You can count on me."

She thanked him and went to knock on the door as he removed her trunk. Mrs. Kent greeted her.

"Right on time, Miss Sawyer," the landlady said. She looked to the driver. "You can have him take your trunk to your room. Breakfast is waiting if you're so inclined."

"Thank you, Mrs. Kent."

The landlady handed Fia the key to her room, and she led the coachman up the stairs. He carried her trunk on one shoulder, seemingly effortlessly. They reached her room, and he placed the trunk on the floor as she put the satchel on the bed. She thanked him and returned downstairs with him, bidding him farewell and joining the others for breakfast.

Mrs. Kent introduced her to the boarders present, telling them that Miss Sawyer was a musician.

"Ooh, do you play at those fancy balls the toffs give?" the man on her right asked.

"I played at Lord and Lady Capwells' ball just last night," she said proudly, seeing that her words impressed her fellow boarders.

After breakfast, she asked to speak to Mrs. Kent privately.

"I know you said the outside entrance is not for your tenants' use," Fia began. "However, because I do play at *ton* events, my hours are quite late. For instance, I did not arrive home until five o'clock this morning."

"Oh, my!" exclaimed the landlady.

"I would not want to beat upon the front door and rouse you from sleep or disturb your tenants due to my late hours. Would it be possible to obtain a key and use the outside entrance? The door is mere feet from my room. Using it would ensure that I would not bother you or anyone else."

Mrs. Kent thought it over a moment. "I suppose I do see your point. Very well, Miss Sawyer. Let me fetch a key for you."

The landlady returned with the key. "Keep it safe, Miss Sawyer. You have a good head on your shoulders. I know you will use it wisely."

"Thank you for this, Mrs. Kent."

Fia returned to her room and claimed her satchel and reticule before leaving the building and hailing a hansom cab, traveling back to Mayfair. If she continued to eat a hearty breakfast at the boardinghouse and then could take a bit of supper at events, she might not have to spend much at all on food.

When she arrived at the townhouse for her first lesson, the butler told her that her services would no longer be required. She did not question the man, knowing he merely relayed the wishes of his employer. It would do no good to berate the servant or try to find out further information from him. She left and walked slowly to her next destination, sitting in the small park in the center of the square until it was almost time for the lesson to begin.

Once again, Fia was turned away at the door by a butler who merely shook his head in apology.

It happened twice more before she arrived at the Capwells' residence. She was shown into the drawing room as usual, greeted by Lady Maisie and Lady Daisy. Their lesson went well. When it ended, she saw Lady Capwell had slipped into the room, which wasn't unusual. She enjoyed hearing her daughters play.

"A word, Lady Fia?" the countess asked.

"Certainly, my lady."

Lady Capwell indicated a chair, and Fia sat.

"I do not know if you have read the newspapers today or not," the countess began.

"No, I did not have time to do so."

A pained expression filled the older woman's face. "The gossip columns are full of you. While most praised your playing, they questioned the fact that you are a working musician."

Fia winced. "I had reason to believe that would occur."

"They suggest that it would be unseemly for you . . . to . . ." Lady Capwell's voice trailed off.

"Teach lessons to children of the *ton*?" Fia completed, understanding the direction their conversation would now take.

The countess flushed. "Yes. That. I know our girls adore you, Lady Fia, but I must think of their future. I do not want them ostracized in any way. The thing is . . . well, we will no longer require your services."

Fia wanted to object and knew it would do no good. Polite Society had spoken. She was no longer fit to teach impressionable children the pianoforte. At least Lady Capwell had the decency to face Fia in person to deliver this news.

"I understand," she said softly, her throat thickening with

emotion. "I do hope you will find another instructor for your girls. They possess a rare talent."

"Oh, they will certainly continue to play the pianoforte and possibly their other instruments," the countess said. "But Lord Capwell and I have discussed it. We do not wish to give them the idea that because they are talented, they should play for . . . money."

"As I do," she said flatly.

"Oh, you are a tremendous musician, Lady Fia," the countess amended. "And we are grateful for all you have done for our girls. But appearances do matter. I am sure you understand my position."

"I would merely ask that you recommend me to your friends, Lady Capwell. That I am open to playing at the events they host."

The countess brightened. "Of course, my lady. I can easily do that."

"Might I say goodbye to the girls?"

The countess frowned. "No. His lordship and I discussed it. We feel it best that a clean break occurs."

"I see." Her heart heavy, she added, "I do thank you for allowing me to accompany you to the country, as well as giving me the opportunity to play at your ball. Good afternoon, Lady Capwell."

Fia didn't bother going to any of her other lessons. She had already walked enough today, and her knee was bothering her. No sense to be turned away again and again.

Hailing a hansom cab, she returned to the boardinghouse.

"A note came for you, Miss Sawyer," Mrs. Kent said.

She took it, seeing it was addressed to Miss Sawyer and not Lady Fia. That meant it came from Margaret. She had told her friend last night as they went up the stairs to communicate with her without using her title. Fia had also mentioned that she would be playing at the next ball.

Going to her room, she opened the note.

My dearest Fia –

I hope you were able to get some rest before you left here this morning. I know your day is full of lessons, and you will be up until the wee hours of the morning, thanks to playing at tonight's ball.

I must inform you that Parkhurst did send a carriage for you today. I had Hampton inform the coachman that you had departed early this morning and had not left word where you went. Hampton was told to say that he assumed you had returned to Lord Parkhurst's residence. We have heard nothing further from your loathsome cousin. He might try and manage a moment alone with you this evening, however, and so I wanted to warn you of that.

Gran has told me that she will insist you dance three times this evening. If I were you, I would acquiesce with whatever she says. Since you will have the list of pieces to be played, you will know best when you might dance. I know Linberry is eager to claim one of those.

I miss you already, Fia dearest, and cannot wait to see you tonight. I am sending this to you via our coachman since he is the only one who knows where you are.

All my love,
Margaret

She held the page to her, willing herself not to cry. Yes, she missed her friend terribly and knew her life would be much more difficult living in this boardinghouse than in the luxurious townhouse of a duke. But Fia also knew she must stay true to herself and her vision for what she wanted in life. After creating a new song this morning, she hoped she would write many more in the years to come. Apparently, she would have her days, after all, in which to compose music since the *ton* had turned their backs on her as far as lessons went.

Placing the letter atop her trunk, she went downstairs and asked Mrs. Kent to wake her at six o'clock. The landlady agreed to do so, and Fia knew that would give her adequate time to dress and arrange her hair before heading to meet the coachman. Mr. Johnson had his musicians gather at eight o'clock on the night of a ball so she would have plenty of time to reach her destination.

She slipped off her gown and left the corset on, not wishing to bother Mrs. Kent again. Her head touched the pillow, and Fia fell soundly asleep.

CHAPTER TWENTY-FOUR

HENRY RECEIVED WORD that Mr. Bankston had arrived in town again and immediately went to see Daniel. The two men immediately set out for the solicitor's office, eager to learn about Fia's situation from her father's solicitor.

When they arrived and gave their titles to the clerk, he almost choked. Henry bit back a smile, knowing it wasn't every day that two dukes came calling without warning.

The clerk showed them into an office, where a portly man sat behind a desk. His brows arched as the clerk managed to get out, "Two dukes, Mr. Bankston. To see you!"

The solicitor rose and thanked the clerk, asking him to close the door on his way out.

"Would you please have a seat, Your Graces?"

They took the two sitting in front of the man's desk and gave Bankston their titles since the clerk had neglected to do so in his excitement.

"We come on behalf of Lady Fia Sawyer," Henry explained. "She has given us permission to look into a delicate matter on her behalf."

The solicitor harumphed. "I suppose this has to do with that detestable cousin of hers. I have known the current Lord Parkhurst since he was a child. He is rotten to the core. I never speak ill of anyone, the exception being the earl."

"We know you were solicitor to Lady Fia's father," Daniel said. "We have questions about her dowry. If it exists, to begin with."

"*If?* Of course, it does. I wrote up the marriage settlements myself, Your Grace. They were quite generous, you know. Lady Fia's dowry was twenty thousand pounds, payable upon her marriage. If for any reason she chose not to wed, the monies were to be delivered to her on her twenty-fifth birthday, which will occur in June."

Henry and Daniel exchanged a glance, and Henry said, "Who is Lord Parkhurst's current solicitor?"

Bankston snorted. "It is a Mr. Williams, who—in my opinion—is as vile as Lord Parkhurst himself. The earl was a bully as a boy, the way he hurt Lady Fia, and runs roughshod over everyone he comes in contact with, from his fellow peers to lowly servants."

"Wait. You say he hurt Lady Fia?" Henry asked, his fists balling at the thought.

"He most certainly did." A worried expression crossed Bankston's face. "Oh, I was never to tell anyone about the incident. Frankly, I hadn't thought about it in years."

"Tell us now," Daniel said, steel in his voice.

The solicitor shook his head. "I promised Lady Fia—"

"I plan to make Lady Fia my wife," Henry stated. "Share what you know."

Bankston sighed. "She told me in confidence. This was years ago. When her parents both grew ill. Lady Fia helped the steward in managing the estate. I came down to Parkwood with some important papers which needed Lord Parkhurst's signature."

"Go on," he urged.

"She was going through the books and had found where Theodore Sawyer, who would inherit the title upon her father's death, had been stealing from the estate. Lady Fia confronted the steward, who admitted to the deception and had kept two sets of estate records. She fired the man on the spot and continued to manage the estate on her own, as well as care for her ailing parents, all when she was only ten and seven."

Pride swelled within Henry, hearing of how capable Fia was even as a young girl.

"Anyway, I arrived just as she ordered the steward out. We went through the books together. I told her that her father must confront his nephew when Mr. Sawyer returned from university during the summer break." Bankston hesitated. "I saw real fear on her face, Your Graces, and asked her why she was so terrified of him. She told me when she was but six years of age, he threatened to rip out her hair if she didn't obey him. He then shoved her down a flight of stairs. She landed hard, breaking both her kneecap and leg. Her cousin warned her never to tell on him—or he would do worse to her."

"My God!" Henry proclaimed.

The solicitor nodded. "Lady Fia told me that she could not confront Mr. Sawyer over the missing funds, especially with her father so near death. She swore me to secrecy. I have never spoken of this incident. When the new Lord Parkhurst terminated my relationship with the Parkwood estate, I was happy to be rid of him as a client. I handed over all documents relating to the estate and the Sawyer family to Mr. Williams. This was shortly after the burials of Lord and Lady Parkhurst."

"Lady Fia believes she does not have a dowry," Daniel told Bankston. "That Parkhurst told her about immense debts her father owed."

"Then he is a bald-faced liar," declared the solicitor. "The funds are there unless he has gambled them away."

Henry rose, rage surging through him. "Thank you for your time, Mr. Bankston."

He strode from the office, not stopping until he was outside, seeing red. Daniel joined him.

"Are you all right?"

"I will kill him," he said. "And it is no idle threat."

His friend grabbed Henry by the shoulders. "You will do no

such thing. You would destroy your good name and reputation. And I doubt Fia would want to wed you."

"She doesn't want to now," he said bitterly. "She told me she never wants to wed. All she wants is to play music."

Daniel shook him. "Listen to me! She probably has in her head that she isn't worthy enough to wed. After all, she's had years of Parkhurst browbeating her. Telling her she is worthless. Making her work day and night for no wages. Forcing her to live in a tiny attic."

Daniel released Henry and stepped away. "She needs you, Henry. She needs a good man and his love to convince her of her worth. Yes, she also needs music. It has been her refuge. But love can conquer all. Do you love her? Do you love Fia?"

"I do," he said. "I do."

"Then we need to see her dowry restored to her. You will also need to take Parkhurst down. Killing him means a few seconds of pain." Daniel smiled. "Ruining him socially and financially? Then he suffers a lifetime of humiliation."

The rage began to subside, clearing his head. "You are right. I want to strip him of everything he has."

"We will go to Bow Street and hire a runner," Daniel said. "Find out everything we can about Lord Parkhurst. All his little dirty secrets. And then we will go and see this Mr. Williams, his solicitor. After all, you will need to be in touch with him to draw up the marriage settlements. He cannot keep you from claiming Fia's dowry."

"All right," Henry agreed.

They took Henry's carriage to Bow Street and met with the head of the agency, explaining how they sought every piece of available information regarding Lord Parkhurst.

"I have just the person for you. That is, if you are openminded, Your Graces," the head of the agency told them.

"As long as we get the information we need quickly, I have no objection to who you select," he said.

"Give me a moment," the man said.

When he returned, a woman accompanied him.

"Your Graces, may I introduce Miss Shelby Slade? *She* will work your case."

Miss Slade smiled. Pulling out a small pad and pencil, she said, "Please tell me everything about Lord Parkhurst that you can, Your Graces—and I will take it from there."

MRS. KENT ASSISTED Fia in dressing, exclaiming over her finery. She had chosen to wear the periwinkle ball gown this evening, thinking with her days now free, she would be able to go to Madame Planche's dress shop and see about dyeing a few gowns to a darker shade so she wouldn't stand out so much among the men playing beside her. She did not want to offend the Dowager Duchess of Westfield, however. The woman had paid for Fia's entire new wardrobe. She realized she walked a very fine line and hoped she could remain in the good graces of the dowager duchess.

"You look like a fairy princess," the landlady told her. "Why, it wouldn't surprise me if one of those toffs swept you off your feet." She paused and then warned, "Don't let one do that to you, Miss Sawyer. You're a pretty one, for sure, but there are men who want only one thing. You shouldn't give it away."

"I understand what you are saying, Mrs. Kent. I will be aware of men who try to flatter me. Truly, though, no one pays attention to the musicians. A ball could not be held without them, yet they are only seen in the background and deemed unimportant by members of the *ton*. Thank you for helping me to dress, though."

"It was my pleasure, Miss Sawyer. I can do so any time."

The older woman left, and Fia retrieved her violin case. Since Margaret was sending a driver, she would leave her reticule behind. Then she thought better of it. Although her room had a lock and her reticule only contained a small amount of coins, she decided she should take it with her. She could place it inside the violin's case while she played tonight.

Leaving the boardinghouse, Fia walked down the block and saw the coachman from this morning sitting atop the dowager duchess' carriage. The vehicle looked out of place in this neighborhood. She thought maybe to ask Margaret if a simple horse and cart could be sent in the future.

A footman handed her into the coach and to her surprise, Fia found the dowager duchess waiting inside.

"Hello, Fia, my dear," the old woman said. "I hope you do not mind sharing with me."

"Not at all, Your Grace," she answered, wondering why the old woman had chosen to come. "After all, it is your carriage we ride in."

The woman patted Fia's arm. "I simply wanted a bit of time alone with you. In private. I wanted to discuss tonight's ball. I wish you to dance this evening, my dear. I know last night was all about establishing yourself as a musician. You played quite beautifully during the supper hour, by the way, although I had thought you were to dine with Linberry."

"Lady Capwell thought it would be a treat for her guests if I played during the supper hour. I informed His Grace of that decision."

"Well, Linberry is a dear boy. We will simply make it up to him tonight. You should dance the supper dance with him and spend the next hour in his company. Unless Lady Danby has also asked you to play your harp during her supper this evening."

Since she had no place to store her harp, Daniel had suggested keeping it at the Westfield townhouse. If a hostess wished Fia to play it at an event, it would be transported there.

"No, Your Grace. Mr. Johnson asked me to play with his musicians this evening, but Lady Danby has not spoken with me. The harp is still at your townhouse."

"Good. Then you'll dance with Linberry. I will want two

other waltzes played since that is the dance you will accept this Season."

"I can check with Mr. Johnson to see how many will be played."

The old woman snorted. "*I* will tell your Mr. Johnson how many to play. During the first waltz, I wish you to partner with Viscount Carstairs. He is a bit on the quiet side, but a lovely man. The second will be with Linberry. The third? I am still thinking on it. I have my eye on an earl that might suit."

"Your Grace, did you read the newspapers this morning? The gossip columns, in particular."

The dowager duchess waved a hand. "I would not give credence to what you read there, my dear."

"You may not—but most of Polite Society does. I have not seen what was written, but I have lived the results of it. I was turned away at every door I went to today. No one wanted me giving their children lessons. I doubt the gentlemen you have mentioned will want to be seen dancing with me. Polite Society has judged me and found me lacking, Your Grace."

Fire sparked in the old woman's eyes. "And *I* say you will dance."

They continued in silence. Fia thought the dowager duchess might bully the gentlemen she spoke of into dancing. Usually, men could get away with a little scandal. But dancing and offering marriage were two different things. Now that the *ton* had decided Fia was not suitable to teach music lessons, they would also deem her unsuitable to wed. In the end, she supposed it was how she wished things to turn out. She would become invisible to members of Polite Society, playing at their events. In return, she would have her freedom and begin composing music in earnest.

When they arrived, the dowager duchess accompanied Fia inside. They went straight to the ballroom, where the musicians were setting up. She introduced her companion to Mr. Johnson.

"I expect three waltzes to be played tonight," the dowager duchess told the conductor.

"Two are scheduled, Your Grace. One at supper and then the final dance of the evening."

"Play another," the old woman commanded. "Early in the evening."

"Yes, Your Grace."

"I will leave you now, my dear, but once guests have arrived, I will introduce you to the two gentlemen who will dance with you. You already know Linberry, so I won't bring him around."

"Thank you, Your Grace."

Fia watched the woman move away, her head held high, her posture beautiful, even at her advanced age.

Mr. Johnson went over the order of music to be played this evening with the musicians and then took her aside.

"I know you said you are teaching during the day, but there is a garden party being held tomorrow afternoon at two o'clock if you could rearrange your schedule to play at it."

"I find my days now free, Mr. Johnson. I would be happy to play with the group."

He gave her the name of the hostess, and Fia tried not to wince. The garden party would be hosted by the viscountess who had sent Fia the horrible note after she had canceled a lesson and offered to double the time and make up the lesson. She only hoped the woman wouldn't notice her as a part of the musicians who performed.

Taking her seat, Fia slipped her violin from its case and placed her reticule inside, closing the case and setting it against the wall with the other instrument cases. Guests began arriving, and the ballroom started to fill.

As promised, the Dowager Duchess of Westfield brought two gentlemen to meet Fia, telling them when they would waltz with her. The gentlemen left, and she began tuning her violin as the other musicians did the same.

Then the ball opened to a lively country dance. She had always loved playing her violin and never more so than when a tune was spirited.

Once the set ended, she caught Mr. Johnson's eye and nodded, letting him know she would slip away for this number.

Lord Carstairs came and claimed her. He was friendly and quite good-looking, and she enjoyed her waltz with him.

But he did not stir any of the wild feelings that had beat within her when she had danced with the Duke of Linberry.

The viscount returned her to the musicians' dais, where Fia once more took up her violin and played until the supper dance. She had deliberately kept her gaze turned from the ballroom floor as she played tonight, not wanting to catch sight of the duke. Not wanting to see which beautiful ladies he danced with.

Then suddenly he appeared before her, just as she removed her bow from the strings. Obviously, he hadn't partnered with anyone during the reel they had just played, else he wouldn't be here so quickly.

He bowed to her as she rose. "Lady Fia. I was told we are to dance the supper dance together."

She wet her lips nervously. "Yes, Her Grace planned my partners for me this evening."

"I saw you dancing with Carstairs." The duke paused. "I didn't like it."

His words—and the look in his eyes—left her breathless.

"Come. Let us have our own waltz."

She took the arm he offered, and he led them to the center of the room. She gripped his forearm tightly.

"I shouldn't be here. Might we go to the edge of the ballroom again?" she pleaded.

"No. You proved the last time we waltzed together that you recall the dance steps well. There is no need to hide in shadows."

Fia met his gaze. "There is every need to do so, Your Grace. Or haven't you read the gossip columns today?"

"I have not."

"I haven't either—but I have learned just what the *ton* thinks of me after they read those reports. Every door I went to today was barely opened to me, only wide enough to tell me I had been dismissed from giving music lessons in that household. As of now, I have no students and am not welcomed in any homes of Polite Society. Thankfully, I have my music to fall back on. Mr. Johnson is most eager for me to play with his musicians. I will do so even at a garden party tomorrow afternoon at Lady Simms' gardens. But it is one thing to play for a *ton* event and quite another to step to the center of the room at one—and with a duke, at that.

"So, please, Your Grace, could we—"

Fia saw the anger in his eyes as he slipped an arm about her and took her hand, and the music began. It was too late for them to move to a far side of the room.

She could feel the stares as the duke twirled her about. She caught sight of matrons whispering to one another behind gloved hands. Her heart sank, and she did not even enjoy the dance as she should have. Fia decided she would not dance with the earl at the end of the evening. It would not be fair to him. Or her. She was on the verge of becoming a social pariah and could not let that occur. If it did, hostesses might even reject her being part of Mr. Johnson's group of musicians.

And where would that leave her? Her dream would be dead—and she would still need to support herself.

The music ended. Fia looked up at the duke, who still held her close. She saw the concern in his eyes.

"I am feeling a bit ill, Your Grace," she lied. "I believe I will go to the retiring room. If I am able, I will join you at supper. Please go on without me."

With that, Fia broke free and moved quickly, retreating to the safety of the retiring room.

CHAPTER TWENTY-FIVE

FIA RUSHED TO the retiring room, praying the Duke of Linberry would not follow her. She reached it and found it empty, save for two lone attendants, and went behind a curtain, her sobs erupting the moment she was hidden from view.

She had known it would be difficult to leave her cousin's household. It had been nice to be spoiled for a while, staying with Margaret and Daniel. She truly did not mind the small room at the boardinghouse she was now calling home because it was all hers. Even though she had prepared herself for being dropped as a music tutor by some of her clients, it had hurt far more than she suspected it would, especially not being able to bid Lady Daisy and Lady Maisie farewell. Now, she would not see any of her pupils, much less be able to defend herself from the lies those children would be told about her.

What worried her more was the fierce gossip which had appeared in the morning newspapers. Gossip had a life of its own and could blaze out of control. She feared it would become so vile that it would prevent her from pursuing her music.

She might die without music in her life.

Brushing away her tears, she prayed that she could return to the orchestra tonight without further consequences. She must never accept a dance again. It pained her to have to tell the Dowager Duchess of Westfield of this decision. Fia planned to pay the woman back for the wardrobe she now wore, even if it took years, which in all likelihood, it would.

She pulled the curtain aside and went to one of the washbasins, splashing cool water on her face and accepting the towel offered by the attendant.

"Are you all right, my lady?" the maid asked.

Fia thought a moment. "I will be," she said with determination.

She left the retiring room, passing two women who eyed her with suspicion and then began tittering the moment they moved past her. Pausing in her tracks, she took a deep breath. She would go to the room designated for the musicians and try to eat a bite.

Then she found her way blocked.

By Parkhurst.

She had not seen her cousin at last night's ball. He rarely attended balls and when he did, he always headed for the card room. His face was now a bright red, indicating how angry he was.

Grabbing her by the shoulders, he shook her violently, so hard it caused the pins to spill from her hair.

"You have made a laughingstock of me," he told her, spitting in her face.

Shocked, she raised a hand and wiped away the spittle.

"First, you run off to that duchess. It's scandalous that she even paints. Then you leave there without informing me where you have gone. And worse, I pick up this morning's newspapers and find them full of you. How you are now working as a musician. By God, I won't stand for it!"

Fia's own fear was only supplanted by her anger. "Enough!" she cried, pushing hard against his chest, breaking the contact between them.

Parkhurst staggered back, stunned she had put her hands upon him. "You will live long enough to regret that."

Her chin rose a notch. "You would kill me?" she asked. "You tried to once before when we were children. Then you tried to kill my spirit, forcing me to live in a cramped attic room and farming me out, allowing me to do the labor, while you collected the fees. I won't bend to your will anymore, Parkhurst. I am almost five and twenty and do not have to answer to you. Yes, I have left your household. I would say left your protection—but you have never protected me. You have used me. Treated me unkindly. Never acted as family toward me. I am done with you."

Hate filled his eyes. "Done with me? I am done with you. You were a spoiled, entitled brat and took all of Uncle's time. He should have taken me about the estate. Not you. I was his heir. His flesh and blood."

"You were a horrible child and have grown into a horrible man," Fia told him. "Papa hated that his title and lands would go to you."

The sting of the slap stunned her. She looked at him. "You are such a small man. Not worthy to hold the title Earl of Parkhurst. Papa would be ashamed to see what you have become and how you have treated me."

Her cousin struck her again, this time with his fist. She felt the pain first and then the blood which trickled from her nose, ruining her gown. She would not be able to return to the ballroom, with her hair streaming down her back and blood covering the front of her gown.

A loud gasp sounded, and Fia turned, seeing the two women from earlier. They took in the scene and hurried by, ready to spread the gossip.

"No one wants you," Parkhurst said. "You are an outsider. Say what you will about me, Cousin, but I hold the title. The power. You are nothing."

His hand rose to strike her again.

And Fia fled.

She raced away, doubting he would follow her as she ran to the foyer, past two startled footmen, and out the door. She ran blindly for a few blocks, only stopping when her knee began to throb. Stopping, she looked at her surroundings to determine where she was.

It would be impossible to return to Lord and Lady Danby's townhouse. Her appearance would frighten everyone away and do nothing for her reputation, which she knew would be in shreds once the two vicious gossips spread the news of the scene they had encountered. Slowly, she began walking in the direction of the boardinghouse. She had left her reticule and violin behind and couldn't retrieve them without running into someone. Hopefully, Mr. Johnson would keep them for her. She wondered if he would even want her at the garden party now. It wouldn't be fair to risk his reputation and that of the other musicians playing at the affair. Yet she needed to show up and collect her things if the conductor thought to bring them.

Fia decided she would go to the garden party and speak to Mr. Johnson. He would let her know if she was still welcome to play or not. If she wasn't, she would go to Madame Planche since she had once spoken to the modiste about being a seamstress. Surely, the dressmaker would hire her because she could work in the back room or even from her own room at the boardinghouse without reflecting poorly on the modiste.

Sighing, Fia continued on her long walk home, her leg and knee both aching.

HENRY LET FIA leave the dance floor and did not try to follow her. Doing so would have brought more unwanted attention.

And Lady Fia Sawyer had had her fill of that.

He had fibbed in telling her he had not read the gossip columns. That had been the first thing he turned to in the morning newspapers. She had seemed concerned about her status in Polite Society, and so he had wanted to investigate to see if those concerns were valid.

Her reputation had been decimated by nameless writers.

They had done more than judge her. They had crucified her. He was relieved to hear that she had not read the columns herself. Henry supposed that is why the Dowager Duchess of Westfield had accompanied Fia to the ball tonight and arranged for her to have a few partners. He had watched her dance with Lord Carstairs and seen the reaction in the crowded ballroom. They watched the couple, waiting for Fia to stumble in the dance. Fortunately, she had performed it with her usual grace and charm. Carstairs had returned her to her fellow musicians and retreated to the card room, not dancing the rest of the evening. The viscount would be able to shrug off the gossip of having danced with Fia one time.

Fia, on the other hand, would not.

The *ton* now had her in their crosshairs—and they could be brutal. It had not surprised him to hear her reveal that she had lost all of her musical students. She must be worried about also losing her newly-earned position in the orchestra which performed tonight. Yet she need not worry about how she would survive. Henry had planned to tell her over supper about the dowry that was hers. If no one offered for her, she could claim it on her next birthday.

It didn't matter. He planned to offer for her. He was a duke, immune to gossip. He would wed the woman of his own choosing.

And that woman was Lady Fia Sawyer.

He allowed the guests to move into the supper room and went to find Daniel and Margaret. They were already seated at a table. He took a seat next to the duchess.

"It's bad, isn't it?" she said, her voice low. "What the papers said of Fia. I have noticed how the crowd tonight has watched her. She did not seem too aware of it during her dance with Lord Carstairs, but I noticed she did not look at any of the dancers as she played tonight."

"But it was different when she waltzed with you," Daniel added. "I caught sight of the two of you. Fia was certainly aware of the looks she garnered."

"She was quite upset. She went to the retiring room and told me to come into supper. I doubt she will join me. I plan to go and wait for her now outside the retiring room. I want to inform her of what Bankston shared with us. She needs to know she has a dowry and that she wouldn't be left destitute."

"You won't let that happen, will you, Henry?" Margaret asked. "If you do not offer for her, I can't think of anyone who would." She hesitated. "Are you willing to stand up to Polite Society and follow your heart?"

"I am," he said firmly. "I will tell Fia tonight that I do love her and wish to make her my wife. We can do it quickly. I can arrange for a special license tomorrow morning."

"We would be happy to host your wedding breakfast," Margaret said. "We can even hold the wedding at our townhouse if you would like."

"If Fia agrees to wed me, then I am certain she would appreciate that. Will you excuse me now? I merely wanted to let you know what was happening."

Henry left the ballroom, determined to persuade Fia of his love for her. He went in the direction of the retiring room, passing two giggling women. Disgust filled him. Instinctively, he knew they had encountered Fia and would want to spread the tale of that encounter.

Suddenly, he saw Lord Parkhurst coming toward him. His gut tightened. Henry believed he must have followed Fia from the ballroom, not wanting to confront her in front of others.

"Where is she?" he demanded as they came face to face.

"Who?" the earl asked gruffly, looking down and fussing with his hand.

"Lady Fia," he said, his jaw tightening as he watched Parkhurst remove a handkerchief and wrap it around his fingers.

Reaching out, he grabbed the earl's hand and snatched away the cloth. He saw traces of blood.

"You *struck* her?" he growled, rage pouring through him.

"If you mean the little whore you were eating ices with, then I would say yes."

Henry slammed his fist into Parkhurst's nose as hard as he could, hearing the loud crunch. Before the earl could cry out, he punched him hard in his gut, and the man doubled over. Henry then grabbed Parkhurst by his elbow and rushed him to the foyer. A quick-thinking footman opened the door before they reached it, and Henry led Parkhurst outside as the footman closed it.

No one else had seen them together.

The earl began sputtering, getting his wind back, blood pouring from his broken nose. He steered Parkhurst to the end of the house and turned the corner before stopping and releasing him.

Holding his nose in his hands, the earl said, "You think because you are a duke, you can do anything."

Henry removed his coat and hung it on the nearby fence before doing the same with his gloves. "I am going to right a wrong done a long time ago. You hurt Fia. Badly. She could have died in that fall."

Parkhurst blinked. His hands fell from his face. "She told you of that?"

"I know how severely her leg was damaged. How even now, years later, it pains her. I know you bullied her. Terrorized her the entire time you were growing up." He paused. "I even know you stole from the estate with the help of the Parkwood steward. So, yes, Parkhurst. I will say that I am a duke—and I can do anything I like. That includes punishing you for all the wrongs you have done to Fia. Forcing her to live worse than a servant. Farming her out and pocketing the monies she brought in from her lessons. Keeping her from society and making her come-out.

"And I also know about the twenty thousand pounds you have withheld from her. The dowry stipulated in the marriage contracts. You lied to Fia. Told her that her father was in debt. I plan to see you make good and give her access to her dowry. After I teach you a lesson you will never forget."

Henry did just that. The years he had spent perfecting his

boxing technique at Gentleman Jackson's gymnasium now came into play. Parkhurst put up little fight. In the end, he was a blubbering mess.

Taking him by the collar, Henry dragged the worthless earl between parked carriages until he located a hansom cab and signaled the driver.

"You are to take this man to his home." Henry tossed Parkhurst into the cab and then retrieved a guinea and handed it to the driver.

To Parkhurst, he said, "You are never to go near Fia again. You are not to talk of this night or the thrashing I gave you. With anyone. Tomorrow, you will write to your solicitor, Mr. Williams, and have him transfer the dowry funds back into Mr. Bankston's care. If this is not done by ten o'clock tomorrow, I will come for you again, Parkhurst. I promise you there will be nothing left of you when I finish. Not a bone will be left unbroken. Not a tooth shall remain in your mouth. Do you understand?"

"Yes, Your Grace," Parkhurst gasped.

Henry stepped back and glanced to the driver. "Be off!"

He then searched for his own carriage after claiming his coat again and slipping into it. His coachman's brows rose, but the man kept silent. Giving him the address of Fia's boardinghouse, Henry then climbed into the carriage as it took off.

His gut told him Fia would not have returned to the ballroom, especially with Parkhurst having struck her. Henry saw red again just thinking of that, wanting to kill Parkhurst. Yet Daniel was right. It would be far more painful to the earl to ruin him. First, he and Daniel would see that Parkhurst received the cut direct from those who mattered in Polite Society. Others would naturally follow suit, not wanting to alienate two dukes.

Then he would take whatever information Miss Shelby Slade came up with and use it to drive Parkhurst into the ground financially. When he was done with the earl, Parkhurst would wish he were dead.

He kept watch out the window. It was past one o'clock in the morning now, and he worried for Fia's safety. Though the streets looked empty, who knew if thieves lingered in recesses or alleyways?

They were almost to the boardinghouse when he spied her a few blocks away, limping along, favoring her left leg. He swallowed down the anger and hatred that rushed through him. What Fia needed now was a gentle touch and compassion.

Tapping the roof, his coachman came to a halt. Henry got out and told the driver to wait for him here. He doubted Fia would enter his carriage. She would prefer to go back to her rented room so no one would see her bedraggled state. He would make sure she got there safely.

And Henry would stay with her. Comfort her. Tell her what was in his heart.

"Yes, Your Grace."

Then he moved to the pavement and hurried to catch up with her, which didn't prove difficult.

"Fia," he called.

She turned, and he closed the distance between them.

"Fia," he repeated, watching as she almost collapsed.

Henry swept her off her feet, cradling her close to him as she began to weep.

"It's all right. I have you, love."

He began walking the last half-block to the boardinghouse. As he approached, he asked, "Do you have a key?"

"No," she said, tears streaming down her face. "I left it in my reticule. It is still at the ball."

"Then I suppose we shall have to knock to be admitted," he said lightly.

Her eyes widened. "Oh, I cannot bother Mrs. Kent. She even gave me a key so I could use a separate entrance and not disturb her or the other renters as I came home from playing at *ton* events."

"We shall go to that entrance. Tell me where it is."

She did so, and Henry climbed the outside staircase with her in his arms. He eased her to her feet.

"Do you have any hairpins left?" he asked.

She felt her hair and produced one, handing it to him.

Henry slipped it into the lock and tinkered a bit. Suddenly, the lock clicked, and he quietly opened the door.

"How did you do that?" she asked, bewildered by his hidden skill.

"An old parlor trick," he told her. "Now, come inside. Where is your room?"

"It is only a few steps inside on the right."

They entered the darkened building, shutting the door behind them. Again, he slipped the hatpin into the lock of her door and jiggled it, freeing the lock. Opening the door, he stepped inside, pulling her with him.

A lone candle burned, and he supposed her thoughtful landlady had left it for her. He faced her and saw the dried blood on her face and on the front of her gown. Tempering his anger, he spied the washbasin and said, "We should clean you up."

"I can do it," she told him, averting her gaze, her embarrassment obvious.

"I know you can, sweetheart. But I want to help."

Henry led her to the bed and had her sit. Going to the washstand, he poured some water from the jug into the basin and pulled out his handkerchief, dipping it into the water. He went to Fia and bathed her face and neck.

"May I feel your nose?" he asked, sitting next to her on the bed.

"It is not broken. I would be in more pain if it were. Parkhurst only hit me hard enough to make it bleed."

"The fact that he hit you at all is appalling."

She shrugged. "It is who he is."

"I know what he did to you all those years ago." He cupped her cheek. "How he pushed you, injuring your leg."

"What? How could you know that? I never . . ." Her voice

trailed off. "I only told one person."

"Bankston. I know. Daniel and I spoke to him. He told us you do have a dowry, Fia. A rather large one. Twenty thousand pounds' worth."

"That's impossible!"

"No, Parkhurst lied to you. Do not worry. I spoke to him tonight. After you saw him," he quickly added, not wanting her to think the conversation had led to her cousin attacking her.

"He . . . lied," she echoed.

"He did. And he will be speaking to his solicitor tomorrow morning. The dowry funds will be returned to Mr. Bankston, who will manage them for you until they are needed."

Henry braced himself, not wanting to keep anything from her. "The dowry can be part of the marriage settlements when you choose to wed. Or they will become solely yours upon your twenty-fifth birthday."

"That is this summer. In June."

His thumb stroked her cheek. "Yes. If that is what you wish. But I wish for something else." He paused, knowing his future hung on what he now said and her reaction.

"I love you, Fia. I want to marry you."

CHAPTER TWENTY-SIX

H E LOVED HER.
The Duke of Linberry loved her.

Elation filled Fia, hearing the words. Yes, she had known he desired her—as she had him—but in her wildest dreams, she had never thought a man such as this might love her.

"I love you, too," she said breathlessly, relieved to have said it aloud.

To love and be loved in return. What more could she ask?

His other hand came up and framed her face now. His hands were large. Warm. Comforting. She felt tears pour down her cheeks.

"What? No more tears, my love," he said gently, his thumbs wiping away the tears that fell. "I love you. You love me. That is all that matters."

He lowered his mouth to hers, his lips softly brushing against hers. Her body remembered his kiss and tightened in response. He kissed her gently for some minutes, soothing her, but she wanted more. Fia clutched his coat's lapels and brought him closer to her.

Then she opened to him, and he answered her invitation, his tongue sweeping inside her mouth and against hers. His hands slid to her nape and pushed into her hair, already freed of its pins. He thoroughly explored every recess, his fingers massaging her scalp. Her nipples tightened, as did her core. She gripped his lapels still, holding him to her, and then decided she simply must touch him.

She released her hold and rested her palms against his chest, slowly rubbing against it, feeling the hard muscle, wondering what he looked like under all those clothes.

Her body heated at the thought, and she wrapped her arms around him. He responded by pulling her onto his lap. Now they were closer than before. She smelled that wonderful spice of his cologne. Felt the slight rasp of whiskers coming in, knowing his last shave had been hours ago. One arm wrapped around her waist as his hand went to her nape, cradling it.

His kisses grew more heated. More demanding. He tugged on her hair, tilting her head back, allowing the kiss to become deeper. More passionate. Her blood grew hot, running through her limbs, her bones dissolving into nothingness. And still he kissed her.

Suddenly, he broke the kiss. "Henry. I am Henry," he uttered before his mouth returned to hers.

He hiked up her gown past her knees, shifting her so that she now straddled him, her knees against the outside of his thighs. As he kissed her passionately, one hand slowly moved up her leg, stroking first her calf, then her thigh, then moving to her core. With her legs wide, he slipped a hand between them, his fingers dancing along the seam of her sex, sending delightful shivers racing through her.

Again, he broke the kiss. "I love you. I want to show you how much. Do you trust me, Fia?"

"Completely," she answered honestly. She had never known this good a man, and she knew he would never harm her.

His thumb dragged along her seam, stroking it, and she felt liquid heat come from her.

"Yes," he murmured. "You are wet for me, love."

Fia had no idea what that meant, only that his touch was driving her wild.

Then he slipped a finger inside her.

"Oh!"

Henry caressed her, and she wiggled on his lap.

"You like that?" he asked.

"I do," she assured him.

He pushed a second finger inside her, causing her to gasp. The caresses came slow and deep, and she began moving against him. He kissed her throat a few times, but his gaze returned to hers.

"I want to watch you as you come."

"Come where?" she asked, not thinking they were going anywhere.

"You'll see," he said, a smile playing about his sensual lips.

As he continued to touch her so intimately, something built inside her, raw and needy.

"Do you feel it? It's like a pressure building," he told her.

"Yes," she gasped, moving against him and meeting his hand.

Then the world exploded in a burst of color and sensations. Fia rode a wave of pleasure so great that she began to call out. Henry quickly covered her mouth with his, muffling the noise. She moved against him until she was spent and collapsed.

He broke the kiss. "Did you enjoy that?"

She chuckled. "What do you think?" she asked, hearing her tone was flirtatious.

"I believe you did."

He kissed her brow. Her eyelids. Her nose. Her mouth. Then he stood and set her on the ground, spinning and turning back the bedclothes. He removed his coat and spread it on the bed before untying his cravat and slipping off his waistcoat. He didn't stop there. He unbuttoned the buttons to his shirt and pulled it over his head, tossing it to the ground.

Her eyes almost popped from her head.

He was magnificent. A chest sculpted of muscle with ridges. She reached out a finger and ran it along them, hearing him suck in a quick breath. He captured her wrist and held it.

"Your touch undoes me, love," he admitted softly. "Let me finish undressing."

"All right."

She eagerly watched as the rest of his clothes came off, staring in wonder at what was revealed. His physique was sleek and . . . beautiful.

Holding out his hands, he asked, "Is this what you desire?"

Fia could only nod, her voice gone.

"If we are to come together and belong to one another, I will need to remove your clothes, as well. May I do so?"

She liked that he asked her. That he didn't assume anything. That told her a great deal about the kind of man he was.

She managed a whispered, "Yes."

Henry didn't rush. He took his time removing her layers, kissing her as he went. He kissed her hands and elbows. Her belly. Her knees. She finally stood before him, unclothed.

Taking her hands in his, he laced their fingers together. "You are so very beautiful, love."

He pulled her to him, wrapping her in an embrace, their bodies flush against one another. She felt his cock move and knew enough to understand that meant he desired her.

Then he gently placed her on the bed, atop his coat.

"Won't your coat get wrinkled?" she asked.

"Leave it where it is," he instructed.

He joined her on the bed, their limbs entwining, more kisses, more heat following. He stroked her back. Her hips. Her breasts. His mouth and lips did wonderful things to her breasts, causing them to feel heavy and crave his touch. After a long time of kissing and touching, he moved over her, brushing his fingers against her sex again, making her grow warm and damp there.

"This might hurt a bit," he explained.

"Go ahead. I want you inside me. I need you there."

Henry grinned. "I need to be there."

He brought his cock next to her sex, brushing it up and down. Then he leaned close and kissed her as he pushed it inside her.

Lifting his head, he asked, "Are you all right?"

She gazed up at him with love. "I am when I am with you."

His lips went to her throat. Slowly, he began to move. Somehow, her body understood it should move with his. They began a dance of love, moving, reaching, shifting. She wrapped her arms around him, never wanting to let him go. Then that interesting, wonderful pressure built within her again as she rose and met his every thrust. The magic happened again, spreading through her, swallowing her whole.

He collapsed atop her, kissing her soundly before rolling to his side. She faced him and as they gazed upon one another, Fia saw the love he held for her in his eyes. Actually, she had felt it in every touch. Every stroke.

"I love you. I will always protect you. You will be my duchess. My great love."

He captured her nape and pulled her close, her ear resting against his chest, hearing each beat of his heart.

His words troubled her, though. Yes, she loved him and believed him when he told her that he loved her.

But he could not protect her from the vicious, wagging tongues of the *ton*'s gossips. She had seen the way they stared at her as she had waltzed with this man. Heard their whispers and knew the horrible things they were saying about her. No matter what Henry said, he could not shield her from the gossip. Polite Society despised her. And they would feel the same about Henry and any children they brought into this world.

Fia could not do that. She couldn't ruin his life and that of innocent children.

In that moment, she realized she could never marry him.

HENRY AWOKE AFTER dozing, reaching for Fia. The bed was empty, but the place beside him was warm. The candle burned low but still allowed him to see Fia, standing by the window, her arms tightly wrapped around her. She wore her dressing gown.

He rose from the bed and came to stand behind her, wrapping his arms around her, nuzzling her neck.

"Come back to bed," he urged, wanting to join with her again.

Their coupling had been the most passionate he had ever experienced. He knew it was because of the love they held for one another. He looked forward to the years they would spend together, years lived in love, their children playing on the lawn at Linfield and growing up, taking their places in Polite Society.

"You should go," she said. "If you are seen leaving my room, Mrs. Kent will throw me out on the street."

Turning her so that she faced him, he lowered his lips to hers for a sweet, lingering kiss in reply. He realized he should go. He had a special license to purchase and needed to stop by his solicitor's office so the marriage contracts could be drawn up. Bankston would need to be sent for in order to represent Fia's interests in the matter. He didn't need her dowry, but it could be used for their oldest daughter instead, for when she wed. Henry hoped they would have several children. Knowing how Fia loved country living, he wouldn't mind spending a good deal of the year at Linfield or one of his other estates, coming to town for the Season each year. His priorities had completely changed. All he wanted now was to be with Fia and make her happy.

Breaking the kiss, he quickly dressed. As he did, he spied one of her instrument cases.

"Would you play something for me before I go?" he asked, wanting to commit to memory whatever melody she played so that it would be with him, and always keep her a part of him.

An odd look crossed her face as she retrieved the case and opened it.

Lifting the instrument, she rested it against her collarbone and then placed her chin atop it. Fia brought the bow up to the strings and then paused, looking at him.

"I wrote this myself. It is for you."

"For me?" he asked, surprised.

"Yes. Anytime I play it, I will always think of you."

He swallowed, his throat thick with emotion as she began to softly play. The melody was achingly beautiful. It amazed Henry that not only did she play incredibly well, but she had also written the music coming from her instrument.

When her bow stilled and the last note hung in the air, he realized tears were streaming down his face. He wiped them away and came to her, enveloping her in his arms.

"This is the most wonderful gift anyone has ever given me, love. I hope you will not tire of playing it, for I will ask to hear it every day."

She stiffened slightly. "I am glad you liked it."

"I treasure it, Fia. Just as I do you."

Henry lowered his lips to hers and gently kissed her.

"I must be off, but I will see you at this afternoon's garden party," he promised.

He opened the door to her room and poked out his head, seeing the corridor was clear. Moving to the outside door, he opened it.

"Lock it behind me," he told her, memorizing how she looked standing in the doorway, her golden waves tumbling about her, her lips still slightly swollen from their many kisses.

He moved quietly down the stairs and to the pavement. The streets were still empty this time of morning, except for his ducal carriage, still waiting for him. Henry hurried toward it.

"Home, please," he told the coachman before climbing inside the vehicle.

They made excellent time, and he was soon back at his town-house, calling for a bath and breakfast to be sent to his rooms. As he waited for the heated water to arrive, he dashed off notes to the two solicitors, requesting they meet with him at his home at eleven o'clock today, telling them to be ready to draw up marriage contracts between him and Lady Sophia Sawyer.

After Ripley bathed and shaved Henry, he sent the valet to deliver the two notes and then breakfasted. Once he had eaten, he called for his carriage and went to Doctors' Commons, having to wait until clerks began to arrive before being admitted. Once they did, he was directed to the office where the Archbishop of Canterbury's representative discussed the matter with him, writing down all the particulars.

After he had handed over the hefty fee for the special license, he was told it allowed him to marry anywhere and at any time without having the banns read. He hoped Fia would want to wed as quickly as he did and not mind not having a smart wedding at St. George's. His heart told him that she wanted him as much as he did her, and they didn't need a hundred or more people to witness their ceremony. Daniel, Margaret, the dowager duchess, and his mother would be enough, along with a clergyman. He would have to ask Fia if she had a man of the cloth in mind who might perform the ceremony. If not, he would find one.

Henry returned to his townhouse and at the appointed time, both solicitors arrived. He welcomed them into his study.

"Have you received word from Mr. Williams this morning?" he asked Bankston.

"I have, Your Grace. Mr. Williams came to my office in person, having come straight from Lord Parkhurst's residence. Lady Fia's dowry has been returned. I don't know how you accomplished such a feat, but I thank you, all the same."

"That is good news, Bankston. Thank you for meeting with Williams and coming today." He smiled. "Shall we get down to it, gentlemen?"

An hour later the language and details had been hammered out. Henry was pleased at what they had accomplished and asked for copies not only for himself but for Fia, wanting complete transparency. She had been deceived by her cousin, and he never wanted her kept in the dark ever again.

He wrote to his housekeeper at Linfield, explaining that he would soon wed and wanted the duchess' rooms to be aired and prepared, explaining he would send word before he and his bride would come down from town. He then called in his butler and housekeeper and told them the same news, wishing the townhouse to be prepared for the arrival of the new duchess.

"When might the ceremony be, Your Grace?" asked Mrs. Orville.

"I have the special license in hand and will discuss things with Lady Fia this afternoon. We most likely will wed at the residence of the Duke and Duchess of Westfield later this week."

"Congratulations, Your Grace," Orville said. "We look forward to meeting Her Grace."

Henry then went to his mother's rooms, wanting to share his good news with her. Her maid told him she was practicing in the drawing room. He went straight there, standing in the doorway and listening to her for several minutes until she concluded the piece.

He began to clap as he crossed the room. "Well done, Mama. I see you and the pianoforte are no longer strangers to one another."

She rose, and he kissed her cheek. "I am most grateful to Lady Fia for that reintroduction. Yes, I have been playing quite a bit this past week. I have also enjoyed catching up with my friends, as well. I think I am ready to begin attending the Season now. I know I have skipped the first two balls, but I am ready to join in the festivities once more."

"You look like you are happy."

She sighed. "As happy as I can be without your father."

Taking her hands in his, he said, "I have some good news to share with you, Mama. I am to be married. To Lady Fia."

Her radiant smile spoke of her approval. "Oh, Henry. That is wonderful. Though rather sudden."

"I love her, Mama. And she loves me. I purchased a special license this morning. The Duchess of Westfield has offered to host the wedding and breakfast. I will speak to Fia today, and we can decide when the ceremony will take place."

Mama kissed his cheek. "You are fortunate that it will be a love match from the beginning, my son. I am happy for you." She paused. "And I will be even happier when I am bouncing a grandchild on my knee."

Henry laughed. "We will work on that, Mama. Hopefully, we will be blessed with many children. Would you like to accompany me to Lord and Lady Simms' garden party? Fia will be there, and you can give her your best wishes in person."

"I shall go and dress."

An hour later, they were in the carriage, making their way to the latest *ton* affair. Henry's heartbeat quickened as they arrived, knowing he would soon see Fia and hear her play. All day long, he had heard the haunting melody of her composition in his head. It had made him miss her, but at the same time, it was as if she had been present with him throughout the day.

Soon, they would be together.

Always.

CHAPTER TWENTY-SEVEN

FIA DRESSED IN one of the five day gowns provided through the generosity of the Dowager Duchess of Westfield. She brushed her hair and then wound it into a chignon with the few pins she had left, hoping it would hold in place. Instead of one of the new pairs of pretty slippers, she laced up some sturdy boots, knowing she had a long way to walk to Lord and Lady Simms' townhouse. A part of her regretted not leaving her reticule and coins at the boardinghouse last night. She had been worried that someone might steal it from her room. Since she had left it behind at the ball, she only hoped Mr. Johnson or one of the other musicians had thought to collect her violin and case for her.

How had the conductor and the other musicians reacted when she hadn't returned to the dais last night? Mr. Johnson knew when she had slipped away for the supper dance. Had he looked for her on the dance floor after supper?

She set out for Mayfair with her viola—in case Mr. Johnson did not bring her violin today—her belly gurgling since she had not gone down for breakfast this morning. Instead of eating, she had returned to her bed after Henry left her, hugging the pillow tightly to her, inhaling the faint scent of his cologne upon it. She had fallen asleep and dreamed of him.

And of a life she could never have.

Fia would need to make that clear to him the next time she

saw him, possibly at this afternoon's garden party. She loved him enough to give him up and would need tremendous strength to stay true to her chosen course. It saddened her to think of him waltzing with his duchess in *ton* ballrooms, a place she would never go after June. Now that she knew she would come into the full amount of her dowry in two months' time, she only had to survive until then. If she were banished from today's garden party by either the hostess or Mr. Johnson, she would go and see Mr. Bankston. Surely, he would advance her a few pounds to live upon until she could access her dowry. If not, she would call upon Madame Planche and hope the modiste might give her a few weeks' work to tide her over.

A secret part of her hoped she was with child. Henry's child. Fia knew she would never marry. Not when she loved Henry as much as she did. She had always wanted children, though. If last night's coupling resulted in a love child, she would happily raise it on her own. Away from London. She had always yearned for the countryside whenever in town, never more than these last few years under Parkhurst's roof. The funds she received would allow her to buy a cottage of her own, where she could live in peace and compose music. And hopefully, raise her child.

Her knee began to ache. Somehow, the pavement in London was harder on her leg than walking on a country lane into a nearby village. She slowed her pace, glad she had left as early as she had, knowing she had a long way to go, wishing she had a few coins to hail a hansom cab and ride the rest of the way. While Margaret said she would send a vehicle to take Fia to engagements, that would have involved sending her friend a note this morning. With no money to pay a messenger to deliver it, Fia had had no way of getting word to the duchess.

Finally, she arrived in the square where Lord and Lady Simms lived. The garden party would start in half an hour, but Fia needed to join Mr. Johnson and the other musicians now. Knowing she shouldn't knock at the front door, she went to the servants' entrance.

A footman answered her knock.

"I have come to play with the musicians for today's garden party," she told him, indicating her viola case.

He frowned slightly but said, "This way, Miss," and led her to the gardens.

Numerous tables had been set up and servants were placing platters of food upon them. She spied Mr. Johnson and went straight to him.

"Mr. Johnson?"

He turned. "Lady Fia! You are here. You disappeared last night. I didn't know what to think." The conductor paused. "Your face. It is bruised."

She winced, not having thought of this. Worry filled her, and she was now fearful Mr. Johnson would not let her play because of the bruises she sported.

"I am sorry to walk out on you without any notice," she apologized. "I had an unpleasant . . . encounter with my cousin. I was very upset and did not feel I could return to the ballroom and play up to your expectations."

His sympathetic smile caused tears to well in her eyes. "Think nothing of it. I did not know if you would show up today, though, so I asked another musician to take your place in the string quartet."

Disappointment filled her, but she asked, "Might it become a quintet, Mr. Johnson? I would be happy to join it if you allow me to do so. Since there are already two violinists, I could play my viola."

He nodded. "I don't see that as a problem." He paused. "Oh. I did bring your violin with me this afternoon. When you did not return, I packed it away and took it home with me. Your reticule was inside the case. I left it there."

Relief flooded her. "Oh, thank you so much."

"Come, join the others. We were about to tune our instruments."

"I am sorry if I disappointed you last night," she told him. "I have no further plans of dancing at any future events."

He halted. "Won't that offend Her Grace?"

"Most likely, it will. But I do not belong in the *ton*, Mr. Johnson. I don't know if I ever did. Music has always filled my heart and soul. I think it best if I merely play and write and leave that world far behind."

Mr. Johnson asked a footman to bring another chair, and Fia joined the others. Soon, she was seated and had her viola in tune with the other members of the quartet. Mr. Johnson had them begin to play as guests started to arrive. She concentrated on her playing and refused to look for Henry. If he came today, she would try to talk with him once the party concluded. The sooner he knew that they would not wed, the more quickly he might recover.

She never would, though. She would love Henry until her dying day.

A hand lightly touched her shoulder and she turned, seeing Margaret standing there with the duke and his grandmother.

"We just wanted to say hello," her friend whispered. "Will you come home with us for tea after the garden party ends?"

Selfishly, she thought she would be able to eat at tea and not have to buy anything from a vendor. Margaret would also send her home in a carriage, saving Fia the long walk back to Mrs. Kent's or spending money on a hansom cab.

"I would be happy to do so."

Her friend smiled and moved away as Fia continued to play. The little group of musicians sounded quite good together, despite the fact she had never practiced with them before.

"You play remarkably well," the cellist told her as the musicians placed new music on their stands.

"You do, as well," she told him. "I also play the cello."

"I would like to hear you do so," he said. "Perhaps we can switch instruments after this next song."

She smiled brightly at him, turning back to Mr. Johnson, who conducted their small group.

Then she spied Henry and his mother over the conductor's shoulder. Henry smiled at her, and his mother waved. Fia bit her lip and smiled weakly, turning her attention to Mr. Johnson, who led them in playing their next piece.

An hour into the party, Fia spied Lady Simms making her way toward them. The viscountess had flitted about as a butterfly during the party, smiling and chatting with her guests. Now, she headed to the musicians, who were seated in a semicircle at the entrance to the gardens. They had just finished their latest selection as she arrived.

"Everything sounds lovely, Mr. Johnson," the viscountess said.

"It is always a pleasure to play for your guests, my lady," the conductor said graciously.

She smiled vacantly and started to turn when she spied Fia.

"*You!*" she hissed. "What is *she* doing here, Mr. Johnson?"

"Lady Fia is playing for your guests, the same as the rest of my musicians."

The viscountess' eyes narrowed. "I count five. I asked for a string quartet, sir. Not a fifth interloper."

Fia winced at being called out.

Lady Simms turned to Fia. "I will not pay for you to play for my guests. In fact, I do not want you here at all. My note to you was clear. You are not welcome here." Turning back to Mr. Johnson, she added, "If you ever want to play at my behest again, sir, it will be without this one among your company. Is that clear?"

"Yes, my lady," the conductor said meekly, looking apologetically at Fia.

The viscountess composed herself and turned away, cooing at a guest and linking her arm through his and leading him away.

Fia opened her case and placed her instrument in it and picked up it and her other case. "I will not cost you or these men your livelihoods, Mr. Johnson. I will make myself scarce now and in the future."

"But I thought you were to play with us at—"

"The well is now contaminated, sir. Lady Simms is a spiteful woman. I can no longer associate with you or those who play for you." She hesitated. "I would like to keep in touch with you, however. I plan to keep composing and hope you might be interested in hearing—and playing—what I write."

She quickly gave him the address of her boardinghouse and, carrying her two cases, skirted the edge of the garden party.

"What happened?"

Fia turned and saw Henry standing there. "Nothing. But I must leave quickly."

"I will come with you," he insisted. "Let me tell Mama to find a way home with one of her friends."

She was too nervous to remain. "I will be waiting in the square. We must talk."

He went to find his mother, and Fia left the party, speaking to no one else. She cut between the numerous carriages and crossed the street to the small, enclosed park that sat directly opposite the Simms' townhouse. Before she opened the gate to enter it, she heard footsteps behind her and turned.

Parkhurst.

His face was mottled with rage, as well as severe bruising. His nose was slightly askew and swollen, as if it had been broken in a fight. Worse, he held a pistol in his hand.

And Henry would be here at any moment.

"If you are going to shoot me, do so, my lord," she said, hoping to provoke him into firing his gun so he would spend his bullet on her and not her beloved.

The earl raised the gun, pointing at her. "You sent Linberry after me. Look what he did to my face. I cannot even breathe from my nose. He forced me to send funds to Bankston."

"You mean *my* dowry? You lied to me, Parkhurst. You said Papa had debts and had not provided for me. Neither was true. You wanted to keep my dowry for yourself. That is why you never allowed me to make my come-out. If any gentleman had offered for me, you would have had to hand my dowry over to him."

"I needed it."

"You did not!" she proclaimed. "You gained my father's earldom. His title. His lands. His wealth."

"Most of it is gone," he admitted.

"You are a gambler," she guessed, disgust filling her.

"I held back. Didn't touch your dowry. It was always in reserve in case I needed it. Then Linberry nearly beat me to death and told me I must return it to Bankston for you. I had Williams send it this morning—but in doing so, I was left practically destitute. If you are dead, then I—your closest relative—will receive it."

Fear trickled through her, but Fia could not risk this man harming—or evening killing—Henry. She saw her beloved now, silently creeping toward them, his eyes warning her not to alert Parkhurst as to his presence.

Then Fia decided she could do something to save herself and Henry. She had her instrument cases in hand. Parkhurst was close enough that she could strike him with one. She swung as hard as she could, hitting his shoulder and knocking him off-balance as a blur swept by her. Seconds later, Parkhurst lay on the ground, someone atop his back.

Henry reached to her. "Are you all right?"

"Yes, but—who is this boy?" Fia asked, even as the pistol in her cousin's hand came up to his temple.

As she cried out, the gun fired, the noise loud on the quiet square. Horses whinnied. She saw several coachmen and footmen scramble from their seats. A few even raced toward them to help.

The boy whipped out a handkerchief and wrapped the gun inside it. Only it wasn't a boy at all. It was a woman, wearing trousers, her hair tucked into a cap.

"Miss Slade!" Henry exclaimed.

"Your Grace," the woman said calmly, slipping the wrapped pistol into the back of her waistband. "I was following Lord

Parkhurst. I had a thorough report to turn over to you and His Grace." She clucked her tongue. "Pity you won't be needing it now."

"Who *are* you?" Fia asked, bewildered.

"Miss Shelby Slade. I'm from Bow Street. I was hired to look into the earl and his affairs. I am sorry I was a bit late in taking him down. You did an excellent job defending yourself, my lady." The woman smiled shamelessly.

Fia found that she liked her very, very much.

Miss Slade looked about at the small crowd of servants that had gathered about them. "Nothing to see here. Please return to your carriages. This accident is a matter for Bow Street now."

Slowly, the men dispersed.

"The noise wasn't loud enough to be heard at the garden party," Miss Slade said. "No one need know the two of you were present when Lord Parkhurst accidentally tripped and his gun discharged, killing him. In fact, I think this will have happened at home, while he was cleaning the weapon."

"So, that will be the story?" Henry asked.

"It will, Your Grace."

"I would still like to hear the findings of the report from you, Miss Slade."

Despite her cousin lying dead a few feet away, Fia knew a marriage to Henry would still be impossible.

"I cannot marry you," she said solemnly. "Think of all the scandal that has surrounded me. What has been written in the newspapers."

"What scandal?" he asked. "Parkhurst is dead. His gun accidentally discharged. That has nothing to do with you. I have the means to keep it out of the newspapers. We will make sure that what is known is that it was an accidental death. You heard Miss Slade. Bow Street can help in this matter."

Miss Slade said, "His Grace is right, you know. Dukes have a great power. Between the two of us, we will be able to keep this incident quiet. I will see that the body is taken back to Lord

Parkhurst's residence."

Fia shook her head. "I still cannot marry you. I refuse to ruin your life. Nor would I ruin that of our children's."

He grinned. "You have thought of our children? That is a good sign."

She furrowed her brow. "You might be able to cover up the circumstances surrounding my cousin's death, Henry, but there still will be talk. The ugly things written about me in the gossip columns will become fodder for the *ton*'s gossip. I do not want you or any children that resulted from our marriage to face that kind of talk."

He took her hands in his. "A duke is almost invincible in Polite Society, Fia, my love. Surely, you know that."

"But the *ton* has already ostracized me. Lady Simms demanded that I leave her garden party."

He kissed her cheek. "That is because you were merely Lady Fia Sawyer. Right now, I have a special license in my pocket that I purchased at Doctors' Commons this morning. You can be the Duchess of Linberry as soon as you like."

Henry smiled, releasing her hands to frame her face, his thumbs stroking her cheeks. "And I know you will use the power that comes with the title for good because that is who you are, my darling. Good, through and through. More than anything, I want you to know that as my wife, you will have my support in whatever you do. If your wish is to continue with your music, both playing and composing, then I shall be your chief supporter."

Still, she hesitated.

Then Miss Slade cleared her throat, causing Fia to look in her direction.

"I say marry His Grace, my lady. He seems quite nice." She paused. "And your children would be quite beautiful and handsome."

Her outrageous statement caused Fia to laugh. "Thank you, Miss Slade. I will take your advice under consideration."

Miss Slade looked to Henry. "I will write and file my report with the office by the end of the day. Do you have time to meet before your wedding tomorrow, Your Grace?" She smiled. "I assume you will wed quickly."

Henry said, "Why don't you bring your report to the Duke of Westfield's townhouse at ten o'clock tomorrow morning, Miss Slade. You can share what you found with Westfield and me and then stay for the wedding at eleven."

He turned to Fia. "That is, if an eleven o'clock wedding suits you, love."

Warmth spread through her. "It suits me quite nicely, Your Grace."

"Oh, Miss Slade," Henry called, motioning for her to return to them. "Why don't you take Parkhurst away in my carriage?"

He called over his two footmen, who had lingered nearby. Her new fiancé gave the servants their instructions, telling them to do whatever Miss Slade asked.

"You are now in charge, Miss Slade."

"Thank you, Your Grace," the woman said. "I will see you in the morning. Should I send the carriage back for you?"

"We will go back inside and meet up with Westfield and his duchess," Henry said. "We can always ride home with them."

He slipped Fia's hand into the crook of his arm and led her back toward the Simms' townhouse.

She balked. "Henry, I cannot go back in there. Lady Simms will throw a fit."

"Leave the viscountess to me."

Only because she trusted him so did she allow him to guide her once more to the garden party.

Lady Simms immediately spied Fia and came charging over. She started to say something, but her jaw fell open, seeing that Fia was on the arm of the Duke of Linberry.

"Oh, Lady Simms. What a lovely day for a garden party," Henry said airily. "I am so happy you chose to host it today." He paused, leaning closer to her as if to share a confidence. "I wanted to ask a favor of you."

She blinked several times. "What might I do for you, Your Grace?"

He smiled. "I have just become engaged to Lady Fia Sawyer and was hoping you would do the honors of announcing our engagement at your event. After all, it is not every day that a duke decides to take a bride. It is certainly the first engagement of the Season. What a feather it would be in your cap to announce our good news."

Lady Simms sputtered a moment, and Henry smoothly said, "My bride-to-be and I thank you for accommodating our wishes in this matter."

Without waiting for the viscountess to respond, he called out in a loud voice, "If I may have your attention, please?"

Conversation at the party ceased. Mr. Johnson and his musicians stopped playing. Henry smiled benignly at Lady Simms.

The woman cleared her throat and then smiled brightly. "I am very happy that I have been chosen to announce the engagement of His Grace, the Duke of Linberry, to Lady Fia Sawyer."

For a moment, there was only silence. Fia's heart stopped.

Then applause began. She looked about the garden party at the very faces who had judged her only last night. Now, suddenly, they showered smiles upon her.

All because she was marrying a duke.

Henry took her hand and lifted it, kissing her fingers tenderly. Smiling, he said softly so only she could hear, "It is not so bad being a duchess after all, is it?"

Fia returned his smile. "I think being *your* duchess will be the best gift of all."

EPILOGUE

London—June 1813

RIPLEY FINISHED TYING Henry's cravat and stepped back to view his work. "You are ready, Your Grace." He paused. "I suppose you will be stopping by the nursery?"

Henry smiled. "Of course," he told the valet. "I must say goodnight to my son."

The valet frowned. "Please, Your Grace, make certain that you place a cloth over your shoulder this time. It is dreadfully hard to get the little lord's spit-ups from your evening clothes. Perhaps you might even refrain from burping his lordship entirely."

"Not a chance, Ripley. But I will remember the burp cloth this time if it is needed."

The valet sighed. "Thank you, Your Grace."

He left his rooms and headed upstairs to the nursery to tell his son goodnight before the musicale he and Fia were hosting began. They had only arrived in town a few days ago, having stayed home for the birth of their babe in March. Still, Henry had pushed for them to return to town in order to show off his wife's musical talents.

This evening, Fia was to play the pianoforte alone and then join Mr. Johnson's string quartet as all pieces played this evening would be original ones written by the Duchess of Linberry. Henry couldn't be prouder of his lovely wife and her burgeoning talent. She had already written a few numbers before they wed. Ever since their marriage, she had become quite prolific. He couldn't wait to hear her perform her own works tonight for their guests, an exclusive list of the most prominent members of the *ton*.

One song, though, would not be played tonight. It was the one Fia had written for him. The one she had first played after they had made love that first time. The piece was only for him. No others would ever hear it.

When he arrived at the nursery, Nanny was nowhere in sight. His mother, however, rocked her grandson.

"Mama, where is Nanny?"

She kissed the baby's head. "I sent her for a cup of tea. She should be back anytime now."

Henry couldn't help but feel happy, knowing how his mother had finally come back to life. No longer did she remain in her rooms. Instead, she spent time with her friends and grandson. She and Fia also got along splendidly.

She rose and handed his son to him. "I must go and get dressed for the evening."

He took her place in the rocker, moving back and forth, talking to his three-month-old son as if the babe could understand every word said.

"Ah, my two favorite men," Fia said, entering the nursery and pressing a kiss to the babe's head before going to claim the violin sitting in the corner of the room. She always left a spare one in the nursery so she might play for the babe.

Removing the instrument from its case, she began to play a soothing tune from Beethoven. Henry watched as his son's eyelids grew heavy and finally closed. He nodded and Fia ceased playing, returning the violin to its case.

She came and stood next to the chair. "Isn't he the most wonderful creature on the planet?"

Looking up, he replied, "I would say the second most. You, love, will always be first."

Rising, Henry took the babe to his crib and placed him in it. He slipped an arm about Fia's waist, and they watched their firstborn sleep.

"Miss Slade was right, you know," he said. "We did make a handsome lad."

He took her in his arms and kissed her lightly. "You look lovely tonight. The azure gown suits you. It makes your eyes an even deeper blue."

"And you look ever so handsome in your evening clothes," she replied, a hint of mischief in her eyes. "Then again, I believe you look wonderful out of them, too."

Henry chuckled. "Do not tempt me, Your Grace. We have guests arriving soon. Millie would have my hide if I ruin your dress or hair."

"Does Millie run this household?" she teased.

"You look too fine. I would not have your maid's efforts go to waste. Now, once our guests depart this evening?" His lips grazed her ear. "Then we will tumble into bed, and I can have my wicked way with you. But first, you must receive all the attention and honor due you, my sweet duchess."

"I am looking forward to debuting my music," she admitted. "I might be the tiniest bit nervous about others hearing it, though."

"Mr. Johnson and his musicians have praised your efforts. All will be well." He paused. "Will you play my song now? Just for the two of us?"

"Of course."

Fia went to the violin case and removed the instrument, bringing it to her shoulder and steadying it with her chin. As she played the haunting melody, Henry counted his blessings.

She replaced the violin in its case just as Nanny arrived.

"Thought I'd find Your Graces in here," she said.

"We will leave things to you, Nanny," Henry said, slipping an arm about Fia's waist and leading her into the corridor.

He stopped before they reached the stairs. "Have I told you how much I love you, Your Grace?"

"Several times today, I believe, Your Grace."

"Know that it will always be true."

With that, Henry kissed Fia one final time and then escorted her to greet their guests.

The evening proved to be a rousing success, with the usually staid applause almost raucous at times. He beamed with pride at the reception to his wife's compositions and admired her playing various instruments with such talent and precision. At the intermission, he stood by his duchess' side, listening to the adoration heaped upon her. As expected, Fia took the compliments with grace and shared a sweet smile for all to see.

When the evening concluded and Fia's admirers departed, Daniel and Margaret remained behind to partake in a final glass of champagne with their hosts in Henry's study.

As he poured the wine, Daniel said, "What a triumphant return to London, Fia! You had the cream of Polite Society agog this evening."

"I simply enjoyed playing my compositions," Fia said. "Though I will admit, it was a thrill to see how well my music has been received."

Henry handed a flute to each of them, and Margaret held hers high, toasting, "To Fia—from one working duchess to another. May we always be fulfilled by the work we do and the men we love."

They clinked their glasses together and sipped the cold champagne, talking about the evening for a few minutes as they finished their drinks. Then the Duke and Duchess of Westfield said their goodnights, leaving the Duke and Duchess of Linberry to climb the stairs and retire for the evening.

Reaching their bedchamber, Fia said, "It was a good night, wasn't it, Henry?"

"It was most definitely a good night." Then he smiled down

at her. "But the best part of the night is yet to come, my love."

Sweeping his wife into his arms, he carried her across the room and placed her gently on the bed, removing each item of clothing she wore and kissing her slowly every time another piece left her body. Finally, she lay gloriously naked before him, and he tore off his own clothes, eager to make love to her.

In the aftermath of their lovemaking, Henry cradled Fia in his arms, telling her, "I am reluctant to close my eyes and have you gone from me, my love, if only for a few hours."

She pressed a soft kiss against his lips. "Then simply dream of me, dearest. Promise we will meet in our dreams."

"I promise," he swore.

And they did.

About the Author

Award-winning and internationally bestselling author Alexa Aston's historical romances use history as a backdrop to place her characters in extraordinary circumstances, where their intense desire for one another grows into the treasured gift of love.

She is the author of Regency and Medieval romance, including: Dukes of Distinction; Soldiers & Soulmates; The St. Clairs; The King's Cousins; and The Knights of Honor.

A native Texan, Alexa lives with her husband in a Dallas suburb, where she eats her fair share of dark chocolate and plots out stories while she walks every morning. She enjoys a good Netflix binge; travel; seafood; and can't get enough of *Survivor* or *The Crown*.